P. C. Doher[illegible]n and educated at Woodcote Hall. He studied History at Liverpool and Oxford Universities and obtained a doctorate at Oxford for his thesis on Edward II and Queen Isabella. He is now the Headmaster of a school in North-East London, and lives with his wife and family near Epping Forest.

P. C. Doherty's previous Hugh Corbett medieval mysteries are also available from Headline.

SATAN IN ST MARY'S
'Wholly excellent, this is one of those books you hate to put down' *Prima*

CROWN IN DARKNESS
'I really like these medieval whodunnits' *Bookseller*

SPY IN CHANCERY
'A powerful compound of history and intrigue' *Redbridge Guardian*

THE ANGEL OF DEATH
'Medieval London comes vividly to life . . . Doherty's depictions of medieval characters and manners of thought, from the highest to the lowest, ringing true' *Publishers Weekly*

THE PRINCE OF DARKNESS
'A romping good read' *Time Out*

MURDER WEARS A COWL
'Historically informative, excellently plotted and, as ever, superbly entertaining' *CADS*

THE ASSASSIN IN THE GREENWOOD

Also by this author and available from Headline

The Mask of Ra
The Haunting
The Rose Demon
The Soul Slayer

An Ancient Evil
Being the Knight's Tale
A Tapestry of Murders
Being the Man of Law's Tale
A Tournament of Murders
Being the Franklin's Tale
Ghostly Murders
Being the Priest's Tale

Hugh Corbett medieval mysteries
Satan in St Mary's
Crown in Darkness
Spy in Chancery
The Angel of Death
The Prince of Darkness
Murder Wears a Cowl
The Assassin in the Greenwood
Satan's Fire
The Devil's Hunt
The Demon Archer

The Sorrowful Mysteries of Brother Athelstan
The Nightingale Gallery
The House of the Red Slayer
Murder Most Holy
The Anger of God
By Murder's Bright Light
The House of Crows
The Assassin's Riddle
The Devil's Domain

Under the name of Michael Clynes
The White Rose Murders
The Poisoned Chalice
The Grail Murders
A Brood of Vipers
The Gallows Murders
The Relic Murders

The Song of a Dark Angel

P. C. Doherty

HEADLINE

First published in 1993
by HEADLINE BOOK PUBLISHING

First published in paperback in 1994
by HEADLINE BOOK PUBLISHING

10 9 8

ISBN 0 7472 4432 4

Printed and bound in Great Britain by
Mackays of Chatham PLC, Chatham, Kent

HEADLINE BOOK PUBLISHING
A division of Hodder Headline PLC
338 Euston Road
London NW1 3BH

Barbara and Rob of 'The Poisoned Pen',
Scotsville, Arizona, USA.
Many thanks for your support and friendship.

Song of a Dark Angel

The sharp, cruel wind swept in across the iron-grey sea towards the white headlands. It caught the tops of the waves and spun the icy foam into white flecks like snow. Those who lived in the villages near the eastern shore pulled their cloaks close about them and edged nearer the fire. The north wind, the Dark Angel as they called it, was making its presence felt. Soon it would rise, turning into fierce buffets. The inhabitants of Hunstanton huddled deep in their beds and hoped the storm would exhaust itself before daybreak. The wind, however, sang on; it tossed the sand and brushed the hairs of the severed head fixed on a pole beside the bloodied corpse sprawled on the shingle and rushed on to tease and play with the corpse of the long-haired woman that swung from the scaffold on the cliff top.

The Dark Angel, singing its sombre song, was accustomed to such cruel sights: this was the Wash, the large, inland sea that thrust into the soft Norfolk countryside – a violent, changeable place with its sudden tides, treacherous whirlpools, mud-choked rivulets and crumbling cliffs. It had seen the landing of the Vikings and the invasion of the Danes and, in the old king's grandfather's time, had witnessed the destruction of a royal army and the disappearance of a king's ransom in treasure. The Dark Angel swept inland, leaving behind its macabre playthings. The woman still danced at the end of the rope; on the deserted shingle, the sightless eyes of the decapitated head continued to gaze into the sea mist which boiled and swirled before it, following the wind inland.

Chapter 1

A week later, on the eve of the feast of St Andrew, Apostle of Scotland, two riders thundered along the cliff-top path. They were determined to reach their destination before the grey November daylight died altogether. As they breasted the brow of a small hill, where the cliff path swung inland round the bay, the leading rider reined in. He waited for his groaning, grumbling companion to do likewise.

'For God's sake!' the man muttered. 'How long, master? My arse is sore, my thighs are chapped and my belly thinks my throat is slit!'

From the shadow of his cowled hood, Sir Hugh Corbett, Keeper of the king's Secret Seal and his special emissary, grinned as he blew on frozen fingers.

'Come on, Ranulf,' he urged. 'At least no snow has fallen and we'll be there within the hour!'

Corbett pulled his hood back. He looked away from his manservant, Ranulf-atte-Newgate, and stared out across the mist-shrouded sea which crashed and broke on the rocks beneath him.

'A cold, sombre place,' he muttered.

Ranulf pulled his own hood back and edged his horse alongside that of his master.

'I've told you this before, Master. I hate the bloody

countryside.' He stared back across the moorland, where the mist's long, cold fingers were beginning to creep. Somewhere in the gathering gloom a dog howled as if protesting at the elements. 'I hate it!' Ranulf repeated, as if to himself. 'Where the bloody hell are we, Master?'

Corbett pointed down to the sea. 'We are on the Norfolk coast, Ranulf. In summer they say it's beautiful. Beneath us lies Hunstanton Bay.'

He pointed across the cliffs. Ranulf glimpsed a faint light winking and made out the outlines of a building.

'Mortlake Manor,' Corbett said. 'And there is the old Hermitage. Can you see it, Ranulf?'

Ranulf strained his eyes and made out the gaunt, rambling ruin, most of it hidden by a high decaying wall.

'Further inland is the village,' Corbett continued. 'And down there in the mist, probably from where that dog is barking, is Holy Cross convent.'

Ranulf looked where his master was pointing and then, beyond the convent, to the sea. If he hated the countryside, Ranulf-atte-Newgate, born in the warren of alleyways that made up Whitefriars, was terrified of the sea – its grey, cold expanse; the mist turning and swirling like a ghost, muffling and making more eerie the hungry, haunting cries of the gulls. The thunder of the waves on the deserted pebble-strewn beach: those lonely buildings, silent as death, nestling on the cliff tops.

'Where was the head discovered?' he asked.

Corbett pointed down to the shore.

'There. High on the beach. The head was neatly severed from the body and placed on a small pole dug into the sand. Beside it lay the corpse.'

'Poor old Cerdic,' Ranulf said softly, blowing into his

hands. He squinted across at his master. 'I knew him, you know. If ever a man rolled crooked dice it was him. He was such a villain he couldn't even walk straight, never mind look directly at you.'

'Well, he's dead now, murdered by a person or persons unknown. But what intrigues me is that there were no signs of scuffling on the beach. How do you account for that, eh, Ranulf? How could a young man as robust and strong as Cerdic Lickspittle have been taken down to a beach and had his head lopped off without a struggle? There are no footprints, of him or of his murderer.' Corbett bit his lip and pulled the hood back over his head. 'Mind you,' he observed drily, 'what I'd also like to know is what Lavinius Monck is doing here. Ah well, we'll soon find out.'

Corbett gathered the reins in his hand and urged his horse forward along the cliff path, making sure he never looked to his right at the sheer drop only a few feet away. Ranulf, still muttering to himself, followed suit. As darkness began to fall the mist grew thicker and Corbett shouted warnings over his shoulder for Ranulf to take care. Corbett reined in as he reached the gaunt, three-branched scaffold that stood between the edge of the path and the cliff top. He stared up at the scrap of rope hanging from a rusting iron hook.

'Is this where they found the second corpse?' Ranulf asked.

'Apparently,' Corbett replied. 'She was a local baker's wife. Disappeared from her home. The next morning someone found her swinging by her neck from the scaffold. An innocent victim executed where murderers are usually gibbeted.' Corbett turned. 'Now, who would do that, Ranulf? Who would murder a poor woman in such a barbarous way? He stared at the scaffold, which rose at least five feet above his head.

'I suppose she was murdered at night,' Corbett continued. 'But why here?'

He looked down at the base of the scaffold and dismounted, throwing the reins at Ranulf, as something caught his attention. He knelt and picked up a bunch of decaying wild flowers from the bare ground beneath the gallows.

'What's the matter?' Ranulf asked impatiently.

'Who put these here?' Corbett asked.

'Oh, for God's sake, Master, the poor woman's husband or her family.'

Corbett shook his head. He sniffed at the brown, rotting stalks.

'No, they have been here for weeks.'

'Perhaps the relatives of an executed felon,' Ranulf hissed through clenched teeth. 'Sir Hugh, for the love of God, I am freezing! I have lost all feeling in my legs and balls!'

Corbett threw the flowers down, wiped his hands on his robe, grasped his reins and remounted. 'Well, well, we can't have that, can we, Ranulf? What a loss to the ladies of London, eh?'

He urged his horse on. Ranulf stuck his tongue out at him and quietly moaned to himself about the buxom little widow – brown-haired and merry-faced, with the sweetest eyes and softest arms he had ever known – left behind in London. He'd had to give her up just because old Master Long Face, riding in front of him now, had been ordered north by King Edward.

'Whose balls,' Ranulf muttered to himself, 'I hope are as cold as mine!'

He followed his master, who had now slowed his horse to a trot, fearful that it might slip or lose direction. The mist had thickened and the angry sea still rumbled and crashed below them. The ruins of the old Hermitage came into sight, mostly hidden by a high sandstone curtain-wall. Corbett caught the smell of wood smoke and the sweeter scent of roasting beef, which made his stomach growl and wetted his dry mouth.

'Shall we go in, Master?' Ranulf whispered.

'No, no.'

Corbett followed the path round, kicking his horse into a gallop. He did not want to stop until he had spoken to Sir Simon Gurney. Ranulf followed suit. He was sure he had heard a shout behind him, but Corbett waved him on and they trotted through the mist towards the lights of Mortlake Manor. At last the path turned inland, then slightly downwards. Ranulf could have shouted with joy as the gates of the manor, with fiery sconce torches lit above them, came into view.

'Maltote had better be there!' he shouted. 'I hope the lazy bugger told them we were on our way!'

'He'll be there,' Corbett replied.

Ralph Maltote, the clerk's messenger, may have nothing in his brains but he was a superb rider with a hunting dog's instinct for threading his way along the twisting roads and paths of England. Ranulf dismounted and hammered on the small postern door in the main gate of the manor.

'Come on! Come on!' he muttered. I'm freezing to death!'

The door swung open. A busy-faced porter peered out and beckoned them into the large cobbled yard that stretched before the fortified manor house of Sir Simon Gurney. Grooms hurried up and took their horses. A servant collected their saddlebags and the porter led them in through the main door of the house. They went down a sweet-smelling, stone-vaulted passageway past the busy kitchen, the smells from which whetted Corbett's and Ranulf's hunger, and into the solar where the grey-haired Sir Simon Gurney and his wife Alice waited to greet them.

The old knight, one of the king's former companions, smiled and rose from his chair by the fire; his petite, sweet-faced wife stood smiling behind him.

'Hugh! Hugh!'

Gurney clasped Corbett's hand. He peered into the clerk's dark, saturnine face and noted the flecks of grey in the hair on either side of his temples and the furrows around his mouth and hooded eyes which had not been there when they had last met at Westminster.

'You look tired, Hugh.'

'A bad day, Sir Simon. Cold and hard. I have had pleasanter rides.' Corbett stared into the knight's weathered face, with its white, bushy brows above eyes that seemed still young, and neatly clipped moustache and beard. 'The king misses you,' he continued. 'He sends greetings and his good wishes to you and' – he turned to Gurney's wife – 'the Lady Alice.'

Alice, who was at least twenty years her husband's junior, came up and offered one soft hand for Corbett to kiss. He brushed her fingers gently and felt a slight tinge of embarrassment as she took his hand and pressed it a little too firmly.

'The same Hugh,' she said in her deep, rather husky voice.

Corbett caught the hint of mischief in her dark brown eyes. He catalogued to himself her still-perfect features – the warm, generous mouth, thin, finely etched nose, the neatly plucked eyebrows and the rich brown hair, now neat beneath a green and white wimple.

'Madame, you are as mischievous as ever,' he breathed.

He prayed Gurney would not take offence. Alice always

made a fuss of him. Corbett, constantly tongue-tied in the presence of beautiful women, never knew whether to be embarrassed or pleased. Ranulf-atte-Newgate had no such reservations. After Gurney had clasped his hand and greeted him with affectionate abuse, remarking that he looked as villainous as ever, Corbett's manservant sank to one knee to kiss Alice's hand. He held it so long that, bubbling with laughter, she pulled it away and walked back to her chair near the fireside.

'Nothing changes,' Gurney observed drily. 'You, Corbett, still as shy as a child in company.' He pushed two chairs between his and that of his wife. 'You, Ranulf, still with all the cheek of a travelling friar. Come on, your cloaks!'

He took them and threw them to a servant. Corbett and Ranulf unhitched their sword belts and hung them carefully on a hook on the wall.

Corbett and Ranulf eased themselves into the chairs, spread their feet and revelled in the fierce warmth from the log fire. A servant brought them posset in pewter goblets with white napkins wrapped round them as the claret had been spiced then heated by a red hot poker. Corbett sipped the wine slowly, savouring each drop as his legs and body thawed out. He felt warm, even drowsy, but did not want to disgrace himself by falling asleep. While Ranulf smacked his lips and crowed with delight, Corbett stared around the darkened solar. It was opulently furnished; woollen cloths and damask hangings covered the walls; the windows were glazed, some of them even tinted; the candelabra held pure beeswax lights – no tallow or cheap oil-lamps here. Corbett felt the carved wooden chair; oak or yew, he reflected, and the same was true of the cupboards and other chairs around the room. Underfoot, the carpets and rugs were of pure wool. As a pageboy hurried to remove his boots, Corbett looked up and saw the black, white and gold of the Gurney arms on a huge shield above the fireplace; beneath this, silver plate glinted and glowed in the candlelight.

Gurney threw another log on the fire. A small pouch of fragrant herbs had been pushed into a split in the log and, as the flames licked the wood, fumes from the hot herbs spread the aroma of summer across the room. Corbett tasted the wine, half-listening to Ranulf's chatter about their journey. On the opposite side of the hearth, Alice watched him closely.

You've changed, she thought. Corbett had always been secretive, taciturn and shy, but now she saw in him a certain hardness; the laughter lines around his mouth were not as pronounced as before and his dark eyes, usually so gentle, had a slightly haunted look.

Alice had heard about Corbett's second marriage to the Welsh princess Maeve and knew how deeply he loved both his wife and his daughter Eleanor. But she had also heard other rumours, of how iron-haired Edward was becoming a harder taskmaster now that he was waging bloody war against the Scots and deeply immersed in a life-and-death struggle with his rival, Philip of France. Corbett, despite his knighthood, his honours and his preferment, looked as if he was paying the price. Alice idly wondered what sights Corbett had seen. She caught his eye.

'Hugh, do you wish to sleep?'

'No, thank you, my lady. Perhaps later. There are matters to be seen to, questions to be asked.'

Alice felt her stomach lurch with fear. Corbett had been her friend. Now, with his sharp eyes, brooding thoughts and clever questions, he was here for other reasons. He would begin to ferret out the truth. Alice, despite the cloying warmth of the room, felt the cold prickle of fear on the nape of her neck. What would this subtle clerk discover? She caught her husband's eyes and gave him a warning look. He saw the glance and looked away. He, too, was apprehensive, fearful of Corbett's visit. All he had wanted was to be free of Edward's court and camp so that he could plough the fertile fields of his manor, raise sheep and export the wool to Flanders for heavy bags of gold. The king's campaigns against the French had stopped all that. Although at this moment Edward and Philip were technically at peace, in practice war still disrupted commerce. Gurney, like others, was suffering the consequences. Now Corbett was here, holder of the royal secrets and, if some men could be believed, custodian of the king's conscience.

'A bloody business!' Gurney blurted out the words before he could stop himself.

Corbett spread his hands out towards the flames and turned to him.

'What is?'

Gurney laughed sourly. 'Hugh, I am your friend. Don't play your subtle games with me.'

Corbett smiled an apology and inclined his head.

'A bloody business,' Gurney repeated. 'A woman found hanging on the gallows. A servant decapitated on the beach. Graves plundered. Stories of black magic, of fires at the crossroads, of strange noises at the dead of night, of demon hags riding the air. And now the bloody Pastoureaux!'

'A time of troubles indeed, Sir Simon.'

Corbett spun round. Lavinius Monck was leaning rather languidly against the door lintel, arms folded. Corbett rose and went towards him.

'Lavinius!' He stretched out his hand. 'It's been some months.'

Monck limply took Corbett's outstretched hand and patted it.

'My dear Hugh,' he lisped, though Lavinius's obsidian eyes never moved.

Corbett stepped back. Why do I always find this man so sinister, he thought? Lavinius, dressed now in black leather, always reminded Corbett of a cruel raven, with his black, greasy hair, smooth-shaven, sour face, beak of a nose and eyes which never seemed to close. Lavinius slapped his leather riding gloves from hand to hand and walked into the room.

'Sir Simon, Lady Alice.'

'You had a good day, Master Monck?'

Gurney got to his feet. From the set of his mouth and his dour look it seemed that he too disliked the secretive, sly clerk of John de Warenne, Earl of Surrey. Monck smiled, or rather twisted his face in a grimace, took off his cloak and threw it on a bench. He took a cup of posset from a servant and sat down in the chair another had pushed up to the half-circle in front of the fire. Monck crossed his legs arrogantly, flicking flecks of mud from his knee. He stared into the fire with an infuriating smile that suggested he was the guardian of some great secret. Gurney refilled his own cup from a jug of claret on one of the aumbries and rejoined his guests, shaking off his wife's warning touch.

'I asked you a question. Did you have a good day?'

Monck smiled and sipped from his cup.

'Sir Simon, for me every day is good. I have ridden around your estates. I have drunk some foul ale at the tavern in the village and I have listened.' His face grew hard. 'I will continue to listen and I will continue to hunt until I find the murderer of my servant Cerdic and see him or her dangling from that gibbet of yours on the cliff top!'

'And the Pastoureaux?' Alice asked.

'Crouching like rabbits,' Monck replied contemptuously. 'They never seem to leave their Hermitage. And you, dearest Hugh, your journey?'

'Hard and cold. The King sends you his greetings, as does the Earl of Surrey.'

Monck moved in the chair, his leather jacket creaking. Corbett realized that the man, despite his heavy clothing, was impervious to the raw heat of the fire.

'And why are you here, Hugh?' Monck peered at Ranulf, who stared coldly back. 'Why do Sir Hugh Corbett, Keeper of the King's Secret Seal, and his loyal but rather lecherous servant Ranulf-atte-Newgate wander the wilds of Norfolk?'

Corbett stared into his cup. He really did hate this man. Lavinius Monck was the Earl of Surrey's principal clerk, spy and professional assassin. Trained in the halls of Cambridge, Monck had won a name for ruthlessness, unwavering loyalty and a cunning that would be the envy of any fox. If John de Warenne was the king's right hand then Monck was a dagger in that hand. Corbett usually kept well away from him, but sometimes, when necessity demanded it, they had to cooperate and share information.

'Why, Hugh?' Monck repeated with mock severity.

Corbett opened the wallet in his belt and brought out a small roll of parchment. Monck grabbed it greedily. He broke the purple wax seal, opened it, leaned forward and studied its contents by the light of the fire.

'Sealed by the king at Swaffham four days ago.' He looked up and grinned, his white, well-set teeth reminding Corbett of one of the king's hunting dogs. 'I see. You are sent to assist me.' He emphasized the phrase. 'Do you understand that, Sir Hugh?'

'I understand,' Corbett replied. 'But assist you in what, Lavinius?'

Monck shrugged, rolled the parchment up and slipped it up the sleeve of his leather jerkin. He leaned back, steepling his fingers, and stared into the fire.

'Ah!' he sighed. 'That's the problem, Sir Hugh. It's best if we each plough our own furrow. My Lord of Surrey was most insistent on that.'

'I thought you were here because of the Pastoureaux?' Gurney interrupted.

Monck smiled. 'Perhaps, Sir Simon, perhaps not. Only time will tell.'

Corbett steeled his features and sipped from the posset, kicking Ranulf gently on the ankle lest his angry-faced servant take up the cudgels on his behalf.

Gurney and his wife sat back in their chairs, Alice's eyes pleading with her husband to remain silent. Corbett tensed in fury. He couldn't abide Monck's smug secretiveness and he was angry with the king, who had despatched him here after telling him as little as possible. Corbett could hardly believe he was here because Monck's servant had been murdered or because a baker's wife had been hanged from a scaffold. The Pastoureaux, however, were a different matter. They were dangerous. His agents in France had reported how these fanatics, with their strange dreams and eerie visions, walked from city to city prophesying the end of the world and launching violent attacks upon Jews, foreigners and all of society's poor outcasts. Now groups of Pastoureaux, literally by the shipload, had arrived in England. Harmless at first, they lurked in the wild and waste places. The group here in Norfolk, however, had grown and attracted the attention of the royal commissioners and, ostensibly at least, Monck had been sent north to investigate.

Corbett shifted uneasily in the chair, ignoring the murmur of conversation that flowed around him. Monck, satisfied that he had emphasized his own importance, now indulged in easy conversation with his hosts about crops, village scandal and the licence to brew ale. Corbett studied the black-garbed clerk. Monck had one weakness – he liked his drink. He could drink claret, beer and ale as a horse munches grass, without any ill-effect. Corbett idly wondered if he, as the king's master spy, should spend some time studying Monck more closely, finding out more about his habits and perhaps discovering other weaknesses. Corbett smiled to himself – Maeve was always teasing him about his own secretiveness, his close scrutiny of the most minor information.

His smile faded. In this matter the king had been sly and secretive. What was Monck really doing here? One of Corbett's spies in the exchequer had reported that Monck had spent days at the Tower going through records and collecting information. That had been some six or seven weeks ago, soon after Michaelmas. Monck had then disappeared from London. Corbett had heard that he was in Norfolk but had dismissed it as unimportant – John de Warenne held estates here and Monck often acted as the earl's steward. Corbett half-closed his eyes. He rolled the cup between his fingers. Why the exchequer? God knows, the treasury was empty. Edward was desperate for money to keep his depleted fleet at sea and wage bloody war against the Scottish rebel William Wallace. Corbett flinched as Monck placed cold fingers on his hand.

'Hugh, Hugh, are you dreaming?'

The clerk rubbed his face and smiled apologetically across at Sir Simon.

'No, no. I'm tired.'

'Not too much, Hugh, I hope.' Gurney said. 'We have a dinner in your honour this evening. I have invited guests – Father Augustine, our village priest, and Dame Cecily, Prioress of the Holy Cross convent. Our physician, Selditch and my man Catchpole will also be there.'

'In which case . . .'

Corbett got to his feet just as Maltote, his hair tousled, his face heavy with sleep, burst into the room and gazed beseechingly at Corbett.

'Master, I am sorry, I did not know you had arrived. I went upstairs and fell asleep.'

Corbett smiled at the man's innocent, open face.

'Don't worry, Maltote.'

Corbett signalled to Ranulf to collect their boots and cloaks. He bowed at the others and allowed Gurney's steward to lead them up the winding staircase to their chamber. Maltote, still heavy with sleep, found it difficult to cope with Ranulf's teasing and without the steward's guidance would not have been able to find his own way back to the chamber they were to share. The steward explained that the house was so full of visitors and guests it was difficult to find a room for everyone. Corbett thanked him, slipped a coin into the fellow's hand and quietly closed the door behind him.

The room contained three beds with thick mattresses and heavy bolsters, probably of swan feather. Woollen rugs were strewn across the wooden floor and so many candles were lit that the chamber reminded Corbett of a church. After his gruelling journey, Corbett found it warm, sweet-smelling and comfortable. A chest stood at the foot of each bed, a large cupboard against the wall. There were two wall-paintings. One was of Christ arguing with Satan, done in brilliant, vivid colours so that in the flickering candelight the black demon seemed to writhe before Christ. The other was more restful; it was of a young lady working on a piece of tapestry beneath a window which looked out on to a light blue sea.

Ranulf and Maltote were already chatting. They sat on the edge of a bed, bemoaning the cold, wild emptiness of the countryside. The servants had already unpacked their saddlebags. Corbett's chancery pouch was, of course, untouched – it was buckled and secured with his personal seal. Corvett walked across the room and unfastened the shutters on one of the windows. There was a small, opening panel in the leaded glass. Ignoring Ranulf's protests, Corbett pushed it open, allowing the cold night air to seep in. The window must have overlooked the cliffs, for he could hear the faint murmur of the sea. The mist parted. He caught a glimpse of water and heard the faint cry of gulls. He closed the window against the cold, just as a huge moth, attracted by the light, fluttered in.

'Why are we here, Master? I mean, why are we really here?' Ranulf spoke up for himself and Maltote.

'I don't know,' Corbett replied. 'All I know is that the king and John de Warenne have some secret stratagem, that is why Monck is here. But time will tell.' He stared at the leaden-paned glass. 'It will be dark in London. Maeve will still be at table. Uncle Morgan will be singing his heart out.'

Corbett chewed his lip. Maeve's uncle had come for a few weeks and stayed almost a year. The boisterous Welsh lord was for ever on the move, drinking in the scenes of London as well as every pot of ale on offer. He'd then stagger home to take his great-niece, the baby Eleanor, and sing her to sleep with some Welsh lullaby.

'I should be there,' Corbett said only half aloud.

'What was that, Master?'

Corbett, not bothering to turn, shook his head. Ranulf pulled a face and winked at Maltote.

'Old Master Long Face,' he whispered, 'is in one of his moods!'

For once, Ranulf was correct. Corbett was worried. He had spent too much time away from Maeve and his daughter. Oh, his wife could more than cope. She ran their business affairs with a shrewdness that made her the terror of every merchant and the manor at Leighton was rich and prosperous in its crops. But the king was growing old, his moods becoming more sharp and cruel. And when he died, what then? Would the Prince of Wales, with his love of hunting, music and handsome young men, still need Corbett's services? The war with France would end – the Prince of Wales was already betrothed to Philip IV's daughter Isabella. In Scotland, Wallace would be beaten – it was only a matter of time before the king's troops hunted him down and either killed him or brought him south for execution.

Perhaps, Corbett thought, I should leave the royal service now – follow the example of Gurney and retire to my manor, raising crops and tending sheep, and turn merchant and sell the wool to the looms of Flanders. He smiled to himself. When he had said as much to Maeve, she had shrieked with laughter, falling back on to the bolsters, her silver hair fanned out around her. She had giggled so much Corbett couldn't even kiss her quiet. 'You a farmer!' she'd teased him. 'I can just imagine that. You'd be drawing reports up on what the rams were doing, how the apples grew and whether the orchard was in the best place.'

'Sometimes I tire of my job,' Corbett had replied heatedly.

Maeve had sobered up. She lay in the four-poster bed, hugging the blankets around her.

'You don't like your job, Hugh? You may hate the tasks the king assigns you but perhaps that's what makes you so good at it?' She leaned over and took her husband's dark face in her hands. 'Whatever you say, Hugh Corbett, you have a hunger for the truth and . . .'

'And what?' Corbett had asked.

Maeve had giggled.

'As Ranulf says, a very long face!'

Corbett looked up as the moth beat against the window pane.

'It's very dark,' he muttered. 'God knows when we will see the light again.'

Ranulf looked at him strangely. He wondered whether his master was talking about the weather or the mysteries that now confronted them.

Chapter 2

Marina was running for her life, eyes wide, heart pounding, mouth dry. The icy gorse caught her legs and clutched at the brown robe she wore. She stopped, chest heaving, cursing the mist. She stared round like a frightened doe.

'Where can I go?' she moaned to herself.

The mist closed in more thickly around her. She crouched on all-fours, sobbing for breath. She had to get to safety. She squatted like an animal, ears straining into the darkness. An owl hunting over the flat headlands made its sombre cry and a vixen prowling near the village yipped in frustration at the mist-covered sky.

The young woman licked dry lips. Where could she go? The villagers would drive her out. Father Augustine? He would only shout at her. Perhaps she should go back to the Hermitage! She might get help there, if she told her friends what she knew. But which way? She looked around, vividly remembering her younger days when she and the other village children used to play along the cliff tops pretending to be elves or fairy queens. They would close their eyes and build make-believe palaces. But what could she do now? She moved forward, then froze as a twig snapped behind her.

'Marina!' a soft voice called. 'Marina!'

She could stand it no longer. She ran blindly, not caring whether she blundered into pool or marsh. As long as she ran she was safe. The ground beneath her feet, however, seemed to take on a life of its own. The briars and brambles clutched like cruel sharp fingernails at her ankles. She saw a light beckoning and could have shouted with joy. Her legs were growing heavy. She ran, but a bramble bush caught her ankle like a noose. She crashed to the hard, cold ground. She was beginning to scramble to her feet when she heard the soft footfall behind her. She half-turned, but the garrotte tightened around her neck.

The loud knocking of the steward summoned Corbett and his two companions down to the manor hall. Gurney's servants had laid the great table down the centre of the room. They'd covered it with green samite cloth and judiciously placed two-branched candlesticks to provide soft pools of light. The place smelt sweet – aromatic herbs had been placed in small pots beneath the table and scattered on the roaring fire and on the small capped braziers that stood in each corner. On the floor lay some of the most luxurious rugs Corbett had ever seen. Costly Turkey cloth, emblazoned pennants and bright banners hung from the hammer-beam roof. The air was thick with fragrant odours from the nearby kitchen and buttery. Instead of the usual hard-baked traunchers and pewter spoons, silver plates, golden knives and jewel-encrusted condiment pots decorated the table.

Gurney and his wife had changed. Alice now wore a murrey-coloured dress whose high collar emphasized her swan-like neck; a gold cord bound her slim waist and a thick white gauze wimple, circled by a silver cord, hid her beautiful hair. Sir Simon was dressed in a russet gown with green hose and brown leather boots. The gown was slashed with green silk on either side of the chest, the sleeves were puffed out with dark-blue taffeta. Corbett hoped he and his party would pass muster. He felt rather dowdy in his dark-brown gown till he glimpsed Monck who, as usual, was dressed completely in black.

Servants ushered them to their seats. The steward blew on a silver horn and, while minstrels played on the gallery at the far end of the hall, Gurney's retainers began to serve the meal. First the steward brought the great silver salt cellar, bowing three times to his master before placing it in the centre of the table. After him came the pantler, with trays of white manchet loaves. He was followed by the cupbearer carrying a great, two-handled ewer brimming with wine which he tasted and placed in front of his master. Gurney and his guests washed their hands in bowls of rose water, wiping them quickly with the towels on the servants' arms. Only then did Gurney introduce his other guests. Father Augustine was a tall, youngish-looking priest with sandy hair and pale face. He had a sharp, green eyes and a slightly bent nose over thin lips and a firm chin. He gave Corbett the impression of quiet authority. The prioress, Dame Cecily, was small and fat, her round face framed by a heavily starched white wimple and a grey-blue, gold-edged veil. A merry soul, Corbett considered, with her dimpled cheeks, small chin and retroussé nose. But her dark eyes were small and shrewd and her mouth firm and Corbett quietly concluded that she could be as commanding as any lord in the convent she ruled. Finally there was Adam Catchpole, Gurney's principal henchman, a veteran of the old king's wars – a hard-bitten, taciturn man with eyes like flint and a face hewn out of granite. Catchpole kept scratching his close-cropped, greying hair and played with the silver plate and knife as if he felt uneasy in such opulent surroundings.

Once the introductions were over, Gurney rapped the table and invited Father Augustine to say grace. The priest delivered it in a high nasal voice. Corbett noticed Father Augustine's command of Latin – he said the prayer smoothly without a second thought. The servants came in and served beef and mutton cooked with olives; broiled venison, the flesh sweetened with brown sugar and flavoured with lemon juice, cinnamon and ginger; and chickens spit-roasted and stuffed with grapes. All the time the servants kept filling the goblet beside each guest. Corbett sipped his wine carefully, though Ranulf and Maltote ate and drank as if there was no tomorrow.

At first the conversation was general. Monck, sitting restlessly beside Corbett, drummed his fingers on the table top. After a few minutes he raised his goblet and looked at Gurney sitting in his high-backed chair.

'Sir Simon, your hospitality is magnificent but tomorrow Sir Hugh and I have business on your estates!'

Gurney put down his own goblet, biting back his annoyance.

'You mean the Pastoureaux? '

His words stilled all conversation.

'Yes, the Pastoureaux.'

'But why now? You have seen them before,' Gurney said.

'I have studied them from afar,' Monck replied. 'And spoken to their leader, Master Joseph. I have never been into the Hermitage.' He smirked and glanced sideways at Corbett. 'Perhaps tomorrow Sir Hugh could change all this?'

'Why are you interested in them?'

Father Augustine leaned forward, chewing carefully on a small morsel of chicken. He had eaten and drunk sparely and so far contributed little to the conversation.

'Why shouldn't I be?' Monck snapped. 'Who else would kill my man Cerdic? I also wager they had a hand in the death of the baker's wife.'

'What proof do you have?' Father Augustine asked.

'Well, someone killed them!' The voice came from the doorway, where a bald-headed, red-faced man of middle years stood, pulling back the cowl of his gown.

Gurney's face broke into a smile as he got to his feet.

'Giles, welcome!'

He beckoned to his steward to pull up another chair and lay a place for the new arrival, who sat down and immediately grabbed a small loaf of bread, hungrily tearing off chunks and popping them into his mouth. He swallowed hard and bowed towards Gurney.

'My apologies,' he spluttered between mouthfuls, 'but babies have the habit of being born at the most ungodly hours.'

'You have been to the village?'

'Yes and I thought I would never make my way back through the mist.'

Gurney clapped his hands softly. 'My apologies, Hugh. May I introduce Master Giles Selditch, family friend and physician. He resides here at the manor, more for my health than his.'

'Tush, man.' The doctor teased back. 'Who else would look after an old physician like myself? Sir Hugh, you come from London?'

'Aye, sir.'

'What news do you bring?' Alice smiled down the table at

Selditch. 'Whose child has been born?'

'The Reeve's. A lusty baby boy. I think they'll have it baptized Simon as a mark of respect to your husband.'

'And the mother?'

'Riccalda. A little weak but her husband's newly found wealth will make sure she is given the best food.'

The physician's words created a stillness as if he had touched upon a sensitive point.

'We were talking about the Pastoureaux,' Monck said abruptly. 'Master Giles, do you have anything to do with them?'

Selditch rested back in his chair and spread his hands.

'A little and, as I've told you before, I can only judge by what I see. I have taken medicines to them – pots of herbs, ointments, a number of poultices.'

'And?' Monck glanced slyly at Corbett. 'Come, educate our new arrivals!'

'They seem God-fearing, quiet people. Their leader is Master Joseph, but the real organizer is Philip Nettler.'

'So, you agree with their creed?' Dame Cecily's tone made it clear that her question was important to her.

The physician shrugged and sipped from his goblet.

'It is, perhaps, different from yours, my lady.'

'But there's men and women together?' The prioress widened her eyes.

'In France,' Selditch replied, 'such houses are common. A group of brothers in one building, a group of sisters in the other.' He laughed and popped a grape into his mouth. 'Sometimes they meet and sometimes they don't.'

'They seem gentle enough to me,' Father Augustine interrupted. 'I have said Mass at the Hermitage on a number of occasions. The Pastoureaux dress simply in brown robes and sandals. They beg for alms and live on the donations given to them. For the rest, they seem to pray and talk a lot.'

'How many are there?' Corbett asked.

The priest pulled a face.

'The number changes as some arrive, some leave, but at any one time no more than fourteen or sixteen.'

Corbett toyed with his wine cup.

'How long have the Pastoureaux been here?' he asked Gurney.

'About sixteen months. Master Joseph and his able lieutenant Philip Nettler came here at the beginning of autumn. They discovered the old Hermitage and asked if they could live there, promising to be no threat to me or mine.' Gurney shrugged. 'So I allowed them to stay. They grow their own herbs and tend a few chickens and pigs. I went there in the early days and saw nothing untoward. They have a makeshift chapel and a communal refectory. When the weather is good, they go along the highways and beg.'

'And the villagers?'

'At first they were suspicious. The Pastoureaux, however, particularly Master Joseph and Philip Nettler, proved themselves to be honest and hard-working, so the villagers accepted them. Some of the young men and women from the village have joined the Pastoureaux and travelled on—'

'Travelled on?' Ranulf interrupted. 'My lord, why should they travel?'

Alice answered him. 'They have a vision,' she said. 'They believe Christ's return is imminent. So, when they have been purified and prepared, they travel to Hull or one of the other ports from where they take ship to Outremer. According to Master Joseph, they are to assemble near the Mount of Olives, where Christ will soon come again in a chariot of fire.'

'And they believe all that?' Ranulf mocked.

'Why shouldn't they?' Alice said. 'I believe there are similar movements all over Europe?'

'But no one questions all this?' Ranulf insisted.

'The Pastoureaux also come to me,' Dame Cecily told him. 'We give them cloth, wine and food. In return they work on our estate, in our gardens and orchards, as they do for Sir Simon. Their community is a changing one, but the young men and women seem full of hope. They stay for a few weeks at the Hermitage, for what Father Joseph calls the period of purification, then he or Master Philip takes them to the nearest port. They are given money, a warrant, a change of clothing, some food, and off they sail.' She shrugged. 'They seem honest enough. They hold everything in common and anything they earn is put into the community treasury.'

She smiled at Ranulf and the manservant glimpsed the lechery in the prioress's eyes.

A hot one there, he thought, and smiled to himself – perhaps a visit to the good canonesses might not go amiss. Ranulf often boasted to Maltote, 'I was born a villain and I can smell villains'. Well, he had smelled them tonight and, as he held the prioress's glance, Ranulf fleetingly wondered what old Master Long Face thought of it all.

'And the women travel abroad as well?' Corbett asked.

'Why shouldn't they?' Father Augustine asked. 'What's a young girl's lot in a peasant village? Hard work, marriage to some lout? Half-dead with child-bearing by the time she's reached her twentieth summer. It's not much better for the young men, they're either chained to the plough or sent off to the king's wars in Scotland.'

'I don't like them,' Adam Catchpole interjected. He carefully placed his thick, muscular arms on the table top. 'I don't like Philip Nettler or even the saintly Master Joseph. They are both idle buggers! I come from a village something like this.' His harsh voice suddenly rose. 'I've seen these movements before! They tell the simpletons that Jerusalem is round the corner or over the brow of the next hill. It never is!' He stared at Corbett. 'And you know that, don't you, Sir Hugh? Otherwise you and Master Monck would not be here.'

'In a way, yes,' Corbett replied quietly. He paused as a servant refilled his goblet. 'The Pastoureaux,' he went on 'originated in France. The name means Shepherds. They were organized some fifty years ago by a renegade monk called Jacob who assumed the strange title Master of Hungary.' Corbett sipped from his goblet. 'According to reports, Jacob claimed to have been told in a vision to organize the poor, like the shepherds of Bethlehem, and send them to the Holy Land to await Christ's return. Unfortunately, he attracted all society's human flotsam and jetsam – apostate clerics, prostitutes, thieves, murderers and wolfsheads. Jacob divided them into companies and, instead of marching to Jerusalem, they began to live off the land like mercenaries. Some who opposed them were cut down by the axe; others, particularly clerics, were stabbed to death or drowned in rivers. These Pastoureaux attacked the Jews and, within years, had decided that their principal task was to wipe out all clerics – priests, bishops, even the pope himself – and found a new Church. Then the movement spread across the Rhine to England. Each group of Pastoureaux is different. Some are violent. Others, like the group at the Hermitage, are peaceful – they lead a simple life and lift their hands against no man. However' – Corbett looked across the table at Father Augustine – the king is concerned. He does not wish to harass innocent people, but a similar group of

Pastoureaux, at Shoreham in Sussex, organized an affray in which a royal official was killed.' He shrugged. 'Hence our arrival at Hunstanton.'

'I still think that those at the Hermitage are trouble-makers,' Catchpole spoke up. 'Far too many strange things have happened in the area since they arrived.'

'Such as?' Ranulf asked in mock innocence, nudging Maltote, who had drunk so much wine he was beginning to fall asleep.

Catchpole was also drunk; his hard face was flushed and he beat his fist gently on the table top. 'Must I speak for everybody?' he asked. He thrust forward a raised hand, thumb up. 'We've had graves robbed, haven't we, Father Augustine?'

The priest nodded solemnly.

'What do you mean?' Corbett asked.

'Graves in our churchyard have been disturbed,' the priest said. 'Coffins buried for years have been dragged to the surface and hacked up, their contents strewn about like offal from a butcher's yard. God knows who does it! Perhaps witches, Lords of the Crossroads, Masters of the Black Sabbath or whatever they call themselves. Sir Simon and I have both organized watches, but the perpetrators have never been caught.' Father Augustine sighed deeply. 'I have warned my parishioners that, if we catch the blasphemers responsible, I will excommunicate them with bell, book and candle!'

'There've been other happenings as well,' Catchpole interrupted. 'I've seen ships coming close inshore at night, lanterns winking. Signals to someone, but God knows who.'

'Do you think the Pastoureaux are involved in that?' Selditch asked.

'In the autumn,' Catchpole continued, ignoring the

question, 'when the evenings were fair, I went out on the headlands. I saw the ships, or rather their lights, but could see no answering signal from the land!'

'But the Pastoureaux never leave their enclosure at night,' Father Augustine asserted. 'These are smugglers.' He smiled apologetically at Gurney. 'No offence, Sir Simon, but the coast is rife with them. Ships from Boston, Bishop's Lynn, Ipswich and Yarmouth. There's a thriving trade. Nonetheless Master Catchpole is right. Strange things do happen here,' – he looked slyly along the table at the prioress – 'such as the death of a member of your community, Dame Cecily.'

The prioress pursed her lips and looked down her nose, as if she did not wish to discuss the matter.

'One of your sisters?' Corbett enquired.

'Aye,' Monck added maliciously. 'It would appear that Dame Agnes, treasurer of the convent was accustomed to taking walks at night along the headland. Apparently she slipped and fell to her death on the rocks below.'

'And, of course,' Selditch interposed, 'there are the murders.' His flushed face and sparkling eyes showed how much he was relishing this litany of disasters. He might perhaps have said more, but at that moment the steward blew his silver horn and the servants brought to the table apples roasted in brown sugar, flavoured with cinnamon and covered with a thick, rich cream as well as plates of sweetmeats, comfits and marchpanes. As Gurney's other guests chattered amongst themselves Ranulf nudged his master. 'A pretty pottage,' he whispered. 'Who would think, Master, that such a collection of notables would have so much to hide?'

Dame Cecily was straining her ears to overhear them so Corbett simply shook his head in reply. But I am not surprised, he thought, staring across the table. Wherever there is wealth, power and the human heart you will find all sorts of crimes, misdemeanours, and sordid affairs. At the king's court high-born wives sold themselves for favours and high-ranking clerics hid in their love-nests a sweet girl or a fresh-faced boy with soft hands and plump buttocks.

At last the servants withdrew. Gurney tried to divert the conversation by asking Corbett about the progress of the war in Scotland, but Selditch, full of wine and mischief, steered the conversation back to the recent murders.

'The murder of the baker's wife,' he said challengingly, 'is a mystery that will tax even you, Sir Hugh.'

'I shall advise Sir Hugh about that and the other deaths in my own time,' Lavinius Monck warned quietly.

'Tush! Tush!' said Selditch. 'It's a macabre mystery. Here is the good wife, a pretty young thing – flaxen-haired and full-bosomed, with generous hips and a mouth like an angel's. She slips out of the house at dusk, leaving her husband behind, saddles their one and only horse and rides out along the headland. The next morning her corpse is found dangling from the old gallows.'

'Giles, stop it!' Alice commanded.

'No! No!' Selditch held up his hand. 'The mystery, Sir Hugh, is that, although the ground beneath the scaffold was wet and muddy, no hoof prints were found of a horse other than her own. And villagers saw the lady riding back to the village, though only the horse made its way all the way home to the baker's shop.'

'Is that correct?' Corbett asked.

'Yes, yes.' Monck snapped. The evidence seems to show that the baker's wife went out to the scaffold and hanged herself and then, somehow or other, rode her horse back to the edge of the village.'

'Then there's the death of your man,' the physician added slyly.

'Ah, yes, poor Cerdic.' Monck gave a sour smile. 'He left here late in the afternoon. The next morning his decapitated corpse was found on the beach, his head impaled on a pole. Again there were no footprints or hoof marks and no signs of violence.'

'Enough!' Gurney rapped the table top and looked warningly down at Selditch. 'Hugh, you left the king at Swaffham?'

'Yes. He and the court were to move on to the Virgin's shrine at Walsingham.'

'And afterwards?'

'The king may stay in the area or he may travel on to Norwich or Lincoln.'

Catching the pleading look in Gurney's eyes, Corbett turned the conversation away from the murders and on to the gossip of the courts. But Selditch, however, was not so easily put off. Ranulf made the mistake of commenting on the physician's ink-stained fingers. Selditch held them up admiringly.

'Oh, yes,' he said. 'I am more of a scholar than a leech. I seek learning' – he preened himself – 'rather than gold.' He smiled coyly at Corbett. 'The king should be careful in these parts,' he said.

Monck sighed in exasperation.

'Why is that?' Corbett asked.

'Don't you know your history, Sir Hugh? The king's grandfather, John, crossed these lands with his army. He was fleeing from his barons with his treasure loaded on sumpter ponies. He attempted to take a short cut across the Wash near the river Nene, but the tide came in rapidly. The king and his lords escaped but the treasure was lost together with its guards and all the sumpter ponies.'

Corbett smiled. He could tell by the look on the faces of the others that Selditch's airing of his knowledge was a constant source of vexation.

The meal drew to an end. Dame Cecily apologized but said she had to return to the convent and Gurney offered servants to escort her. Father Augustine accepted an invitation to stay the night. Alice withdrew with the thanks and plaudits of her guests ringing in her ears. Gurney escorted Dame Cecily out. The rest pushed back their chairs, accepting the servants' offer to refill their cups. Corbett whispered to Ranulf that he should take the now sleeping Maltote up to their chamber. Once they'd gone, Monck grinned sourly at Corbett.

'A penny for your thoughts, Sir Hugh. Or shall I tell them for you, eh?'

Corbett glanced across the table at Father Augustine, then at Selditch, who sat in his chair cradling his cup like some fat, cheerful goblin.

'Tell me,' Corbett murmured.

'A pretty mess.' Monck replied.

'Why was your servant killed?' he asked directly.

'I don't know,' Monck replied. 'But I blame the Pastoureaux. Cerdic was not the most talkative of men but he was eager as a ferret in searching out gossip. One thing I have established is that he visited the good sisters at the convent. Dame Cecily says that it was only a courtesy call and that Cerdic left just before dusk. Where he went then, or how his decapitated corpse came to be on the beach, I simply don't know.'

'What happened to his horse?' Corbett asked.

'God knows! We never found it. But Father Augustine is

right. This countryside is a nest of thieves, smugglers, horse-copers and tricksters. Perhaps we should recommend to the king that he send his justices in Eyre to turn over a few stones and squash whatever crawls out.'

'Is that really necessary?' Selditch snapped. 'Sir Simon is a loyal subject of the Crown. He maintains the king's peace on his lands, but he cannot be held responsible for every one of his tenants or, indeed, for the Pastoureaux.'

'He allowed them to settle here,' Monck jibed.

'And they have done no wrong,' Selditch replied flatly.

'The baker's wife?' Corbett tactfully intervened. 'What was her name?'

'Fourbour, Amelia Fourbour. The poor thing now lies buried in our churchyard, though whether she's allowed to rest in peace is another matter.'

'Did you view the corpse?' Corbett asked Selditch.

'Yes, I did. She died by hanging.'

'No mark of any other violence.'

'Such as?'

'Was she struck on the head? Were her hands pinioned?'

'No.' Selditch smiled sadly. 'She was brought to the death house and I examined her. Some of the villagers believed she committed suicide. They said a stake should be driven through her heart and she should be buried under the scaffold.'

'Harsh words for a poor woman,' Corbett observed.

'Amelia was not local born, she was pretty and she had her airs and graces. And tell me, Sir Hugh, have you ever met a popular baker?'

Corbett smiled and shrugged.

'Fourbour's no different,' Selditch continued. 'What he makes others have to buy. With a pretty wife too he was hardly the most popular man in Hunstanton.'

'Could it have been suicide?' Corbett asked.

'Perhaps. I viewed the woman's corpse from head to toe. I examined the back of her head but found no contusion. And I found no sign of any opiate or poison.'

'Nonetheless you think it was murder?'

'I don't know, of course,' Selditch said. 'But why should a pretty young woman hang herself? Father Augustine asked the same question of his parishioners and, thankfully, Amelia now lies buried in God's acre.'

'Yet,' Monck interrupted, 'no one else was at the scaffold. No marks of violence, no hoof prints of another horse or boot marks, were detected.'

Selditch stirred in his chair. 'That is true. But if it was suicide why should someone ride a horse back to the edge of the village, sitting sidesaddle as if it were poor Amelia?'

'You think it was the murderer who rode the horse back? ' Corbett asked.

'Yes, I do.'

The physician's eyes narrowed and Corbett realized that, despite his bluff manner Giles Selditch was a shrewd man, and one not easily swayed by popular opinion.

'Who saw the horse return?' Corbett asked.

'Two villagers. They recognized the baker's horse. The rider was sitting sidesaddle. Of course, it was dark and the villagers stood aside, lowering their eyes because, as I have said, neither the baker nor his wife was popular in the village.'

'Where was this?' Corbett asked.

'On the trackway just outside Hunstanton. But, before you ask,' Selditch continued, 'by the time the horse entered the village the mysterious rider had disappeared. That's why we think it's murder.' Selditch smiled at the priest. 'I thank you for your support, Father. If it had not been for you, those ignorant buggers would have desecrated the poor woman's corpse even further.'

'Don't be so harsh,' the priest said. 'Hunstanton is an isolated place and its people live in each other's pockets. What happens in one house is soon known in another. But they are a close and secretive people. I have been here, oh, almost two years, and I am still not fully accepted.'

'So, you are not from these parts, Father?'

'No, no, I am not. I was born and raised in Bishop's Lynn.' The priest smiled sourly. 'His Grace the Bishop of Norwich has sent me here for my sins. Now, I really must retire . . .'

Monck got to his feet. He stretched till his muscles cracked and yawned loudly. Father Augustine rose also. Corbett, heavy-eyed, bade both of them good night and went up to his own chamber. Ranulf and Maltote lay on their beds snoring blissfully. Corbett pulled a rug over each of them then went and stood by the window. He stared out into the misty, cold night.

'Strange murders,' he murmured. 'People with secrets.' He remembered the physician's ink-stained fingers. I must talk to Selditch,' he muttered. 'He seems to know the secrets of these parts.'

He undressed hurriedly and slipped into his own bed. He pulled the blankets high – despite the merrily spluttering charcoal braziers the room felt cold. Before he drifted into sleep he reflected that it was more than just an investigation into the Pastoureaux that had brought Monck to Hunstanton.

Chapter 3

Corbett was awakened early by the tolling of the manor bell. This also roused the servants, the signal for the daily life of the manor to begin again. Corbett rose and threw a blanket around his shoulders as a servant knocked on the door and brought in large, steaming earthenware jars of hot water to fill the basins and laid out fresh napkins and towels. Once he'd left, Corbett shouted at Maltote and Ranulf to rouse themselves and hastily shaved and washed. Then he broke the seals of his chancery bag and set out his writing instruments on the table. His two companions were hard to wake, so Corbett pulled aside the shutters of the window and opened the small casement. The cold morning air seeped in. Ranulf and Maltote staggered out of bed cursing and muttering. Corbett, however, ignored them and stared through the window. The mist still lingered.

Corbett felt more comfortable and relaxed than the night before. He finished dressing; he made sure he wore long, thick, woollen hose and a brown, serge gown over his shirt tied at the neck and cuffs. He pulled on Spanish leather riding boots, took his military coat and a quilted pair of gloves. He recalled the mysteries of the night before and wrapped his sword belt around him, telling Ranulf and Maltote to do the same.

'Hurry up!' he barked. 'We must leave early!'

He ignored Ranulf's mutterings and went out into the gallery, where a servant took him down to the manor chapel – a small, white-washed room, black-timbered with a simple altar under the window. Father Augustine had already begun to say Mass. Gurney was there with his henchman Catchpole. Afterwards they went down to the hall, colder and not so welcoming as the night before. There they were joined by the others, including Ranulf and Maltote still heavy-eyed with sleep and glowering at their master. Alice was still abed but Selditch came down, chattering as merrily as the night before. Servants brought them ale, freshly baked bread and strips of meat heavily coated with malt. Corbett urged Ranulf and Maltote to break their fast quickly.

'I'll take you to the Hermitage,' Gurney offered.

Monck insisted on going with them, although Gurney argued that Catchpole's presence would provide sufficient protection.

The physician and the priest also wanted to go – 'Just in case,' Selditch said, glancing quickly at Gurney.

Corbett studied both men closely. They seemed friendly enough to him, but a little more guarded than on the previous evening and he wondered what they had to hide. Monck remained as taciturn as ever; he tapped his leather gloves against his thigh, impatient to move on. A groom announced that their horses were ready and they swung their cloaks about them and went out into the yard. The sun, surprisingly strong for November, was burning up the mist. Corbett looked back at the old manor with its dressed-stone ground floor and half-timbered upper storeys.

'How old is Mortlake?' he asked.

'It dates from before the Conqueror's time,' Gurney replied, 'but my great-grandfather pulled the Saxon house down and rebuilt it, using the best stone and finest oak.'

Corbett stared appreciatively. Mortlake Manor was a long, rectangular building well defended by a curtain wall within which was a small village of barns, stables and smithies.

'And the land?' he asked.

Gurney grinned. 'It extends as far as you can ride, but some of the soil is salt-soaked, though further inland it yields good crops. However, it's the sheep that make us rich. But come!'

The rest had already mounted their horses. Ranulf and Maltote were trying to hide their smiles at the sight of the fat physician being bundled into the saddle and Father Augustine looked decidedly ill-at-ease on a rather sorry-looking roan. Corbett and Gurney mounted. The gates were thrown open and they followed the trackway out of the manor and across the moors. In the distance, Corbett could hear the thunder of the surf. Now and again rabbits, startled by the hoofbeats, darted across the gorse in a flurry of fur; short, fat-tailed sheep scattered, bleating, before the horses. The mist was still thick and Gurney shouted to them to keep together. At one time they had to rein in as he led them around a small, weed-fringed marsh.

'It's treacherous country,' he said from the depths of his cowl. 'Hugh, be wary where you go. Try and keep to the paths. The same applies to the beach. The tides are fickle. Sometimes they come in slowly like the night, at others they will rush in to catch the unwary.'

'Which is the point of my story last night,' Physician Selditch spoke up. 'The whole coastline of the Wash is treacherous. Sudden tidal surges can make trickling streams into full-grown rivers, as King John found to his cost.'

'Was the gold never recovered?' Ranulf asked, intrigued by the prospect of a royal treasure lying nearby, waiting to be discovered.

'There are many legends,' Selditch replied. 'Some say that beneath Sir Simon's land a royal ransom waits to be collected.'

He broke off as they cleared the marsh and Gurney urged them forward. Corbett realized that Gurney was leading them further inland, along a well-beaten path; they were travelling south, keeping the coast to their left. He pushed his horse alongside Gurney's.

'What is the Hermitage?' he asked.

'It's really an old farmstead, a small outlying manor. The soil around it is rather poor. In my father's time it fell derelict. Sometimes it was used by shepherds and the people of the roads, travelling friars, anyone.'

'And why did you give it to the Pastoureaux?'

Gurney pulled back his cowl and wiped the sweat from his brow.

'Why not? They seem God-fearing and hurt no one.' He smiled. 'No, don't think of me as a saint, Hugh. In return they provide free labour on my farms.' He pointed through the shifting mist. 'See the light, we are almost there.'

Gurney broke into a gallop. The mist, as if expecting them, suddenly cleared and the Hermitage came into full view. However, as Gurney reined in, all Corbett could see was a high wall, a stout oaken gate and, above this, a tiled roof and the thatch of other dwellings.

'Who goes there?' a voice called.

Corbett, squinting his eyes, saw a man standing on one of the gate pillars. A tinder was struck and a torch flared.

'Who goes there?' the voice repeated.

Gurney gestured to his companions to stay still as he edged his own horse forward.

'Sir Simon Gurney!' he shouted, standing up in the stirrups, 'with the king's emissary, Sir Hugh Corbett.'

'Wait there!' the voice called.

The figure put the torch down and disappeared. Corbett urged his own horse forward.

'But, Sir Simon, you said this was your land and property?'

Gurney shrugged. 'Yes, but I gave the Pastoureaux the same rights as any other religious house. You just can't ride in as you please. Don't forget, Hugh, the countryside is plagued with wolfsheads and outlaws who would help themselves to anything – food, drink, not to mention any woman under sixty!'

He stopped speaking as the gates swung open. Two men came through and walked towards them. Corbett watched them curiously.

'The older one,' Gurney whispered, 'is Master Joseph. The other is Philip Nettler, the abbot and prior, you might say, of the house.'

The two men drew near. Master Joseph was about fifty, rather small, with a sun-tanned face and light-blue eyes which crinkled as he smiled at Gurney and bowed towards Corbett. Sharp-eyed, Corbett thought – he looked more like a military commander than a cleric. Philip Nettler, the younger man, had black tousled hair, a thin narrow face, hooded eyes and tight lips. He seemed more wary, and his eyes strayed beyond Corbett to where Monck sat like the figure of death on his horse.

Master Joseph smiled up at Gurney. 'Good morrow, Sir Simon.'

'This is the king's emissary here, Sir Hugh Corbett,' Gurney said.

Master Joseph stretched out his hand to Corbett, who clasped it. It was smooth and warm.

'And may I introduce Master Philip.'

Again Corbett shook hands, but this time he felt a slight unease. Nettler's face was guarded and he refused to meet Corbett's eyes.

'The king's emissary, Sir Hugh?' Master Joseph voiced his companion's concern. 'Why are you here? You've not come to interfere or move us on?'

Corbett smiled and shook his head.

'Master Joseph, you are blunt so I'll be equally honest in return. The bishops are concerned about any new communities and have conveyed their anxieties to the king. He is' – Corbett chose his words carefully – 'interested in what you do, though at the moment more intrigued by the recent deaths in the area.'

'Aye, I thought so.' Master Joseph's voice suddenly betrayed a country burr.

'We have nothing to do with those.' Nettler spoke up, his voice high, rather waspish. 'Sir Simon knows we keep ourselves to ourselves.'

Monck suddenly urged his horse forward. 'Are we to stay here and freeze?' he asked.

'Sir Simon,' Master Joseph said flatly, 'you gave us the Hermitage and your solemn word that, as long as we lived here in peace, we had the right to say who came or left. We are an enclosed community. We cannot allow anyone, without a by-your-leave, to ride in and ride out.'

He stared at Gurney's other companions. Corbett saw the shift in attention and noticed a slight worry in the Pastoureaux leader's eyes when he caught sight of Ranulf.

Master Joseph, as though he had made up his mind, took a step back. 'Sir Simon, you are welcome, as always. So are Sir Hugh Corbett and Master Monck. Surely the others can wait outside?'

Gurney agreed, and he, Corbett and Monck rode forward, leaving Ranulf and Maltote to converse with an aggrieved Father Augustine and a rather disappointed Selditch. At the gates all three dismounted and followed Master Joseph and Nettler into the wide enclosure. Corbett stared around. It looked to him like any other small farm. There was a low one-storeyed house surrounded by a number of outhouses. Two dogs lay dozing at the entrance to a small barn near a well and some scrawny chickens pecked on the cobbles. He saw a small pig-sty and, on one side of the farmhouse, a small grassy hillock which probably served as a rabbit warren. Master Joseph followed his gaze.

'We are largely self-sufficient,' he said. 'We have plenty of water, we have fresh meat, and we grow our own herbs. Sir Simon pays us in cash or in kind for our work. And the sisters of the Holy Cross are generous to us, as are some of the more prosperous farmers.'

Corbett stared around. The place looked shabby yet well kept – the Pastoureaux had apparently worked hard to build their refuge.

'It's very quiet,' he said.

Then he heard the faint sounds of singing and Nettler pointed across to the farmhouse.

'The community is at prayer.'

'Then perhaps,' Monck said tartly, 'you should have allowed Father Augustine to enter.'

'The community rule is quite precise,' Master Joseph said.

'No more than three visitors are allowed at any one time. Father Augustine will understand.'

Corbett remembered the sour look on the priest's face and thought otherwise.

'You pray often?' he asked, tapping his feet on the ground and wondering if the Pastoureaux would take them in from the cold.

'Our rule is sweet but light,' Master Joseph replied.

Corbett looked quickly at him; he was sure he detected a note of sarcasm in the man's voice.

'What we do,' Master Joseph continued hurriedly, 'is rise, say prayers, study, do some work and return for community prayers and a meal at night.'

'And you never leave here?' Monck asked.

'Only for our journeys to Bishop's Lynn.' This time it was Philip Nettler who replied. 'Father Joseph and I go there when, now and again, we need supplies and when a period of purification is over.'

'Purification?' Monck asked innocently as if that was the first time he had heard the word.

'We are the Pastoureaux.' Master Joseph enthused. 'We are Christ's good shepherds. We accept young men and women of good standing and prepare them in our rule.' He cleared his throat. 'When they are ready we take them to a port, in our case, Bishop's Lynn. We secure passage for them abroad, to our house at Bethlehem, where Christ will come again.'

'You really believe that?' Monck asked, not bothering to hide his sneer.

'Don't you?' Master Joseph asked, blue eyes widening in surprise. 'Don't you, Master Monck, accept the Church's teaching that Christ will come again?'

Monck sensed the theological trap opening for him and drew back.

'It's just strange,' he muttered.

'I have been there,' Joseph said. 'And so has Philip. The Lord is coming.'

Monck returned to the attack. 'But in France and on the Rhine the Pastoureaux are ungodly!'

Master Joseph spread his hands. 'Are we to be held accountable for that? Surely some of your priests are not what they should be?' He lowered his voice to a mock whisper. 'They even say that not all friars, monks, bishops – even popes – are what they should be.'

Philip Nettler, who had been busy hobbling their horses, now came back, wiping his hands on his brown fustian robe. He looked squarely at Gurney.

'Sir Simon, have we ever done any wrong? We never knew Master Monck's servant, who was so barbarously murdered, or the poor baker's wife. We very rarely go down into the village. We cause no trouble.' He pursed his lips. 'But now we have troubles of our own.'

'What troubles?' Corbett asked.

'One of our sisters is missing. Marina.'

Gurney, concerned, looked at Master Joseph.

'You mean Marina the tanner's daughter?'

'Yes, she left last night wanting to visit her father, Fulke. She has not yet returned.'

Master Joseph saw Corbett rubbing his hands together against the cold.

'Come in! Come in!' he urged.

He led them across the yard into the farmhouse. The kitchen was a long, low-beamed room. A small log fire burnt in the great hearth; beside it an oven, where bread was baking, turning the air sweet and moist. The room was clean but furnished sparsely – some chests, shelves with a few pots and pans, and a long trestle table ringed by stools. Master Joseph offered some wine or ale, but Corbett refused. They gathered around the hearth, taking their gloves off and warming their fingers. A door at the far end of the room opened and the rest of the community came in. Corbett looked at them with interest. There were sixteen of them – ten men and six women – all young. They looked cheerful enough. The men had their hair cropped, the women had theirs gathered high under simple blue wimples. All wore brown robes, bound by a cord around the waist, over hose or leggings and stout leather sandals or boots. Corbett idly wondered how discipline could be maintained among people so young but dismissed his thoughts as unfair. Such mixed communities were common in France and 'double' houses of men and women were favoured in the order Gilbert of Sempringham had founded in England.

The community sat down around the table. Master Joseph went over to say grace before ale and bread were served. The Pastoureaux chatted quietly among themselves, almost oblivious of the visitors watching them.

'Are they all local?' Corbett whispered.

'It depends what you mean by local,' Nettler replied. 'There are about four from the local village, others from further afield.'

Corbett studied the young men and women. He knew the life of back-breaking work they had escaped from and wondered what they'd think of the Holy Land after the cold dampness of England. He also caught their concern and heard the name Marina whispered. Gurney walked over and began a conversation with one young man whom he recognized. Nettler moved across to hover anxiously. Suddenly Master Joseph straightened like a hunting dog, ears straining.

'What's that?' he asked.

The room fell silent. Then Corbett heard it too – a pounding on the outer gate and Ranulf's voice. Master Joseph hurried out. Nettler told the other Pastoureaux to stay where they were. Corbett, Gurney and Monck followed Master Joseph out. They hurried across the yard. Master Joseph unbarred the gate. Ranulf pushed him aside.

'Master!' he called. 'Sir Simon!'

'What's the matter, man?' Gurney snapped.

'One of your servants – a huntsman or a verderer – has found the body of a girl. She's been murdered!'

'Oh, Lord help us!' Master Joseph's face paled. 'Oh, God forfend that! Master Nettler, stay here!'

Gurney had already hurried on to where Father Augustine and the physician stood by their horses. With them was a man dressed in a dirty brown leather jacket and leggings pushed into high riding boots. Gurney turned to him.

'Thomas, what is it?'

The man turned. His usually tanned, bearded face was now pale, his eyes had a haunted look.

'Further along the moors I was out looking for poachers' snares. There's a girl's body.' The man hawked and spat. 'You'd best come and see!'

He took off in a long loping run, Master Joseph hurrying behind him. The rest collected their horses and followed. They travelled about a mile across the moor and there, in a dip in the land just before a small copse, lay the girl's corpse. Her brown robe was thrust back over her young breasts, her legs spreadeagled, her hose pulled down about her ankles.

The physician dismounted and went over to study the corpse. Corbett went with him.

'She's been raped!' Selditch said as they knelt beside her. 'Look at the bruises on her thighs.'

Corbett glanced fleetingly, then turned his attention to the thin rope tight around the girl's neck. He used his knife to cut it loose. He brushed back the girl's long, lustrous, black hair with a gentle hand and stared pityingly at the pathetic face, mottled and bruised, a trickle of dried blood at the corner of the half-open mouth. The eyes were wide open, staring blindly into the gorse. Corbett looked over his shoulder at Master Joseph, who was staring, pallid-faced, down at the corpse.

'This is Marina, isn't it?'

Master Joseph nodded.

'Then God help her!' Corbett whispered. He forced the girl's eyes shut and pulled down the long robe to cover her nakedness.

Ranulf, standing behind him, said sadly, 'She must have been beautiful.'

'Aye,' Corbett replied. 'A terrible death for a lovely girl. Sir Simon, she has to be moved.'

Gurney nodded. Telling Thomas the huntsman to control the horses, which were becoming nervous at the smell of death, he walked over and knelt beside the girl. He turned her face towards him.

'About sixteen summers old,' he murmured. 'I remember her baptism. Her father, Fulke, will be beside himself with grief.'

Father Augustine, whose sorry nag had found it difficult to keep up with the rest, finally arrived. He dismounted, studied the corpse and swallowed hard. He pushed the cowl of his robe back, knelt down and whispered absolution into the girl's ear, sketching a blessing above her. He got to his feet, wiping the wetness off his robe.

'We have to take her home,' he said. 'Master Joseph, do you have a cart?'

The Pastoureaux leader nodded and hurried back towards the Hermitage. Corbett went over to where Selditch was taking a generous swig from Gurney's wineskin before passing it to Ranulf.

'Master physician,' he asked Selditch formally, 'the girl was raped and then garrotted?'

Selditch lowered the wineskin. 'Aye, that's bloody obvious.' His face softened. 'I'm sorry,' he muttered. 'But the girl was an angel.' He looked at Gurney. 'I'm not sure whether she was raped and then killed or whether she was first strangled and then brutally abused.' He turned and looked towards the mist-shrouded woods and back at Corbett. 'Whatever you are here for,' he said dully, 'find out the truth about this. For the devil's come to Hunstanton!'

Corbett looked up at Monck. The black-garbed clerk had neither dismounted nor made any attempt to approach the girl's body. His face was more pallid than usual and Corbett saw a muscle twitching high in his cheek. He went over and touched Monck's ungloved hand. It was cold as a block of ice.

'Lavinius?'

Monck just stared at the corpse.

'Lavinius!' Corbett hissed. He grasped the man's arm and squeezed it. 'Master Monck!'

Monck broke from his reverie and stared down at Corbett, as if seeing him for the first time. His lips curled.

'Piss off, you bastard!' he hissed.

Corbett's hand fell away. He stepped back, appalled at the

fury blazing in Monck's eyes, and spread his hands in a gesture of peace.

'She's dead!' Monck whispered hoarsely. 'She's dead! And there's nothing that bloody priest or the bloody Pastoureaux can do to bring her back!' And, tugging violently at the reins of his horse and digging his spurs in, he turned and rode off in the direction of the manor.

'Master!' Ranulf hurried over. 'Master, what's wrong?'

Corbett merely shook his head. 'It's nothing.' Corbett declared. 'Nothing at all.'

And then he recalled the stories he had heard about Monck – tittle-tattle from the clerks in the chancery, fragments of gossip around the court.

'The man's mad!' Ranulf muttered.

'Perhaps.' Corbett replied.

Master Joseph came back, leading a donkey pulling a flat two-wheeled cart. Maltote and Ranulf placed the girl's body gently on the cart. Gurney sent the huntsman on into the village.

'Tell them what has happened,' he ordered. 'Father Augustine will take the body to the church.'

The sad little procession made its way back, the cart bumping and jolting along the trackway that led down to Hunstanton. They skirted the manor and, a short while later, entered the village. The main thoroughfare was broad and rutted. The cart jolted, giving a strange life to the corpse which lay sprawled under the blanket. As they entered Hunstanton, Corbett saw a small crowd gathering. The women and children were first, then men came running from the fields, their tunics and breeches stained and heavy with dark clay. Small boys, carrying the slings they used to drive away marauding crows, trotted behind. Corbett looked at their red, raw faces, bruised by the cold, salty wind. He felt a pang of compassion at the fear in their faces. They wordlessly gathered around the cart and looked askance at their lord. Gurney pulled his hood back, shook his head and dismounted. He raised his hand, stilling the low moans and muttered curses.

'Marina, God rest her,' he announced, 'has been foully murdered out on the moors. I swear, by God and the king, her murderer shall be found and hanged!'

'What was she doing there?' someone shouted.

The question went unanswered as a heavy, thickset man, an anxious-faced woman in tow, hurried up and pushed his way through to the cart. He took one look at the body and turned away, clutching his chest, his fingers pressing deeply into the leather apron he wore. He tried to stop his wife from seeing what he had seen, but the woman struggled free and stood for a long moment looking down at the body. Then she slumped on to the cobbles beside the cart, mouth open, and gave the most wretched cry Corbett had ever heard. 'My baby!' she moaned. 'Oh no, not my Marina!' The cry was all the more pathetic in its thick rustic burr. She began to bang her head against the wheel of the cart. Her husband tried to raise her to her feet but again she fought free of him, the hood slipping back from her wispy, grey hair. She flung herself at Gurney, grasping his robe.

'Who would do it?' she cried. 'Who would do that?'

Her terrible sobbing stilled all clamour. Gurney looked at her husband.

'It is Marina?'

The man nodded, tears streaming down his face.

'I want justice, my lord,' he whispered.

'You shall have it.'

He looked up at the priest. 'You'll bury her, Father?'

'Aye, Fulke, I will, in God's acre.'

Fulke pushed his way forward to where Master Joseph stood silently watching.

'You said you'd look after her,' he said bitterly.

Master Joseph stood his ground, ignoring the dark mutterings that had broken out around him.

'Fulke, I did. But Marina insisted on returning to the village last night. She had to see you, or so she told me. Perhaps she wanted to visit someone else? '

'Where's Gilbert, the witch's son?' someone shouted.

'He's not here,' someone else replied.

Corbett leaned over. 'Father Augustine, who is this Gilbert?'

'The girl's sweetheart. Or at least he was sweet on her. A simple lad, a woodcutter's son. He and his mother live on the edge of the village beyond the church, as you go out towards the headland. She's a wise woman. She knows simples and cures, remedies and potions.' Father Augustine lowered his voice. 'But you know how it is Sir Hugh – there's gossip that she dabbles in the black arts and, at night, rides the wind with other demons.'

The crowd's mood had suddenly turned ugly. Gurney remounted and shouted for silence. Then: 'There is no proof against any man!'

'Well, who else could it be?' a voice asked.

A tight inner group of villagers had gathered around Fulke and his wife. A small, pot-bellied man stepped forward from amongst them. His wart-covered face was sour, the anger spots high on his cheek bones. He walked with a swagger, running thick fingers through wispy blond hair. He took up position before Gurney's horse.

'You know the custom, Sir Simon, and the ancient usage? I, Robert Fitzosborne, reeve of this village, demand that a jury be assembled and the murderer named!'

So this was the reeve. Corbett studied the man carefully, remembering the gossip of the night before. He noticed how Fitzosborne's boots and jerkin were of a better quality than those of the other villagers. The reeve now extended his arms and half-turned towards the villagers. 'We demand it,' he shouted. 'It is the custom and the law.'

The crowd of villagers shouted their approval. Corbett felt beneath his cloak for the hilt of his sword and glanced warningly at Ranulf and Maltote. The villagers moved forward. Corbett turned at the sound of hoof beats on the track and saw Catchpole and other liveried servants galloping towards them. Gurney's henchman had been astute enough to guess what might happen for, beneath his cloak, he wore chain mail and the five servants who accompanied him were also well armed.

At their arrival, Robert Fitzosborne lost some of his arrogance, though he refused to be cowed.

'Sir Simon, the manor's custom is well known,' he shouted defiantly. 'One of your tenants has been murdered, brutally. You have the power.'

Gurney turned to Corbett and smiled weakly at him.

'Fitzosborne is right,' he said. 'I have the power of sword and gallows. But you are the king's representative here, what do you advise?'

Corbett looked at the throng of peasants milling by the cart with its pathetic burden. He felt the justice of Fitzosborne's demand. A young girl had been brutally murdered. Moreover, if a jury was empanelled and he was present, he might discover more about this mysterious place with its strange murders. More than one type of mist hid the place, not only from the eyes of men but from the eyes of God as well. He looked at Gurney.

'A jury,' he declared firmly, 'must be summoned!'

Chapter 4

Within the hour Marina's corpse had been removed to the death house on the edge of the village. At the same time the nave of the long, solidly built church had, according to custom, been turned into a court. Corbett stood outside, staring up at the squat tower, at the base of which yawned the main door to the church. He admired the sculptures over the door and round the windows. These were carefully carved with animals, flowers and strange beasts. He looked over his shoulder at the priest's house, a large cottage with plastered walls and a thatched roof. Corbett shivered; a place of secrets, he thought, why had this village now become a place of shadows and sudden death? Ranulf, Maltote and he walked around the church and stared at the gorse, weeds and creeping brambles.

'A sad place,' Ranulf remarked.

Corbett studied the battered wooden crosses and crumbling headstones. He wondered what any grave robber would find so interesting there and walked back into the entrance of the church. Father Augustine came bustling from the death house, wiping his hands on his robe, his thin face creased in concern. Corbett and his companions followed him in to the church. Staring up, they admired the wooden ceiling, painted in bright lozenge patterns. The walls and pillars of the nave had also been painted, with bizarre, gaudy zig-zag or dog-tooth designs and the flickering cresset torches revealed vivid scenes from the life of Christ painted on the transept walls.

The church was quiet now. A long trestle table had been placed in the nave. Six men sat on either side of it. At the far end Gurney sat enthroned in the heavily ornate sanctuary chair, which had been moved from beneath the rood screen. At the near end Father Augustine, who also served as parish clerk, had laid out parchment, inkhorn and pumice stone ready to record the proceedings. Behind Gurney stood a forbidding-looking Catchpole, Giles Selditch and Master Joseph. Villagers squatted on the ground around the table. Gurney waved Corbett forward, indicating a stool on his right.

'Sir Hugh, you will be my witness to the proceedings.'

Gurney got to his feet and formally pronounced the court to be in session.

Corbett watched fascinated. He had often acted as a royal justice or commissioner, but he had never seen a serious matter dealt with in a manor court.

'The death we are here to enquire into,' Gurney began, 'is that of Marina, daughter of Fulke the tanner, who was barbarously murdered out in the moorlands. She had been raped and strangled' – he raised his hands to still the clamour – 'by a person or persons unknown. Now,' he continued hurriedly, 'you know the ancient customs and usages. First, the death may be recorded. Secondly, if enough information is brought, a person or persons may be indicted.' His voice rose. 'If the latter is the case, then such a person or persons must be arrested and given fair trial before their peers at the next assize.'

A low chorus of protests greeted his words. Gurney wiped

his hands nervously on the edge of his gown. He looked down the line of jurors on either side of the table, staring hard at Robert the reeve.

'You have all sworn the oath on the book of the gospels.' He pointed to the heavy tome on the table. 'Anyone who wishes to give evidence must swear on the gospels. I need not remind you that perjury can be a capital offence.'

Gurney's last words rang like a death knell through the church, a harsh reminder to his tenants of the danger of lying on such an important occasion.

After that the questioning began. Gurney's huntsman took the oath and described how he had found the girl. Next came Giles Selditch, who graphically described the girl's wounds. Corbett glimpsed the ugliness in the faces of the jurors and the rest of the villagers.

'When do you think the girl was killed?' Gurney asked.

The doctor, standing at the far corner of the table, shrugged.

'Her flesh was cold, covered in frost, she must have been slain last night.'

'What was she doing out on the moorland?' one of the jurors asked.

Gurney told the man to shut up.

Master Joseph was called next. 'Marina was a member of our community,' he began. 'No one forced her to join us.' He stared around, nodding at the murmur of assent that greeted his words. 'No one forced her to stay.' He held one hand up. 'Indeed, the very fact that she was out on the moorland proves she had the freedom to move as she wished.'

'Why did she leave?' Gurney asked harshly.

Master Joseph stared back, waiting as Father Augustine's squeaky quill recorded the question.

'She said,' he finally answered, 'that she wished to see her father. I was reluctant to let her go but had no right or cause to prevent her. However, I got then the impression that she was lying to me – that it was really someone else she was meeting.' He looked over his shoulder at Fulke the tanner, who was squatting at the base of one of the pillars, his arm around his sobbing wife. 'I don't know who. Marina was due to leave us soon. Her purification was complete and, at the end of the month, we hoped to secure her passage to Outremer. She could have been in Bethlehem for Christmas.'

Corbett whispered to Gurney, who said quickly, 'Sir Hugh Corbett would like to ask a few questions.'

Corbett got to his feet. 'Master Joseph, while Marina was at the Hermitage, did anyone from outside attempt to speak to her?'

'Yes, Gilbert, the old witch's son.'

'And did Marina go to the gates to speak to him?'

'She did on two occasions. But the last time she refused to see him.'

'And how did Gilbert receive that?'

'Angrily, a little hurt, but he left peacefully enough.'

'Master Joseph,' Corbett smiled faintly. He was aware that the villagers were looking at him intently, nudging each other to draw attention to this important man, the king's representative, whom they regarded with a mixture of admiration and awe tinged with a deep suspicion of any outsider.

'Master Joseph,' Corbett repeated. 'I must ask you this. Last night, did anyone else leave the Hermitage?'

'No. Master Nettler can swear to my presence there as I can to his, and all the other members of the community can vouch for each other.' Master Joseph looked directly at Gurney. 'Sir

Simon, we have been on your lands for over a year and, as you know, when spring comes we may move on.' His words provoked a deep sigh of disappointment from the watching villagers. 'Never once have we abused either your hospitality or that of this village; never once told a lie or been involved in any fraudulent trickery. I make this assertion now so it can be challenged.' He paused and stared around the now quiet church. 'Good!' he said, and added quietly, 'And I tell no lie now, on my oath!'

Corbett nodded and sat down. Master Joseph was dismissed and quietly slipped out of the church. Fulke the tanner was called next. He identified his daughter's corpse. He said that Marina had been happy at the Hermitage. Then he told the court that a small amber-bead necklace, a gift from him and his wife, was missing from the girl's body.

'She always wore it,' he said flatly. 'And now, like her soul, they have gone.'

The villagers clapped when he returned to his place. Others were called to give evidence. They named Gilbert time and again, telling how, in the village tavern, he had bitterly attacked the Pastoureaux for taking Marina from him, how he had missed her and how, on one memorable occasion, he had boldly asserted that she would never leave Hunstanton.

Corbett could see Gurney's unease deepen as other witnesses began to hint that Gunhilda, Gilbert's mother, now described as a well-known witch, had tried to help her son. Perhaps she was also the perpetrator, the blasphemer who had been pillaging graves in the village churchyard?

'The use of dead men's skulls and bones,' one reedy-voiced villager intoned, 'is well known to the Masters of the Gibbet and to the night hags!'

Father Augustine was then called. 'I cannot say,' he replied to a question from Gurney, 'whether Gunhilda or her son were responsible for robbing the graves. It has been going on for the last year and seems to have neither rhyme nor reason.'

'Why do you say that?' Corbett asked.

'Because the graves that are pillaged are never recent ones but often decades old. Nothing remains except a few bones.'

'And has anything been taken?' Corbett asked.

'To my knowledge, nothing.'

The church began to grow dark as the day died. Gurney gave a pithy summary of what had been said. The jury retired, but came back a short while afterwards. They trooped in behind their reeve, Robert, who looked, as Ranulf whispered to Corbett, as important as a cockerel on a dung heap.

'You have a verdict?'

'We have, my lord. We find that Marina, daughter of Fulke the tanner, was murdered by Gilbert with the connivance and support of his mother Gunhilda. We demand that they both be arrested to stand trial for their lives.'

Gurney held up his hand. 'They will be arrested,' he promised. He looked warningly down the table, then at the other villagers clustered in the nave, who were murmuring threateningly amongst themselves. 'They are to have a fair trial,' he said firmly. 'They must be given a fair trial.'

There were mutinous sounds from the villagers. 'The business of this court is concluded,' Gurney said. He dug into his purse and placed two silver pieces on the table. 'This is for Fulke the tanner, to pay for his daughter's funeral Mass. I shall also give Father Augustine a chantry fee for Masses to be sung for the repose of her soul between now and Easter Day.'

The villagers, humming like an overturned beehive, swarmed around the jurymen, slapping them on the back as they left the church. Father Augustine, murmuring he had other business to attend to, left his record of the proceedings with Gurney and hurried after his parishioners.

Gurney beckoned Catchpole forward. 'Take some men,' he ordered, 'and go and arrest Gunhilda and Gilbert. Pray God that we do so before the villagers, now thronging in the taproom of the Inglenook, become so full of ale they take the law into their own hands.'

Catchpole hurried off. Gurney rose, stretched and looked at Corbett.

'Well, Hugh, a bloody day's business.'

'Aye, and it won't end well.' Corbett pursed his lips and looked down at the door of the church. Your tenants, he thought, want justice and blood.

'Are you going back to the manor, Hugh?'

'Perhaps in a while. The day is drawing on. I would like to see more of the countryside before darkness falls.'

Corbett excused himself and, accompanied by a taciturn Ranulf and Maltote, collected the horses idly grazing in a small paddock behind the priest's house. They rode back through the village. Corbett, going ahead, stared around at the white-washed, thatched cottages, each standing in its own little plot of land. A prosperous, thriving place, he thought. Nevertheless, he felt the heavy hand of violent death. The place was deserted. The women were indoors with their children, the men in the tavern opposite the village green with its now ice-covered pond.

Some of the villagers standing at the door caught sight of Corbett and shouted greetings. Corbett raised a gloved hand in reply. He saw Robert the reeve leave his house, a freshly painted, half-timbered building, and wondered about the reeve's newly found wealth. Further along was the baker's house, with its small, gaudily painted sign depicting three white manchet loaves on a silver platter. Corbett would have stopped, but the house was shuttered and closed, as if the young girl's death had reminded the baker of his own tragedy. Corbett rode on out of the village, taking the path towards the cliff edge.

The darkness was drawing in and the mist seethed above the angry waves sweeping in at low tide. The haunting cry of sea birds sounded above the low, moaning wind. Corbett sensed the desolation of the moors. He recalled legends of the place. Someone at Swaffham had called the wind the Dark Angel and told Corbett how this part of Norfolk had once been ruled by an ancient tribe which had rebelled against the Romans and drenched the land in blood. Corbett almost jumped as Ranulf pushed his horse alongside.

'Master,' he began cautiously, glimpsing Corbett's close-set face. 'Maltote and I were wondering how long we are to stay here?'

Corbett smiled. 'How long is a piece of rope, Ranulf?'

Ranulf changed tack. 'The villagers have already made up their minds who killed that girl. Sir Simon is right – if Gilbert falls into their hands they will kill him.'

Corbett pulled on his reins and stared at Ranulf. 'Do you know Master Joseph?'

Ranulf scratched the stubble on his chin. 'I've been thinking about that. He certainly recognized me and I think I recognized him.'

'From where?'

'I don't know. I can't remember.'

'What do you make of the Pastoureaux?' Corbett asked.

'Cranks and tricksters.' Ranulf grinned. 'My old mother told me to beware of religion. It attracts few saints and many, many rogues.'

'You think the Pastoureaux are rogues?'

'I think we should talk to the young men and women of their community.'

Corbett nodded. 'When we have finished here, you and Maltote will take my compliments and condolences to Master Joseph. See if you can talk with the community.'

Ranulf closed his eyes. 'Master, I'm cold and I'm hungry!'

'Aye, and when you return there'll be a warm meal and a good bed and you and Maltote can play dice.' He held up an admonitory finger. 'But not with Sir Simon's servants.'

Ranulf blinked innocently at him.

'I mean that,' Corbett insisted. 'And you aren't to gull them into buying the medicines you try to sell whenever we come into the countryside, the strange concoctions and elixirs handed down to you from the ancient Egyptians.'

Ranulf swallowed hard and stared guiltily at Maltote. How did old Master Long Face know about his little leather bag and the remedies he was always ready to sell to the gullible?

'Now,' – Corbett urged his horse forward – 'let's look at the gallows.'

They rode along the cliff edge until they came again to the three-branched scaffold. It soared up against the darkening sky, only about seven yards from the cliff edge. Corbett gathered the reins and tried to keep his skittish horse still. He looked up at the great iron hook in each of the scaffold branches.

'I suppose,' he said, more to himself than to his companions, 'if some poor unfortunate's to be executed, he's brought out here, pushed up a ladder, the ladder's turned and he's left to hang. But that's not what happened to the baker's wife.'

He stared down at the ground, where the grass had long

been worn away. His horse was so nervous that he wondered whether someone was buried there – it was, he knew, the custom to bury suicides and excommunicants beneath a scaffold. Why, he wondered, had the baker's wife come out here? Why had she allowed someone to place a rope round her neck? How was it that the murderer had left no sign? And who had ridden the baker's horse back to the village?

The sound of hoof-beats made him look round in alarm. Monck came galloping out of the mist; with his black cloak billowing out, he looked like some evil raven. Corbett nodded a dismissal at Ranulf and Maltote.

'Go to the Hermitage,' he ordered. 'I'll meet you back at the manor.'

Ranulf and Maltote galloped away as Monck, his mount slowing to a trot, came up beside Corbett. He pulled back his hood and Corbett saw that his face and hair were soaked. Had he been on the beach, staring into the stinging spray? Monk gestured towards the scaffold.

'A mystery, eh, Corbett?'

'You saw the corpse?' Corbett asked.

'Yes, nothing but a noose mark around her neck. Not like the poor girl we discovered this morning.' Monck pushed his horse closer. 'I thought you'd be either in the village or here. I came to find you.'

Corbett stared at him. 'Why?'

Monck wiped his mouth with the back of his black-gloved hand.

'I came to apologize.'

For a few seconds Monck's face relaxed and Corbett glimpsed a younger, pleasanter man. Monck stared out at the mist-covered sea and spoke softly.

'You've heard the gossip?'

'Aye,' Corbett replied. 'I've remembered. You had a daughter.'

'She was sixteen,' Monck said, still looking out to sea. 'She was pretty as a summer's day. Every time I looked at her I thought of her mother, who died giving her birth. It happened so quickly. My Lord of Surrey had organized a small banquet. It was a most beautiful day. Caterina, my daughter, said she wished to go for a walk in the nearby woods. I was stupid, I let her go. We were on the earl's estates. I thought she'd be safe. An hour passed and she didn't return. I became anxious. I went searching for her. She was like that girl we found this morning, just lying there.' Turning to face Corbett for the first time, he blinked away tears. 'She had been attacked, raped, then choked to death. And there was nothing I could do. I kept talking to her.' His voice faltered. 'I even took my dagger and cut myself in case I was dreaming. My Lord of Surrey was most kind, but the murderer was never found.'

Corbett leaned across and touched him gently on the arm.

'I am sorry, Lavinius. Truly sorry.'

'There were suspects, though,' Monck continued.

'There were Pastoureaux on the other side of the wood. They occupied an old ruined church. They swore they had nothing to do with Caterina's death.'

'The same group?' Corbett asked. 'The people we have here now?' Monck shook his head. 'I don't know. I was prostrate with grief. My Lord of Surrey brought in the sheriff's men but they could discover nothing.'

'Do you think the Pastoureaux killed Marina?'

Monck's face twisted into a sneer. 'That's for you to prove, Corbett! I don't give a damn who murdered Marina. But one day someone is going to pay for my daughter's death!' Monck grasped the reins of his horse and leaned over, pushing his face to within a few inches of Corbett's. 'I know what you think of me,' he whispered. Corbett saw the murderous hatred blazing in his eyes. 'You think I've no scruples, no principles, no morals. But how can you have these, Corbett, when you have no soul? My soul, my life, died the day my daughter was murdered. God took away my wife, then he took Caterina. I don't listen any longer to the mumbling of priests!' Monck threw his head back and stared up at the grey skies. A strangled sound came from his bared lips. 'I'll curse and I'll curse till the day I die!' Monck tugged at his horse and galloped back towards the manor.

Corbett watched him go. He felt uncomfortable. He had judged Monck but had not realized the nightmares and ghosts that haunted the man's soul. He felt a surge of compassion for a man who had made his daughter's life the centre of his being and then had that life so barbarously removed. Corbett spurred his horse forward at a leisurely pace along the path. What else had the gossips said? Hadn't there been suspicions that Monck's murdered servant, Cerdic Lickspittle, had been too sweet on the girl? Monck had certainly blamed his manservant for not keeping better care. Corbett stared down at his horse's bobbing head. What if Monck had asked for this assignment? What if he had come into the wilds of Norfolk to settle a number of grievances – with the Pastoureaux and with his own servant? Had there been any link between Monck and the baker's wife? His horse's whinny jolted him from his reverie. He looked up and saw he was only a stone's throw away from the gate of Mortlake Manor.

In the courtyard, an ostler took his horse. Corbett walked through the main entrance. The hall and solar were deserted and a servant told him that Sir Simon was with his wife in their chamber. Corbett snatched something to eat from the buttery and carried a pewter cup of mulled wine to his own chamber. Once he had warmed himself by the small fire he lit candles and placed them on the table. He took out quill, inkhorn and parchment and tried to make sense of the mysteries that faced him.

First he drew a rough map, showing the line of the coast and the location of different places. Then he began to list the people concerned, starting with Sir Simon Gurney. Corbett chewed the end of his quill and considered. Sir Simon was nervous, slightly withdrawn and fearful – but of what? Then there was Giles Selditch, the physician: an enigmatic figure. Next, Catchpole, Sir Simon's henchman: he was loyal, disliked strangers and deeply resented the Pastoureaux. Next, Lavinius Monck: insane or simply motivated by malice and revenge? His name led to all kinds of questions. What is he really doing in the area – investigating the Pastoureaux, seeking personal vengeance, or pursuing some other, secret aim? Who killed his servant, Cerdic Lickspittle? What was Cerdic doing out on the moors? Why was he murdered in such a barbaric fashion – head cut off and stuck on a pole on a misty, cold beach? How had the assassin managed to leave no signs, no clues?

Then there were the Pastoureaux? Were they fanatics, simpletons or saints? Would it be worthwhile writing to the chancery or the exchequer about them? He began to list names. First there was Master Joseph. Who was he? Why did Ranulf recognize him? Next, Marina, daughter of Fulke the tanner: why had she left the Hermitage and what was she doing out on the moors?

Corbett's list of names began to seem endless. He added Amelia Fourbour, the baker's wife. Why did she go out to the scaffold? Why hadn't she struggled? Why were there no signs of another horse at the scene? Who had ridden her horse back to the edge of the village?

Corbett wearily rubbed his eyes and sat staring for a while. He sighed, sipped from his cup of posset and continued writing.

Father Augustine: a stranger in the area, not really at home with the people of his parish. Dame Cecily: shrewd but luxury-loving. Robert the reeve: what was the source of his newly found wealth? Corbett put his pen down. He folded his arms on the table and studied his list of names. Other questions jostled in his mind. Who was disturbing old graves in the churchyard? How had Dame Agnes fallen to her death? He rose from his chair and stared into the shadows at the far end of the room. One question in particular kept nagging him. Why had he and Monck been sent here? What was so important that the king should send a trusted and confidential servant to assist the Earl of Surrey's right-hand man in, ostensibly, the investigation of a few admittedly bizarre murders?

Corbett returned to sit at his desk and thought back to his last meeting with the king. Edward had refused to meet his eye, but had kept shuffling from foot to foot, more engrossed with a peregrine jingling its jesses on a perch. John de Warenne, Earl of Surrey, had also been present. Bland-faced, he kept stroking his mouth as if concealing a grin or some secret joke.

That had been at Swaffham. Now, Corbett knew, Edward and his young French queen, Margaret, would be at Walsingham.

'I'll wait,' Corbett muttered to himself. 'I'll wait a little longer. If Monck doesn't tell me the truth, I'll ride to Walsingham and demand it from the king myself!'

Corbett went and lay down on his bed. Closing his eyes, he drifted into sleep. Outside darkness fell and the rising song of the Dark Angel began to be heard above the roar of the sea.

Chapter 5

'Master!'

Corbett opened his eyes. Ranulf was bending over him.

'Master, the steward is summoning us to supper!'

Corbett swung his legs off the bed. He stared at Ranulf and Maltote, who were still swathed in their cloaks, the raindrops glistening in the flickering candlelight.

'We went to the Hermitage,' Ranulf said. 'Master Joseph was surprisingly friendly. He allowed us to come in. He, too, thinks he's seen me before, though he can't remember where.'

Corbett rubbed his face in his hands.

'Did you talk to any of the community?'

'Yes, although Nettler and Master Joseph were always in attendance. Everyone we spoke to said that Marina was a happy girl. But they all agreed that, in the days before she died, she became withdrawn.'

'And?'

'She had nightmares. The women – they sleep in one dormitory and the men in the other – heard her calling out the name Blanche in her sleep.'

'Who is Blanche?'

'A childhood friend of Marina's. She was the reeve's

daughter, one of the first to enter the community. She left over a year ago.'

Corbett sighed. He got up and went to the lavarium, where he bathed his hands and face and dried himself on a towel. Ranulf and Maltote took off their cloaks and boots, slipped on soft leather buskins, washed and followed Corbett down to the main hall.

The evening meal was a desultory affair. Gurney was taciturn, still worried about the girl's death and the events in the village. Alice caught her husband's mood and only picked at her food. Monck, smiling strangely to himself, ate in silence. Corbett watched him and wondered again whether his mind was slipping into madness.

They were still at table when Catchpole strode into the hall, damp and muddied, his bad temper apparent.

'God damn them all!' he swore. 'There's no sign of Gilbert or his bloody mother! They have fled!' He brought his hand from beneath his cloak. 'I found this in their house.' He opened his hand to show glistening amber beads.

'That is Marina's necklace,' Selditch said immediately. He smiled self-consciously. 'I knew the girl well. So it seems that the villagers are right. Gilbert is the murderer.'

'I passed through the village,' Catchpole said. 'The hot-heads are still drinking in the Inglenook tavern. There will be violence.'

Gurney shook his head. 'Adam, I thank you. But enough is enough. Change, join us for supper. Tomorrow's another day.'

Corbett took the opportunity to excuse himself. He left Ranulf and Maltote drinking and went back to his own chamber to study the notes he had made. He waited until he heard the others leave the hall, then went out into the passage and found a servant to take him to Monck's chamber. He knocked and, deliberately, opened the door without waiting for an answer. Monck was seated at a table, his back to the door. He whirled round and saw Corbett. Hastily he gathered up the manuscripts spread out on the table in front of him and rose, that strange smile still on his face.

'What is it?' he asked. 'What can I do for you now?'

Corbett went into the room, closed the door behind him and sat down on a stool. Monck carefully kept himself between Corbett and the manuscripts on the table.

'Why are you here?' Corbett asked him.

Monck shrugged. 'Because of the Pastoureaux.'

'And how did Lickspittle die?'

'I have told you. He went out on the moors and never returned. His decapitated corpse and severed head were found on the beach.'

'A strange way to die,' Corbett observed.

'Dying is always strange.'

'You know what I mean, Lavinius. To kill a man is one thing, to mutilate his body another.'

'This is a strange place,' Monck said. 'According to our fat physician, the Iceni who once lived in this area used to take the heads of their enemies and expose them in public – just as our king does now on London Bridge.'

'What was Lickspittle doing on the beach?'

Monck shrugged.

'He went to the convent. There's a path from there down to the beach, though why he should have followed it, if he did, is a mystery. He was certainly taking a risk.'

'Why's that?'

'The tides here are fickle. After a heavy rainfall the waves come swirling in, they could take a man unawares.'

'And you'll tell me nothing else?'

'I cannot tell you anything.'

Again that crooked smile. Corbett got to his feet and went to the door. With his hand on the latch he paused.

'Lavinius!'

'Yes?' Monck half-turned in his chair.

'You should tell me the truth. I assure you of this, more murders will occur.'

Monck just went back to his papers and Corbett left, closing the door quietly behind him. He went along the passage and stood at the top of the stairs. He could hear Maltote and Ranulf laughing below. He hoped that the precious pair had not enticed anyone into a game of dice. He went back to his chamber. Outside the wind was howling, beating on the windows and rattling the shutters. Beneath the wind's sombre song Corbett could hear the waves crashing on the rocks as the sea poured into the Wash. He knelt down, made the sign of the cross, and said his favourite prayer: 'Christ be in my head and in my thinking, Christ be in my eyes and in my seeing, Christ be at my left hand and my right.'

His mind drifted. Was Maeve well in London? And baby Eleanor? He shook himself and went back to his prayers, but he found it difficult to concentrate. He gave up, crossed himself and lay, dozing, on the bed. After a little while he undressed, got into bed properly, pulled the blankets about him and went instantly to sleep, dreaming about running across a lonely beacon, pursued by dark, hooded figures.

When he awoke the next morning, Ranulf and Maltote, still fully dressed, were lying on their beds looking, as Ranulf would have put it, as happy as pigs in a mire. Corbett opened the shutters. The wind had dropped, the mist had almost gone and he glimpsed an ice-blue sky. Rubbing his hands against the cold, he washed, shaved, dressed and went down to the buttery. The hour candle on its iron spigot made him realize how late he had slept, for the flame had already reached the tenth circle. Gurney came in, cheery-faced, stamping his feet and blowing his hands.

'Good morning, Hugh. Why do horses always give trouble in winter?'

He poured himself some mulled ale and hungrily snatched mouthfuls of bread and meat as he walked up and down the buttery. Alice came in with Selditch. They stood discussing the day's events, the atmosphere jovial because Monck had already gone walking.

'By himself as usual,' Gurney added wryly. 'Never have I met a man who liked his own company so much.' Then he put his tankard down as a clamour came from the front of the house. With a clatter of boots Catchpole came rushing into the buttery.

'Sir Simon!' Catchpole leaned against the door jamb to catch his breath. 'Sir Simon, Sir Hugh, you'd best come, now!'

'What's the matter?' Alice asked, her voice high.

Catchpole wiped the sweat from his face. 'I've been down to the village. They've caught Gilbert and his mother.'

'Oh, Lord save us!' Gurney grabbed his cloak and shouted at the servants to prepare the horses.

'What are they doing?' Corbett asked.

'They are pressing Gilbert to plead – the old way, under a heavy oaken door with weights on top.'

'And Gunhilda?'

'They have brought out the ducking stool.'

Gurney hurried from the buttery. Corbett went back to his

own chamber. He put on his sword belt, boots and cloak, and looked despairingly at his two servants. They were still snoring their heads off. Corbett hurried down to join Gurney and Selditch who stood, booted and spurred, in the yard, shouting for their horses. They left the manor a few minutes later, accompanied by six of Gurney's burlier servants and thundered down the path towards the village.

The green in front of the tavern was full of people milling about. For a while all was confusion; mud, dung and even a few rocks were thrown at Gurney's party. Gurney's retainers, using the flats of their swords and their whips, eventually imposed order and forced their way through. The scene at the edge of the pond was terrible. Gilbert lay pinned beneath a heavy door on which boulders and iron weights had been placed. The flaxen-haired young man was semi-conscious, quietly moaning to himself. Fulke the tanner was kneeling beside him, shouting at him to confess. Further along, the villagers had rolled a massive tree trunk to the edge of the pond and, over this, slung a long pole with a small chair at one end. To this was strapped a pathetic old lady, tied like a sack of straw. Her ragged clothes were soaked, her long, grey hair slimed with pond water. A group of burly villagers, under Robert the reeve's direction, swung the poor woman in and out of the icy water whilst the crowd, women and children included, simply shouted: 'Confess! Confess! Confess!'

'This is murder!' Corbett shouted.

He strode over and pushed the reeve away. Behind him Gurney and the rest began to clear the weights and the heavy door from the prostrate young man.

'You have no authority here!' The reeve's face was ugly and red, swollen with anger and ale.

Corbett drew his sword.

'I am Sir Hugh Corbett, the king's representative here. And that woman will be tried only by due process of law!'

A low grumble of protest greeted his words. Emboldened, Robert the reeve took a step forward. Corbett, gripping the hilt two-handed, raised the sword.

'What are you going to do, Robert?' he said softly. 'Attack me?'

The reeve hastily stepped back.

'Bring the bitch in!' he shouted over his shoulder.

The ash pole was pulled back and the ducking stool lowered into the shallows at the edge of the pond. Corbett splashed up to it.

'Oh, Christ, have pity!' he breathed.

Gunhilda's dirty grey hair was clamped to her lined, seamed face. Corbett took one look at the heavy-lidded, half-open eyes and the sagging jaw and knew it was too late. He felt for the blood beat in her neck and her scrawny wrists, but there was not even a flutter. Drawing his dagger, he slashed the woman's bonds and took her up in his arms. She was as light as a child. He walked back up the muddy green.

'You bastards!' he roared.

The reeve quietly slunk away. Gurney and Catchpole came up.

'Corbett, what's the matter?'

'The old woman's dead!' Corbett answered. 'Murdered by these bastards!'

He walked on and placed the old woman's corpse on a table that stood outside the tavern. He arranged the body carefully, pulling the dirty skirts over vein-streaked, spindle-like legs. He listened once more for her heart beat.

'Dead from drowning or from shock.' He stared at Gurney. 'Either way, Sir Simon, this woman was murdered.'

Two of Gurney's men brought the blond young man towards him. Corbett went over to him, put his hand gently under his chin and raised his face. Gilbert was obviously slightly simple, slack-jawed and heavy-eyed. An ugly swelling had closed one eye and bloody bubbles frothed at the corner of his mouth. He was also a mass of bruises from head to toe.

Corbett took a wineskin from one of Gurney's retainers and forced it between the young man's lips.

'He is a murderer!' Robert the reeve shouted. With a throng of villagers behind him he had rediscovered his defiance.

Corbett glared at the reeve's fat, pompous face.

'You and your friends are murderers!' he shouted. 'Gunhilda is dead and her blood is on your hands!'

Gilbert's strangled moan echoed Corbett's words.

'This man,' Corbett shouted hoarsely, 'must be tried by the due process of law before the king's justices. He is now my prisoner.'

Father Augustine pushed his way through to the front of the crowd. Gurney, standing now beside Corbett, beckoned him forward.

'Father, couldn't you have stopped this?'

The priest's eyes flickered from Gurney to Corbett. He licked his thin, dry lips and stared shamefacedly down at the old woman's corpse.

'I tried to,' he muttered, 'but their blood lust was up. You can't blame them, Sir Hugh. Marina's corpse lies cold in my church. Who will answer for her death, eh?'

Gurney snapped his fingers at his retainers. 'Take the woman's corpse to the church. Father, I'll pay the burial dues.'

'And the young man?' Corbett nodded towards Gilbert,

who was straining at his captor's arms and staring slack-mouthed at his mother's bedraggled body.

'Take him to the manor!' Gurney told his men. 'Get Master Selditch to tend his wounds!'

Corbett stared round at the villagers.

'The king and his court lie nearby at Walsingham. He will not be pleased to hear of this violence and disorder. And any person who lifts his hand against Gilbert puts himself beyond the king's peace.'

'Sir Hugh speaks the truth,' Gurney confirmed. 'A terrible evil stalks this place. More violent deaths have occurred in the last few months than in living memory. So, go! Disperse to your homes!'

They went. There was some grumbling from hot-heads, but already wiser minds were beginning to prevail. The crowd broke up, the women hustling their children back to their cottages, the men remembering that ploughing and harrowing had to be done. Gilbert was bundled into the saddle of one of the retainer's horses and a taciturn Gurney led them back to the manor house. Just before they entered the gates, he pulled his horse alongside Corbett.

'Hugh, I thank you.'

Corbett looked at him.

'I know what you are thinking,' Gurney said. 'Perhaps I should have shown more force, but these are my people. I held Marina at her baptism.'

Corbett patted him gently on the arm.

'Sir Simon, I'm not your judge,' he said. 'Gilbert may well be guilty and if he is he should hang for that terrible crime. But he may be able to help us. You have dungeons?'

Gurney nodded.

'Then take him to them, but make him comfortable.'

Gurney agreed and they clattered into the yard.

Alice and her maids hurried out and Gurney hastily explained what had happened. Alice led them into the hall and the kitchen boys brought in stoups of ale, bread, cheese and salted bacon. Monck was already sitting before the fire with a heavy-eyed Ranulf and Maltote. He seemed a little calmer than the night before and listened patiently while Corbett described what had happened in the village.

'You will question Gilbert?'

Corbett nodded.

'Good!'

'But shouldn't you do so?' Corbett asked. 'Surely Marina's death is linked to the Pastoureaux? She was a member of their community.'

'No, no.' Monck shook his head and played with the pommel of his dagger. 'You deal with Gilbert.'

Corbett hid his annoyance. 'Tell me, where is Lickspittle buried?'

'In the village cemetery.'

'Did he leave any effects?'

'Yes, some papers, geegaws, daggers, swords, the clothes he died in. Selditch prepared the corpse, though that was done hurriedly enough. A decapitated body is not something to linger over.'

'May I look at these effects?' Corbett asked.

'In time.' Monck got to his feet. 'Now I am busy with the venerable sisters of the Holy Cross convent.' He patted Corbett patronizingly on the shoulders. 'You take care of the rustics, Corbett. Leave other matters to me.' He walked out of the hall.

Corbett winked at Ranulf and Maltote. 'And how are my lively lads?'

Ranulf groaned. 'Too much wine, too little water,' he said. 'It's Maltote's fault – he invited Catchpole to a drinking contest.' He stopped speaking as Catchpole himself came into the hall.

'Sir Hugh, the prisoner is in the dungeons.' The old soldier grinned. 'It's a long time since we had a prisoner.'

'Is he comfortable?'

'Aye, but fearful of being hanged.' Catchpole smiled. 'But, there again, aren't we all?'

Corbett finished his ale and walked out to the courtyard. He watched as Monck mounted his horse and galloped out through the gates. Corbett went back up to his own chamber and took a special key from his saddlebag.

'Every self-respecting housebreaker has one, Master,' Ranulf had once explained. 'All locks are similar and this key fits most.'

Corbett hastened down the gallery towards Monck's room. He slipped the key into the lock. It turned easily.

'Well,' Corbett said to himself, 'Ranulf was right.'

He opened the door and stared around the chamber. The stools were precisely positioned around the table, the blankets neatly arranged on the bed. Monck's tidy mind, Corbett thought. Monck's saddlebags lay tidily under the window, but they were securely strapped and buckled. Corbett went across to the small table beside the bed. A thick beeswax candle stood there and the wax had dripped down, forming a brittle crust on the table.

'I wonder?' Corbett whispered to himself.

Monck might be a strange character but he was still a clerk. Perhaps he, like Corbett, would sit in his bed late at night poring over parchments, scribbling notes on his writing tray. Corbett knelt, felt beneath the bed and smiled in triumph as his fingers caught hold of three pieces of parchment.

He pulled them out carefully and sat on the edge of the bed to study them. The first appeared to be a list of precious objects. Corbett examined it closely; these items were not mere baubles but silver plate, cups, even a cope. It was difficult to decipher the writing because Monck had used many of the personal abbreviations so beloved of chancery clerks. Corbett put the list on the bed and studied the second piece of parchment. At first he could make no sense of the strange lines drawn on it. He smoothed the parchment out and then realized he was looking at a crude map of the Hunstanton area. It was very similar to the one he had drawn. He traced with his fingers the coastline of the Wash, as drawn by Monck, and found the crosses that marked Holy Cross convent, Hunstanton village, Mortlake Manor, the gallows and the Hermitage. It was more detailed than his own map and covered a wider area, including Swaffham, the area around the Wash and the river Nene. It was here that Monck had done the most scribbling, with dotted lines criss-crossing each other. On the third piece of parchment was a crude drawing of the coastline and a sketch of a cog under sail.

Corbett tried to memorize every detail of all three parchments before pushing them back under the bed. He got up and, making sure everything was in its place, walked across and looked out through the unshuttered window which, like his, overlooked a grey, sullen sea.

Whatever brought you here, Monck, he thought, it's not the Pastoureaux!

He left the chamber, locking it securely behind him, and went down to the others sitting in the hall.

'Sir Simon, may I see the prisoner now?' he asked.

Gurney nodded. 'Catchpole will take you down. Selditch is already with him.'

Catchpole escorted Corbett along a passageway which ran by the kitchen. He stopped before a metal-studded door, opened it and revealed steps leading down into a cavernous darkness relieved only by the flickering light of a few sconce torches. At the bottom of the steps was a long passageway hewn out of the rock. Corbett touched the wall in surprise. Catchpole, leading the way, stopped. 'Didn't you know, Sir Hugh, that Mortlake Manor is built on a warren of passageways and tunnels? It used to be a ferry point for those who wanted to travel across the Wash.' He pointed to the ceiling. 'Some people say the Romans had a watch tower here with a beacon to guide their ships. After that the Saxons, then old Duke William of Normandy built a keep. You should talk to physician Selditch, he knows the history of the place. But, come.'

They continued down the narrow sloping passage. Corbett felt a flicker of panic and tried to control his breathing. Maeve and Ranulf always teased him about his horror of enclosed spaces. At last Catchpole stopped before a heavy timber door with a small grille at the top. He unlocked it and mockingly ushered Corbett through.

The dungeon was no more than a bare, cavernous storeroom, though Gurney had tried to make his prisoner comfortable. Gilbert was sitting on the edge of a cot bed with Selditch on a stool opposite him. The physician was washing the prisoner's face with a mixture of water and wine and applying an unguent to the large bruise around his eyes. A small, three-branched candelabra provided a pool of light. Gilbert hardly looked up but stared morosely at the rush-covered floor whilst Selditch, busy with his medicines and potions, mumbled a greeting. At last he finished.

'There!' He smiled at Corbett. 'No real injury, some bruising on his chest and legs. But he'll live to stand trial.'

'They murdered my mother!' Gilbert muttered.

'They say,' Corbett replied quietly, 'that you murdered the girl.'

Selditch got to his feet. 'I'll wait for you outside, Sir Hugh.'

Corbett nodded, sat on the stool and waited for the physician to close the door behind him.

'Gilbert!' he ordered. 'Look at me!'

The young man lifted his podgy, slack face and rubbed his wavering, watery eyes. Could this man, Corbett wondered, clumsy, slightly dim-witted, catch and murder the young fawn-like Marina? He closed his eyes – an idea had occurred to him but it flickered like a weak flame and he lost the thread. Something about Marina being out on the moors? Corbett stared down at his hands. Yes, that was it! Marina was a local girl. She knew the area well. If she was threatened, why not try and return to the Hermitage? Or had she gone to meet, not her father in the village, but someone from the manor? The visitors – the Prioress and Father Augustine – had, obviously, been abroad that night. Selditch had arrived late at table. But anyone could have left the manor – Catchpole had mentioned underground passages. Had someone used one of them to slip out of the manor?

'I didn't murder the girl,' Gilbert mumbled.

Corbett pointed to the scratches on the man's hands and wrists as well as the few on his face.

'Where did you get these?'

'When I was running away, the brambles tore at me.'

'And what about the amber necklace found in your house?'

Gilbert shook his head blankly. He stared unblinkingly at Corbett.

'I wouldn't hurt Marina. Gilbert loves Marina. All Gilbert wanted to do was stroke her soft hair.'

Corbett studied the young man. You are no murderer, he reflected, but you are someone's catspaw.

'Gilbert, the necklace was found in your hut.'

'Somebody put it there.'

'And Marina refused to meet you.'

'No, she didn't.'

Corbett's head snapped up. 'What?'

The young man smiled so slyly that Corbett had to pinch himself. Perhaps Gilbert was more intelligent, more cunning than he had thought.

'You met Marina?'

'Yes, at our usual place, the old oak on the moors. Marina met me twice. I put something there. When we were young we used to play there. Marina, me and Blanche.'

'The reeve's daughter?'

'Yes, the reeve's daughter.' Gilbert suddenly grasped Corbett's knee. 'Why did they kill Mother? Is she really dead? Will she go to heaven?'

Corbett gently removed the man's hand; it felt weak, slack.

'Are you in good health, Gilbert?' he asked.

'Will Mother be in heaven?'

'Yes, of course, she died with her face towards God. But, Gilbert, are you injured? Your hands are weak.'

'They have always been,' the young man replied. 'Mother said it was because of my birth. I am not as strong as I look. That's why Marina always trusted me.' Gilbert drew himself up and smiled. 'That's why I took the package to the old oak.'

'The package?' Corbett asked.

'Well, yes, a small letter, a scroll. A pedlar brought it from Bishop's Lynn. It had Marina's name on it because I read the markings. Every day I took it to the oak tree. Marina didn't come.' He smiled. 'But I did talk to her when I went to the Hermitage, even though they refused to let me. I told her I had a present for her.'

Gilbert's jaw fell slack. Corbett looked around the room. A jug of wine stood in the corner. He filled a battered cup and thrust it into Gilbert's hand.

Gilbert gulped some wine and went on, 'Marina came to the oak and I gave it to her.'

'The package?'

'Well, as I said, it was really a small scroll.'

'Did you know what was in it?'

'No, Marina put the scroll beneath her robe, kissed me on the cheek and left.'

'And you don't know what was in it?'

'No, Master, I don't. Will I hang?'

Corbett got to his feet and patted the prisoner on the shoulder.

'Don't worry, Gilbert, you won't hang. Someone will, but you won't. However, it's best if you stay here for your own protection.'

Corbett hammered on the door. Catchpole and Selditch were waiting for him. They went back along the passage, up the steps and back into the hall. Corbett tried to draw Selditch into conversation about the history of the house but the physician became strangely evasive. He shrugged, fluttered ink-stained fingers and refused to meet Corbett's eye. Corbett strode impatiently away to look for Gurney. He found him in his writing chamber. Gurney looked up as he strode in.

'I want the baker brought here,' Corbett said without preamble.

'Fourbour?'

Corbett drummed his fingers on the desk. 'Yes, and Robert the reeve also. I want to question them.'

'Why?'

'Because, Sir Simon, none of these mysteries will be solved until honest answers are given to honest questions!'

Chapter 6

By noon Fourbour and the reeve were at Mortlake Manor. Corbett saw the baker first. Brushing aside the man's protests at being taken from his work, Corbett waved him to a stool in the corner of the great hall and sat opposite. He studied the man's silver hair and pasty skin, which made it look as though the baker had been tinted by the flour he used. Fourbour was small and thin, with darting eyes and a flickering tongue. A muscle high in his cheek twitched nervously.

'I want to talk to you about the death of your wife,' Corbett said brusquely.

Fourbour's nervousness increased.

'Her name was Amelia?'

'Yes,' Fourbour whispered.

'And how long had you been married?'

'Six years. She was ten years my junior.' The man's eyes filled with tears. 'She was very pretty, Sir Hugh.' His eyes flitted round the empty hall. 'But she was never at home in Hunstanton.'

'Where did she come from?'

'She was a miller's daughter from Bishop's Lynn. I used to go there to buy my flour. Her maiden name was Culpeper.'

Corbett glanced away. A miller in a place like Bishop's Lynn would be very prosperous. Why had he allowed his daughter to marry a village baker? Fourbour seemed to read Corbett's mind.

'Amelia had been involved in scandal. She became pregnant, but the child died.' The words came out in a rush.

'And you asked for her hand in marriage?'

'Yes, yes, I did. Her father was only too pleased. He bestowed a large dowry and Amelia did not object. At first our marriage was happy but, about eighteen months ago—' Fourbour pushed his fingers through his thinning hair. 'Yes, I think it was then, Amelia became secretive and unhappy. She would go for long walks or ride out on the moors. I would object but she said the villagers didn't like her, she had to get away.'

'Do you know where she went?'

'Sometimes, I think, as far as Holy Cross convent.'

'Didn't she have any friends?'

'No, not really. On May Day and Holy Days she tried to join the rest of the women on the green, but they always ignored her. The same was true when she went to church.' Fourbour licked his dry lips. 'Amelia said she used to be jostled.'

'Did she see the priest?'

'Twice. But Amelia said she didn't like Father Augustine. She found him rather cold.'

Corbett nodded understandingly. 'And the evening your wife was killed?'

Fourbour rubbed his face in his hands. 'Amelia had been agitated,' he replied slowly. 'Just before dusk she saddled our horse and said she would ride out on the moor.' The baker's voice broke. 'The horse came back by itself. I and my apprentices went out to search. We found her there, hanging from a rope that had been thickly coated with pitch. Lord knows, it was black as soot out here. If it hadn't been for the white of her face, we wouldn't have glimpsed her. One of my apprentices saw her first. He saw her hanging. I said not to approach her. I just couldn't believe it.'

'Didn't you want to cut your wife's body down?'

Fourbour looked away.

'I couldn't,' he stuttered. 'I just went cold. One of the apprentices ran to Mortlake Manor. Sir Simon, the physician and that strange man, Monck, came. Monck carried a torch. He and the physician went forward. Monck searched the ground beneath the scaffold then remounted his horse to cut Amelia free. Afterwards he said there was no sign of any other hoof marks or boot prints.'

Fourbour paused. He seemed to be thinking. 'The next morning,' he said at last, 'the headless body of his servant was found on the beach. At first, I thought the deaths were connected.'

'Did you?' Corbett asked. 'Why?'

'Oh, because they happened at the same time.'

Corbett touched the man gently on the back of his hand. It felt like a sliver of ice.

'They were murdered, Master Fourbour. Cerdic Lickspittle and your wife were murdered. Do you know why?'

The man shook his head.

'Can you tell me anything which would explain your wife's death?'

Again the shake of the head.

'Or who rode your wife's horse back to the outskirts of the village?'

'I don't know,' Fourbour whispered. 'The villagers who saw it thought it was Amelia, but the night was dark and the rider wore a cloak.'

Corbett chewed his lip. He heard Robert the reeve outside the door, complaining loudly about being kept waiting. Corbett ignored him.

'You saw your wife's body?' he said gently.

Fourbour nodded.

'And there was no other mark of violence on her?'

'No,' the baker whispered.

'And did you discover anything amongst her possessions – a letter, a note – that might explain her death?'

'No, I didn't.' Fourbour looked away. 'Amelia was a caring, loving young woman. She had been grievously hurt by the desertion of her lover and the death of her child. And, before you ask, never once did she mention him.' For a moment he looked as though he were going to say more, but clearly he thought better of it.

'What were you going to say?' Corbett asked quietly. 'Please tell me.' He leaned forward and gripped the man's wrist. 'I apologize for my blunt questions. Your wife may have had a sad life but she had a tragic death. She met her murderer out on the moors. Are you going to allow him or her to walk away scot free?'

Fourbour opened his wallet and brought out an ivory necklace. It glinted and shone in the candlelight.

'It's beautiful,' Corbett murmured. 'And rather costly.'

'It was Amelia's,' Fourbour said. 'And, although she never said, I always believed it was given to her by her lover. No reason, it's just that she carried it everywhere.'

'Anything else?' Corbett asked.

'Once, just once, I went out after her on the moors. Amelia began complaining about the villagers. I told her they were poor people. Amelia looked at me and laughed. She said Hunstanton might be richer than I thought.' He shrugged. 'I didn't know what she meant. Do you, Sir Hugh?'

'No.' Corbett got to his feet and held out his hand. 'Master Fourbour, I thank you for seeing me. And, if necessary, I will come back to you again.'

Fourbour heaved a sigh of relief and left the hall as Gurney's steward ushered Robert the reeve into the room. Robert looked surlily at Corbett, who waved him to the empty stool. The reeve pulled his cloak about him, his fat face suffused with a malicious arrogance.

'I am a busy man, Sir Hugh. Ask your questions but, before you threaten me, may I remind you that Gilbert and his mother were found guilty of murder by the court. And we did not intend to kill her.'

Corbett leaned across. 'Master Reeve, you are an assassin and a bully. A man full of his own pride who acts to hide his own secrets.'

The reeve paled.

'What do you mean?' he stuttered.

Corbett smiled to himself. The reeve had forgotten the insults he had thrown at him in his alarm at being accused of harbouring a secret. The reeve's black button eyes watched Corbett anxiously.

'Secrets!' he exclaimed. 'What secrets?'

'Your newly found wealth.'

'It was a bequest. A legacy.'

'From whom?'

'A distant relative.'

'Where did this distant relative live?'

The reeve looked away.

'Master Robert,' Corbett murmured, 'I can order your arrest and send you south to be questioned before the King's Bench. Now, you do not wish that, do you? Your wife has recently given birth to a child and you are, quite rightly, an important man in this community. You could spend months in London.'

The reeve looked sullen and bit at a dirty fingernail.

'I was given the money honestly.'

'Who by?'

The reeve sighed.

'I want the truth, Robert,' Corbett persisted.

'A pedlar came to Hunstanton. He brought a message from Edward Orifab, a goldsmith in Bishop's Lynn, saying that he held certain monies for me. I went there and was given five silver coins and one gold piece.'

Corbett narrowed his eyes. 'And you didn't ask who would bestow such wealth on you?'

Robert shook his head. 'The goldsmith was most insistent. He would tell me nothing.'

Corbett watched the reeve carefully. You are lying, he thought.

'You are sure of that, Robert?'

'As God made little green apples, Sir Hugh.'

'And your daughter, Blanche?'

Robert smiled. 'She joined the Pastoureaux and left.'

'You seem pleased.'

'I miss her, but I have seven mouths to feed and what could Blanche do? She was too poor for the nunnery and whom could she marry? Someone like Gilbert? I am a poor man, Sir Hugh. Blanche will be happy.'

Corbett nodded. He thanked and dismissed the reeve, then sat staring at the wall. 'Bishop's Lynn! Bishop's Lynn!' he repeated to himself.

'Master?'

Corbett looked up. Ranulf was standing over him.

'Sit down, Ranulf. Do you feel better now?'

'Aye, it's a wonder what a walk in God's fresh air will do.'

'Good! Listen, Ranulf, we are just whistling in the dark here. Monck scurries around the countryside doing God knows what. It's time we did a little work ourselves. I want you and Maltote to go to the village tomorrow and see what you can find out. And talk to Gilbert – he roams the moors and may have seen something.'

Ranulf pulled a face. Secretly, though, he was delighted at the prospect of working independently, for once not under the eye of old Master Long Face.

'Anything else, Master?' he asked innocently.

'No, just use your native wit and discretion,' Corbett said. 'Help me to clear up this mystery because, I assure you, the devil stalks the moors of Hunstanton!'

'And you're going to Bishop's Lynn, Master?'

Corbett shook his head. 'No, not yet. I'm off to Walsingham. If Monck won't tell me the truth then I'll ask the king himself. He'll either tell me or we'll leave and let Monck find out what is happening here.' Corbett rose. 'And you still can't remember where you have seen Master Joseph before?'

Ranulf shook his head.

'Oh well. Let Maltote know what's happening.'

Corbett walked out of the hall and back to his own chamber. He filled his saddlebags, collected his boots, cloak and sword belt and stared through the window. It was a fine day, but still misty. He would visit the village and speak to Father Augustine about the desecrated graves, then ride on to Holy Cross convent and, from there, to Walsingham.

Corbett found the priest busy in his church preparing the altar for the funeral masses of Gilbert's mother and of Marina. The two coffins stood on wooden trestles before the rood screen; Father Augustine was trimming the purple funeral candles that flanked the two coffins. He put the knife down as Corbett walked up the nave.

'Sir Hugh, not more tragic news?'

Corbett shook his head.

'Where is everyone?' he asked. 'I found the village empty.'

Father Augustine waved him over to one of the benches in the transept.

'My parishioners are making up for lost time. Whatever happens the fields still need ploughing, the soil always remains.'

'You said you were born in Bishop's Lynn, so you're not a countryman yourself?' Corbett said.

'No, my father was a trader. But come, you are a busy man, you are not here to ask me about my past.'

'No, Father, I came about the disturbed graves. Perhaps you could show me?'

Father Augustine led him out into the overgrown churchyard.

'My predecessor,' he explained, 'Father Ethelred, was very old and infirm. That's why the bishop sent me here. When spring comes, I'll tidy this place up.'

Corbett looked around at the crumbling headstones and at the weather-beaten wooden crosses – all of which had been freshly coated with black pitch.

'I did that,' Father Augustine said. 'The parish council were concerned at how quickly the wood rots. But let me show you the graves that have been disturbed.'

He took Corbett across the churchyard and pointed to where the wet earth had been freshly turned.

'This is the most recent.'

'Who is buried here?' Corbett asked.

Father Augustine squatted down on the wet grass and peered at the weathered headstone.

'Yes, I remember this,' he said. 'When I checked the burial book I found that this is the grave of some unknown person. Church law is strict about this,' he explained. 'If a stranger dies, he has to be buried in the nearest parish with the word *Incognitus* – "Unknown" – and the date of his death on the tombstone.'

'And the other graves?' Corbett asked.

The priest took Corbett round, pointing out the disturbed graves. Corbett quietly realized there was a pattern to the desecration. All but two of the pillaged graves were of persons unknown – the exceptions were both old ladies. And they were all of old people who had died between the years 1216 and 1256.

'And you have no idea who is the perpetrator?'

'None whatsoever,' Father Augustine sighed. 'I have set guard, as did Robert the reeve and members of the parish council. It's always the same.'

'When is it done,' Corbett asked. 'At night?'

The priest nodded. 'Though on one occasion the desecration occurred late in the afternoon. Only the good Lord knows what they were after.'

'Amelia Fourbour, the baker's wife,' Corbett asked abruptly, 'she visited you?'

The priest shrugged. 'Yes, she did. A very unhappy woman. Amelia complained about the villagers, but there was little I could do.' Father Augustine looked up at the overcast sky. 'I cannot explain her death and was unable, God forgive me, to assist her when she was alive. You've met my parishioners, Sir Hugh, they are as hard as the earth they till!'

Corbett agreed and thanked him. He went back to the

lychgate, mounted his horse and rode through the dusk towards the Holy Cross convent. He followed the cliff path, now and again stopping to stare out at the grey angry sea. At last the convent came into sight. As soon as he entered the gates, Corbett sensed the wealth of the foundation. The doors were freshly painted, opening soundlessly on well-oiled hinges. The outhouses were tiled, the woodwork fresh and gleaming and the yard neatly cobbled. A groom took his horse and a lay sister led him into the convent. Here again the wealth of the sisters was apparent. The walls were panelled, the furniture well polished and beautifully carved statues stood in recesses. At the end of the passageway, above an arched door, was a superb triptych. The air smelt sweetly of wood, resin and incense.

'You admire our convent?' the lay sister asked, pausing as Corbett stopped to gaze at a large cross carved and painted in the Byzantine style.

'It is quite beautiful,' Corbett replied.

'Only the high-born are admitted here, the daughters or widows of nobles,' the lay sister explained. 'They bring rich dowries – and, of course, there's always the profit from the sheep.'

Corbett remembered the flocks he had seen on the moors.

'The convent exports wool?' he asked.

'Oh, yes, it goes by the cartload to Whitstable, Boston, Bishop's Lynn and Hull.' The lay sister straightened up. 'It is high-quality wool, much in demand by Flemish weavers.'

Corbett took one last, lingering look at the crucifix and followed his guide along beautifully furnished passageways to Dame Cecily's chamber. The prioress appeared pleased to see him. She ordered wine and sweetmeats and escorted Corbett to a large throne-like chair before a roaring fire.

Corbett sat down and stared around. Even the queen's chamber at Westminster couldn't rival such riches – woollen rugs, golden tapestries, silver oil-lamps, precious candelabra, paintings and silver ewers, cups and dishes adorned the room.

'Before you ask, Sir Hugh,' said Dame Cecily, placing a goblet of wine beside him. 'We sisters of the Holy Cross do not take a vow of poverty. We are a foundation dedicated to good works and prayer and to providing a refuge for women of good standing in what can only be termed a violent world.'

Corbett murmured his thanks and stared at the fire. Such foundations were common, he reflected, built on generous endowments and constantly financed by a regular source of income.

'How long has the convent been here?' he asked.

'Sir Simon's great-grandfather issued the first charter. The building was completed in 1220. I am the fifth prioress and our community is sixty strong.'

'So you have no objection to the Pastoureaux. You don't see them as rivals?' Corbett said, half-teasingly, as the prioress lowered herself gracefully into a large, quilted chair.

Dame Cecily shook her head.

'Of course not. We give the Pastoureaux every help we can. We are only too pleased to accept their labour in our stables, farms and orchards. They cause us no problems.'

'You have heard of the murder?' Corbett abruptly asked. 'The girl Marina?'

Dame Cecily nodded. 'Of course, poor girl. She did apply to this convent, wishing to come to us as a lay sister, but . . .' Dame Cecily shrugged elegantly plump shoulders, with such a look of contrived sorrow on her face that, in any other circumstances, Corbett would have laughed.

'Has Master Monck been here?'

'Yes, this morning.'

'Why?'

'He came about his servant, Cerdic Lickspittle, the one who was found murdered on the beach.'

'And?' Corbett asked testily.

Dame Cecily became flustered. 'Well, specifically, he wanted to know if Lickspittle visited here the day he died. I said yes.' Dame Cecily played with the pleats of her woollen gown. 'But his visit was very short. He was a nuisance – our sisters were for ever seeing him riding out along the headland and staring out to sea. Master Monck is no better.'

'Perhaps they were concerned?' Corbett suggested.

'About what?'

'About one of your order, Dame Agnes, who fell from the cliff top.'

Dame Cecily became visibly agitated.

'That was an accident!' she snapped.

'But Dame Cecily,' Corbett persisted, 'what on earth was one of your sisters doing out on the headland at the dead of night?'

'I don't know. We are a foundation for noble ladies, not a prison. We guard against intruders, but do not prevent our sisters from leaving as they wish. I can only suppose that Sister Agnes wished to go for a walk.'

'On a stormy cliff top,' Corbett said disbelievingly. 'In the dead of night?'

Dame Cecily spread her plump little fingers.

'Sister Agnes was a hardy soul.'

'What position did she hold?'

'She was our treasurer.'

'Did you investigate her death?'

'Yes. Sir Simon came, as did Master Monck. They

examined the headland, but found no marks to suggest anything but that Agnes slipped and fell.'

'So there was nothing suspicious about her death?' Corbett asked.

'Nothing whatsoever. We found her corpse on the rocks below and she now lies buried in our graveyard, God rest her!'

'And Cerdic?'

'Oh, he came one morning. He stayed for Mass, saw round our church then left.'

'Is that all?'

'Of course.'

'And the baker's wife,' Corbett asked. 'Amelia Fourbour?'

'Poor woman, she would often ride past our gates.' Dame Cecily played with the gold bracelet around her plump wrist. 'But we knew nothing about her.'

Corbett sensed he would get no further. He finished his wine and placed the goblet gently on the table beside him.

'Dame Cecily, I ride to Walsingham. His Grace the King will be pleased at the hospitality you have offered me.'

Dame Cecily's lips smiled, but her eyes were puzzled.

'I would like to stay here,' Corbett explained, 'in your guest house.'

The prioress clapped her hands girlishly. 'Of course, you will be our welcome guest.'

Corbett thanked her, withdrew and went back to the stables. He told the groom that he would be back in the hour – he needed to ride, relax and marshal his thoughts. Once outside the convent he turned his horse's head in the direction of the headland, determined to make use of the dying day's light. First he found the long, winding path leading down to the beach. He hobbled his horse and went downwards.

However, the mist was growing thicker and the tide was racing in, beating against the rocks at the foot of the cliffs. He went back and led his horse along the cliff edge, turning his head sideways against the buffeting wind. He walked carefully because the ground was treacherous. He passed the convent where it nestled in a small hollow, a sprawling collection of buildings behind its curtain wall. He continued along the headland and gazed out over the sea. The wind was even stronger here. His horse became nervous, so he left it to crop the grass, and went back to the spot where Sister Agnes must have stood. Darkness was falling. He was glad that he had a warm bed to go to – the night would be black, without stars or moon, and the wind, which snatched at his hair and stung his eyes, would grow stronger.

He stood for a while. He could understand how Sister Agnes could have slipped, but what was a middle-aged nun doing out at night staring across the sea? Just what were the mysteries of these parts? Why had Monck and Cerdic come here? Corbett was about to turn away when he glimpsed a faint light on the sea. He stared and realized that, in spite of the mist and the loneliness, the sea roads beyond the horizon would be very busy, with cogs and fishing smacks sailing to and from Hull and other eastern ports and the many fishing villages clustered along the coast. Corbett walked further along, away from the convent, noticing how the cliffs turned in a series of little bays and natural harbours. Satisfied, he collected his horse and went back to the convent. He watched the groom unsaddle and stable the horse for the night and slipped the man a coin.

'Take good care of my horse,' he urged. 'Tomorrow I have to travel far and fast.'

'Where to, sir?'

'Walsingham.'

The man scratched his head. 'You'd best go back to the village and find the road from there. If you keep to it and the weather is fair, you should be at Walsingham by the afternoon.'

Corbett thanked him. 'Oh, by the way, Sister Agnes, the nun who fell—'

'God rest her, sir, I knew her well.'

'Did she often go out for walks along the cliff top?'

'Oh no, just occasionally. Always very careful she was, carried her staff and lantern but, there again, she was such a busy woman.' The groom gave a gap-toothed grin. 'A busy hive this convent, what with its farms, its sheep and its wool.'

'But there was no pattern to her leaving?' Corbett asked.

'Why?' The man became more defensive. 'Sister Agnes came and went as she pleased. I tell you this, sir, I was born in these parts and they be treacherous. The cliffs are made of chalk and can crumble. On the moors be marsh which will trap a horse and rider. And above all there's the tides – after heavy rain and in high winds the sea can race in faster than a greyhound.'

Corbett thanked him and went back into the convent. One of the sisters showed him to the small guest house opposite the chapel and brought to him a savoury meat pie and a small jug of the best claret he had drunk in months. After which Corbett retired. However, as he lay dozing on the bed, his mind kept returning to that lonely, windswept headland and the figure of the nun resting on a stick, holding a lantern, staring out across the midnight sea.

Chapter 7

'Your Grace, I demand to know why Lavinius Monck is at Mortlake Manor.'

Corbett stood in the royal chamber in the Augustinian priory of Walsingham and glared at the king, who was slouched in a window seat staring moodily out of the window.

On the other side of the room, sprawled in a chair before the fire, the hard-faced John de Warenne, Earl of Surrey, shifted his bulk uneasily and slapped mailed gauntlets against his knee.

'Master clerk,' the earl called over his shoulder, 'you do not make demands of your king!'

'Oh, shut up, Surrey, and don't be so bloody pompous!'

Edward of England glared across at his boon companion and faithful friend. He wished the earl would keep quiet. De Warenne was fine leading a charge against the Scots but when it came to intrigue he had all the tact and diplomacy of a battering ram. Edward stared at Corbett and hid a grin. Usually so calm and poised, Corbett now was travel-stained, covered in flecks of dirt from head to foot. He was unshaven and his usually hooded eyes blazed with anger. The king extended his hands.

'Hugh, Hugh. Why all this excitement?' He indicated the

chair beside him. 'Sit down, man.' Edward smiled, his craggy, leonine face suffused with charm. 'I've come to the blessed shrine to seek peace and the wisdom of God.'

Corbett walked over and took the seat. You are a liar, he thought. He stared at the king's falcon-like face. The silver-grey beard, shoulder-length hair, open, frank eyes and generous mouth were all a mask. Edward of England was a born plotter who loved intrigue and took to it as easily as a duck to water. Corbett, however, wasn't in the mood to be played with. He had ridden all day from Holy Cross convent, arriving at Walsingham just as darkness fell.

'Why,' the king asked, 'are you so concerned about Lavinius?'

Corbett seized his opportunity and explained in pithy sentences what was happening out at Hunstanton. Edward scratched his beard, becoming more and more embarrassed at the picture of Corbett, his principal clerk, blundering amongst the salt marshes and watery meadows of Norfolk.

'I thought,' he said when Corbett had finished, 'that you might help Lavinius, particularly after the death of Cerdic.' He nodded towards de Warenne, who stared moodily into the fire. 'And Surrey agreed with me.'

'Lavinius is a good clerk!' de Warenne said.

'My lord,' Corbett replied, 'Lavinius is mad.'

The earl swung round in his chair, but Corbett's gaze did not falter.

'You know that, my lord,' he continued quietly. 'The man is driven mad with grief.'

'And the Pastoureaux?' Edward asked quickly.

'Your Grace, I would recommend that, when you next meet your council at Westminster, you issue a decree to all sheriffs, bailiffs and port officials, as well as leading barons and tenants-in-chief, banning the Pastoureaux from your realm.'

'On what grounds?'

'Public order and the maintenance of the king's peace.'

'Why? Do you think these Pastoureaux are responsible for the murders?'

'They might be. But I am uncomfortable at strangers moving into an area and enticing the young people away with dreams of foreign travel.'

Edward nodded.

'But Monck's not there for the Pastoureaux,' Corbett went on. 'Your Grace, are you going to tell me the truth or do I surrender my seals of office and, like Sir Simon Gurney, retire to my manor?'

Edward leaned forward and grasped Corbett's knee in a sudden gesture of affection. His blue eyes brimmed with tears. Oh, God, no! Corbett thought. Not the role of Edward, the ageing monarch, abandoned by his friends. He knew what the king was going to say.

'Hugh.' The king's voice was throaty. 'You are tired.'

'Accept his resignation!' de Warenne jibed.

'Piss off, Surrey!' Edward bellowed. 'Just piss off and shut up!'

He got to his feet, his mood altering violently, and went to stand over de Warenne.

'This is your bloody mess!' he roared. 'I told you that. But oh, no, you had to send Monck!'

De Warenne gazed back. The king winked at him. The earl sighed – ever since they were lads he had been the king's whipping-boy; he would just have to accept this latest pretend tirade. Corbett stared out of the window and schooled his features. He knew the king and de Warenne were play-acting but he relaxed, knowing that now he would be given at least some of the truth.

Edward went across to the table, filled three goblets with white wine and served Corbett and de Warenne. He then sat sideways in the window seat and slurped noisily from his goblet, glaring at Corbett from underneath bushy eyebrows.

'I'll have letters issued this evening,' he said. 'You will take over from Monck.' He smacked his lips. 'Now, my Lord of Surrey, tell my good friend Hugh here what Monck is doing at Mortlake Manor.'

De Warenne got up and dragged his chair over. He patted Corbett on the shoulder.

'No offence, Hugh.'

'As always, none taken, my lord.'

De Warenne stared into his cup. 'The story begins in October 1216, in the last year of the reign of King John, our present lord's most noble and puissant grandfather.'

'Less of the bloody sarcasm!' Edward intervened.

'Well, the story is as follows. John spent most of his reign fighting his barons, moving around the country, trying to bring this earl or that lord into submission. He died at Newark-on-Trent. Some people think he was poisoned, others that he died of a broken heart after losing all his treasure and regalia in the Wash.' He smiled at the change in Corbett's expression. 'Ah, so you have heard the story. Let me refresh your memory. John was travelling north from Bishop's Lynn. He had his whole household with him and a long line of pack horses carrying his treasures. He was trying to cross the estuary of the Nene when, according to the chronicle, he lost all his wagons, carts and pack horses with the treasures, precious vessels and all the other things he cherished.' De Warenne paused and licked his lips. 'According to the chronicler Florence of Worcester, whose writings my clerks have studied, the ground opened up and violent whirlpools engulfed men, horses, everything.'

'What happened,' Edward explained, 'is that dear grandfather tried to cross the estuary too late in the day. You know the area? There was a sudden tidal surge, the waves rushed in and the treasure train was lost.' Edward shrugged. 'Dear grandfather went to Swynesford Abbey to console himself with fresh cider and rotten peaches and then on to Newark, where he gave up the ghost in something akin to the odour of sanctity.' Corbett smiled – 'Dear grandfather' had been the black sheep of the Plantagenet family; he had neither lived nor died in anything akin to sanctity.

'What was the treasure?' Corbett asked.

'A king's ransom,' Edward replied slowly. 'Dozens of gold and silver goblets, flagons, basins, candelabra, pendants and jewel-encrusted belts. The coronation regalia—' Edward sighed. 'And, what is worse, the coronation regalia of dear great-great-grandmother Matilda when she was Empress of Germany: a large jewel-encrusted crown, purple robes, a gold wand and the sword of Tristram.' Edward rubbed his stomach and groaned. 'A fortune,' he murmured. 'A bloody fortune lost in the sea!'

'Was there any attempt to search for it?'

'Well, you can imagine the confusion that broke out after grandfather's death. It was every man for himself and the devil take the hindmost. Father was only a child. He had difficulty keeping the crown, never mind looking for lost treasure!'

'And how does Monck come into this?'

'Well,' de Warenne replied. 'My family have always felt deeply ashamed about King John's disaster at the Wash. You see, *my* grandfather was in charge of the pack train.'

He glared at Corbett, daring him to smile – planning and other intellectual skills had always been a rarety in the Surrey family. Corbett refrained from comment.

'Good!' de Warenne breathed. 'Now, the treasure's lost. John dies. Everyone more or less forgets about it until a year ago, when Walter Denuglis, a leading goldsmith in London, purchased from a pawnbroker an ancient gold plate with John's arms on it.' De Warenne rolled his goblet in his fingers. 'Denuglis brought it to the exchequer. Then two other, very similar, pieces of plate were found. The clerks of the exchequer scrutinized the records from John's time. Sure enough, all three pieces had been part of John's treasure.'

'But,' Corbett interrupted, 'I thought everything was lost. Is it possible that these pieces were thrown up on some marsh, found by a pedlar and brought to London to be sold?'

'That isn't likely,' the king said. 'If it was a mere pedlar he hid his tracks very artfully. More importantly, Corbett, there's a legend in court circles that King John's disaster at the Wash was planned. Not even dear grandfather – who, admittedly, could be as dense as a forest – would try and cross the Wash without guides. Now a local man was hired, we know this from the records, called John Holcombe. He knew the estuary well. The accepted account says that he died in the tragedy.' Edward pursed his lips. 'But local legend has it that he escaped with a string of pack horses.'

'And if so, what happened to him?'

'We don't know,' de Warenne answered. 'Our clerks have searched the records of both central and local courts. There's no record of any John Holcombe surviving.'

'Are you sure?' Corbett insisted. 'Surely, after John's death the exchequer would have investigated such rumours thoroughly?'

'They did,' de Warenne replied. 'And could report nothing except for a very garbled story that Holcombe had been seen somewhere to the north of Walpole St Andrew, between that village and Bishop's Lynn. After that, he disappears from history.'

De Warenne paused as the bell of the priory began to ring for Vespers. Corbett reflected on the scraps of history he had been told.

'Did anyone survive the disaster of the Wash?' he asked.

'Oh, yes,' de Warenne said. 'Only the treasure train was lost. The king, the court and the escort escaped.'

'Was there a Gurney amongst them?'

Edward grinned. 'I wondered when you'd ask that! The answer is yes. Sir Richard Gurney, Sir Simon's great-grandfather, followed the king to Swynesford Abbey where he witnessed a charter. After the royal army dispersed, Gurney went home.'

Corbett chewed at the quick of his thumbnail.

'And so,' he concluded, 'Monck was sent to Mortlake Manor, not to investigate the Pastoureaux but to look into the possibility that this treasure, or part of it, is hidden in the area?'

The king nodded.

'But why Mortlake Manor?' Corbett asked. 'Why not the countryside around Bishop's Lynn?'

'It's a wild guess,' de Warenne said, 'based upon a scrap of information about the guide John Holcombe. He was seen riding north away from Bishop's Lynn. The only possible port could be Hunstanton, if he intended to flee abroad.'

'There's another reason Monck was sent,' the king interrupted. 'Whoever sold the plate in London knew where to go. They didn't blunder into just any goldsmith's shop. No, the three pieces were sold in different parts of the city. One near the Tower, another in Southwark and the last to some grubby pawnbroker near Whitefriars. Now that requires planning. It also means someone who knows the city well.'

'You mean Sir Simon Gurney?'

'It's possible, but we suspect the Pastoureaux. Their leader is a man called . . .' Edward closed his eyes.

'Master, Joseph,' Corbett reminded him.

'Yes, Master Joseph. And he regularly visits London. He may have been born there. Now, when we looked at Hunstanton, we asked ourselves what of significance had happened in the area about the same time as the gold appeared.' Edward smiled. 'The arrival of the Pastoureaux could not be ignored.'

'But how would Master Joseph know?'

'That, my dear clerk,' de Warenne answered, 'is a matter of conjecture. However, what a marvellous way of searching for the gold and silver, posing as a leader of a religious community!'

'And what has Monck discovered?' Corbett asked.

'Very little,' the king replied sourly. 'That's why we sent you. Monck was furious.' The king grasped Corbett's wrist. 'Will you do this for me, Hugh? Will you go back and find grandfather's treasure?'

Corbett nodded. The king heaved a sigh of relief. He got to his feet and clapped Corbett on the shoulder.

'In which case, we will leave you to your thoughts. It's Vespers and I must have a few words with God.'

The king beckoned to de Warenne to follow him. Corbett heard the door close behind them. He went over and absent-mindedly refilled his cup. Thank God, he thought, that Edward had not asked him about his suspicions, which were many and included more than just the Pastoureaux. Corbett sipped at his wine. Is that why the graves have been dug up? he wondered. Could the treasure be buried in the church-yard? Did it explain the ostentatious wealth of the Holy Cross convent? What about Robert the reeve? Had he stumbled upon something? And what of the Gurneys? Sir Simon was a rich man. Finally, the Pastoureaux – were they really searching for gold? Was that why Marina had died? And did Ranulf remember Master Joseph because he had come across him in London? Corbett sat back in his chair, closed his eyes and drifted into sleep.

He returned to Mortlake late the following evening to discover Gurney fretting because Monck had not returned from the moors.

'When did he leave?' Corbett asked, doffing his cloak and easing off his boots in front of the fire.

'Yesterday afternoon. I have made enquiries. He was seen last night galloping through the village. I told Catchpole and some of my servants to go out and search the moors, but they can't find him.'

'And Ranulf?' Corbett asked.

'He and Maltote have retired. They said they were exhausted.'

Corbett nodded and stretched his aching feet towards the fire. He glanced across the hearth to where Alice and Selditch sat drinking mulled wine.

'Did Monck ever tell you,' Corbett quietly began, 'why he was really here?'

'He said it was because of the Pastoureaux.'

Corbett rose, went across and closed the hall doors. He came back but this time he did not sit down but stared at Gurney, his wife and the sly, secretive face of the physician.

'Lavinius Monck came to Mortlake Manor,' Corbett explained, 'not because of the Pastoureaux but because of more ancient history, the lost treasure of King John.'

Corbett hit his mark. Alice looked up startled. The physician's head went down to conceal his features. Gurney's hand immediately went to his face as if he wished to smooth away his anxious frown. Corbett sat down.

'You knew, didn't you? You knew, or at least you suspected?'

'Aye.' Gurney shrugged. 'Of course I did. As soon as they arrived here, Monck and Lickspittle demanded to search the manorial rolls and court records.'

'Why?' Corbett asked. 'Is there anything there about the lost treasure?'

Gurney shook his head.

'Sir Simon,' Corbett persisted. 'You know the story. Your great-grandfather accompanied King John when he crossed the Wash. He journeyed with the king as far as Swynesford Abbey before returning here. You must have heard the legends about John Holcombe, the guide who may have escaped with some of the treasure. The king is determined to find this treasure. Did Monck tell you why?'

Again Gurney shook his head, but his eyes never left those of Corbett.

'Because some of the plate, which is supposed to lie under the sands of the Wash, has recently surfaced on the London markets. Somebody knows where that treasure is hidden and is already selling it.'

His three listeners sat frozen in their chairs.

'I believe,' Corbett continued, 'that someone in this manor is selling the treasure. I want the truth. Terrible deaths are occurring, horrible murders. Now, Sir Simon, on your allegiance to the king, do you know anything about the treasure?'

'No, he doesn't. But yes, I do!' Selditch sprang to his feet.

'Giles, there's no need!' Gurney said.

The physician rubbed his face with his hands. 'I'd rather tell Corbett than Monck. It's best if charges were not laid against you.'

'Master Selditch!' Gurney ordered. 'Sit down and keep quiet!'

The physician looked at Corbett.

'You'd have found out sooner or later,' he said. 'You, with your sharp eyes and silent ways. I sold the plate in London.' He laughed sourly. 'After all, I am a physician; I go to London regularly to meet friends as well as to purchase goods, those potions and powders that can only be bought there. I was also born in London, a fact you would have soon discovered, so I know the city well.' Selditch's voice was edged with bitterness. 'Especially the pawnbrokers. I was born poor. My parents could ill afford my education, so those tawdry little merchants knew me well.'

'There's no need for this,' Gurney interrupted quietly.

'I am sorry, Sir Simon, there is. Every need.' Selditch took a deep breath. 'Sir Hugh, I entered Sir Simon's household. He proved to be a generous lord. When we left the king's service his home became mine.' The physician paused and stared around the richly furnished hall. 'I became fascinated with the place. I searched every nook and cranny. I read every document in the manorial archives until I discovered

Mortlake's great secret.' Selditch looked at Gurney. 'It's best if Corbett sees what we know.'

Gurney quickly agreed. He told his wife to stay in the hall whilst he and Selditch led a bemused Corbett down into the underground passageways. Torches were lit. They continued along the hollow, cavernous passage past Gilbert's cell. Corbett peered through the door's spyhole, but the young man was fast asleep on what appeared to be a most comfortable bed. At the end of the passage, the physician pulled away a large beer barrel revealing a narrow doorway. He took a key from his belt and unlocked the door and they entered a long tunnel. The air was much colder and Corbett was sure he could hear the rumble of the sea. With the physician in front and Gurney behind, Corbett realized how vulnerable he was and wished Ranulf was with him. He put his hand on his dagger and, as the ground underfoot became slippery, wished he had not changed his boots for soft leather buskins. His heart began to pound and the sweat broke out on his brow, for the passageway was narrow, so tight it almost felt as if the walls were closing in on him. Corbett breathed deeply. He fixed his gaze on the spluttering torch Selditch carried and quietly prayed for a speedy end to their journey. Suddenly, Gurney and the physician turned a corner. The passageway became broader and led into an underground chamber. Corbett breathed more easily as Selditch lit the torches fixed in the walls of the cavern. The place flared into light. Selditch began to claw at a pile of boulders and stones in the far corner. Gurney went over to help him and Corbett watched fascinated as they pulled out a long pinewood coffin. Gurney undid the clasps and pushed the coffin forward. Corbett gazed at the yellowing skeleton that lay there. He looked up in surprise.

'Who is this? And what is this?'

He glimpsed a leather pouch at the foot of the coffin. He bent down to pick it up, but Gurney was faster. He plucked it out and held it tightly against his chest.

'Who is this?' Corbett repeated.

The hair on the nape of his neck began to prickle. His hand fell to his dagger.

'Oh, Hugh, Hugh,' Gurney murmured. 'We are not your enemies. We are only frightened of what you might do.' Gurney pointed to the skeleton. 'This is John Holcombe, once a native of Bishop's Lynn. My great-grandfather, Sir Richard Gurney, hired him to lead King John's convoy across the Wash.' Gurney tapped the decaying coffin with the toe of his boot. 'Instead Holcombe took it to its destruction – or at least part of it, the royal treasure train. Apparently, before King John left Wisbech, Holcombe had seen the treasure piled high on sumpter ponies and mules. In the blackness of his soul he devised a murderous plan. The king's convoy was in three parts – the king and the court first, the treasure train and then the foot soldiers. Holcombe was to go in front but on that day he held back. He also, using a heavy mist as his excuse, deliberately delayed the crossing.'

'The rest you know,' Selditch interposed. 'The tides began to sweep in. The treasure's escort panicked. Holcombe rode back. He seized a string of mules and, using his knowledge of the secret paths and routes, escaped with some of the treasure, leaving the rest to be washed away and its guardians drowned.'

Gurney took up the story again. 'Now, when my great-grandfather reached Swynesford, he began to think about what had happened. He was no fool and, in the last confusing days of King John's reign, he decided to leave the court and hunt Holcombe down. It's a long story.' Gurney played with the leather pouch he held. 'It's all contained in here.'

Corbett held his hand out and Gurney gave him the pouch.

'For you only, Hugh. I don't want that bastard Monck seizing these documents!'

Corbett nodded. 'We'll see,' he murmured. He gestured down at the coffin. 'How did Holcombe end up here?'

'Well, to cut a long story short, my great-grandfather caught him and hanged him on the gallows, the ones you passed on Hunstanton cliffs. Once the flesh was decomposed, he had his corpse placed in a special casket and buried it here.'

'But he told no one?' Corbett asked.

'No, he was ashamed. After all, it was he who had hired Holcombe and he had his enemies. The malicious would whisper that he and Holcombe were accomplices.'

'And what about the treasure?' Corbett asked.

'Ah, that's where the mystery begins. You see, Sir Richard had few sensibilities in the matter. Before he was hanged, Holcombe was tortured in the dungeon you have just passed. He refused to disclose his hiding-place but did admit he'd had an accomplice, a second guide named Alan of the Marsh, the steward here at the manor. According to Holcombe, Alan knew where the treasure was hidden. However, according to my great-grandfather's confession, dictated to his son, this Alan was never found nor the whereabouts of the treasure.'

Corbett pointed to Selditch. 'But you sold three pieces in London?'

'Ah!' Gurney knelt and placed the lid back on the coffin. He looked up at Corbett. 'The disaster at the Wash happened in the October of 1216, but it wasn't until the following February that great-grandfather caught up with Holcombe. When he did, out in the wilds of the moors, Holcombe carried a leather bag containing those three plates. According to my great-grandfather's confession, he thought Holcombe was probably heading for one of the ports to take ship to London or even abroad to sell these pieces.' Gurney got to his feet. 'Now, my great-grandfather had caught Holcombe with a very small portion of the treasure. What could he do? If he handed him over to justice Holcombe might, out of sheer malice, insinuate that my great-grandfather had been an accomplice in his terrible crime. And what could Sir Richard do with the plate? Send it to the exchequer in London and say he had found it? No. He buried it in Holcombe's secret grave in this hollowed-out cavern. No Holcombe, no grave, no treasure. Sir Richard dictated his confession but did not tell his heir where either Holcombe or the precious plate was buried.'

As Gurney finished speaking Corbett looked at Selditch. 'And your part in this?'

Selditch blew his cheeks out in a long sigh.

'I became interested, as I have said, in the history of Mortlake Manor and all its mysterious legends. I opened up the passageways, found this cavern and realized that the stones in the far corner had been disturbed. I pulled out Holcombe's coffin. Inside I found both Sir Richard's confession and three pieces of plate. I told Sir Simon. He said I should put the plate back where I found it. I did, because I wished to protect his good name. But then the king's wars interfered with trade. Sir Simon fell into the hands of moneylenders. I remembered the plates. I took them out, went to London on some pretext and raised enough gold and silver to pay off his creditors.' Selditch spread his hands. 'What I did was wrong. Sir Simon was only told after I returned.' The physician smiled. 'He was angry, but what could he do? The plate had been sold, his creditors paid off.' The physician shrugged his shoulders. 'And I'd settled a long outstanding debt.'

Corbett stared at him.

'What will you do, Hugh?' Gurney asked.

Corbett pulled a face. 'What's the use of going back to the king?' he replied slowly. 'After all, he now has the three pieces of plate. What troubles me is who else could be looking for the rest of the treasure? Are all these mysterious deaths connected to it?' Corbett pushed the leather bag into his belt, stretched out his hand and clasped Gurney's. 'Why should I punish you, Sir Simon? The king wouldn't believe it. As for your physician, a foolish but well-meaning mistake.' He held his hand up. 'But these documents are mine and Monck must not be informed.'

Gurney's gratitude, as well as Selditch's, was almost too embarrassing to tolerate. Once they had all sworn that no one other than Alice, Ranulf and Maltote would be told, Corbett was relieved to be out of the tunnels and back in the privacy of his own chamber. He was exhausted after his journey and the rather tense confrontation in the underground passageways. Corbett glanced at his companions snoring blissfully in their beds and settled down to study the manuscript he had taken from Gurney.

At times Corbett found it difficult. The parchment was yellow with age and the writer, Sir Richard's son, had recorded his father's confession in a scrawling, almost illegible hand. Corbett read the opening sentence: 'In the name of the Father, the Son and the Holy Ghost, I, Sir Richard Gurney of Mortlake Manor, confess this in secret, but tell the truth. I call on Christ, his blessed Mother and all the saints to be my witnesses.' The confession then rambled on about the crossing of the Wash, Holcombe's treachery, Lord Richard's shame, his secret pursuit of Holcombe and the latter's capture, torture and slow death by strangulation on the gibbet. Most of the details Corbett already knew, but one statement towards the end caught his attention. It was that Holcombe's accomplice, Alan of the Marsh, was thought to have gone into hiding somewhere in the vicinity of Hunstanton.

Corbett studied the manuscript again, rolled it up and hid it in his saddlebag. He then paced up and down the room, trying to probe the mysteries. What had happened to this Alan of the Marsh? Where was the treasure? Was Sir Simon telling the truth? Did Robert the reeve know something? Or Master Joseph of the Pastoureaux? Corbett breathed deeply. He lay down on his bed and wondered where Monck fitted into all of this.

Chapter 8

Corbett sat up and stared across at Maltote and Ranulf sleeping soundly on their beds. Had they discovered anything during his absence? He wanted to shake them awake, but that would be harsh. He got off the bed, sat at the table and reflected on his recent meeting with the king. What would have happened if he had tendered his resignation and Edward had accepted it? Where would Ranulf go? Could they all settle down on a manor and become farmers? Ranulf was now a clerk and had achieved his ambition. Corbett idly wondered if he should take Maeve's advice and delegate more of his work to Ranulf-atte-Newgate.

'Such matters can wait,' Corbett murmured.

He put his head on his arms for a few seconds and drifted again into sleep. He was dreaming of Leighton and the green fields behind the manor which stretched out to the river Lea. Other images tangled his dream. He could hear someone shouting his name. He opened his eyes and looked up. Ranulf was standing over him, grinning from ear to ear.

'Master, you returned late last night?'

Corbett groaned and stretched his aching limbs. He stared at the window.

'Lord save us, it's morning!' he murmured.

'Aye,' Ranulf agreed. 'Maltote and I have already been to Mass.' He preened himself, full of virtue. 'We thought of moving you to your bed but you seemed so comfortable. We would have waited up for you,' Ranulf continued, 'but I was teaching Maltote a new game of dice. We had a jug of wine. Two of the maids from the kitchen joined us.' Ranulf shrugged. 'You know how things are, Master?'

'Yes, I bloody well do!' Corbett retorted, getting to his feet.

Behind his back Ranulf pulled a face at Maltote sitting on the edge of his bed.

Corbett stripped, shaved and washed whilst Ranulf laid out fresh robes and linen. As he dressed, Corbett tersely told them what he had discovered the previous evening and described his meeting with the king.

Ranulf's eyes danced with merriment. 'The miserable Monck,' he crowed, 'will eat his heart out!' He handed Corbett his sword belt. 'So there's treasure here?'

'Aye, Ranulf, the king's treasure. And, if we find it, every last penny goes back to the exchequer.'

Not if I can help it, Ranulf thought.

'Isn't there a law?' he protested, looking at Maltote for support.

The messenger nodded wisely, though he had no idea what Ranulf was talking about.

'What law?' Corbett snapped.

'That if you find treasure trove, a quarter of it can be kept by the finder? That's what happened when old Leofric, you know the half-mad priest who lives in chambers by the Tower—'

Ranulf paused as they heard shouting from below and the

sound of running footsteps. A servant hammered on the door and burst into the room.

'What's the matter, man?'

'Sir Hugh, you'd best come now! Catchpole has returned. He's brought Master Monck!'

'What do you mean?'

'Monck's dead. A crossbow bolt in his chest!'

Corbett and his two companions hurried down into the yard. Sir Simon, Catchpole and other retainers were grouped just inside the entrance to the barn. Corbett pushed his way through. Monck's corpse lay on a pallet of straw, arms and legs flung out, head back. The heavy-lidded eyes were half-closed. The left side of his mouth was stained with dried blood, the crossbow bolt deeply embedded in his chest.

Corbett knelt down and stared at the white, waxen face.

'What happened?'

'Yesterday,' Gurney replied, 'Master Monck left late in the afternoon. He visited Father Augustine at Hunstanton before going on to the Holy Cross convent.'

'Last night he was seen thundering through Hunstanton village,' Catchpole added, 'riding his horse as if pursued by Satan and all his demons.'

'Where did you find him?'

'Out on the moors, just sprawled on the grass. No sign of his horse. That could be anywhere.'

'Where on the moors?' Corbett asked.

'Oh, on the wasteland area. And, before you ask, Sir Hugh, there were no other marks of violence or any sign of a struggle. Just Monck's corpse and the hoof prints of his own horse. The beast must have galloped off after his master's fall.'

Corbett glanced at the red-eyed physician; his face was

drawn and unshaven. Sir Simon also looked as if he hadn't slept the previous night. Did you tell me the truth? Corbett wondered. If so, why didn't you go to bed? What kept you up all night?'

'Is anything wrong?' Selditch asked.

Corbett forced a smile. 'Oh, master physician, what do you think? Perhaps you could examine Monck?' Corbett got to his feet and studied Monck's boots, leggings and cloak, which were coated with mud. 'Where's his sword belt?' he asked.

'It was rather loose,' Catchpole explained, 'so I took it off and put it over my saddle horn.'

Corbett nodded and glanced down at the dead man's face.

'God rest you, Lavinius,' he murmured. 'Perhaps you'll have peace now!'

He walked out of the barn to inspect Monck's sword belt, slung across Catchpole's saddle horn. The belt was rather rucked. Corbett eased the sword and dagger from their sheaths. These were gleaming clean so he pushed them back again.

'What's the matter, Master?' Ranulf whispered.

Corbett shook his head and walked across to the water butt to wash his hands, drying them on his jerkin. He put his finger to his lips and led Maltote and Ranulf back into the hall. Servants were laying bread, cheese and slices of cured ham on traunchers so the household could break its fast. Corbett slid on to the bench, Ranulf next to him.

'Why did you look at the sword belt, Master?'

'Monck was a born street-fighter,' Corbett explained. 'He was a good sword-and-dagger man and he was no fool.' He bit absent-mindedly at a piece of cheese and stared up at the great shield above the hearth bearing the Gurney coat of arms. 'I think he went out to meet someone, and that someone carried a crossbow. Now, Monck's sword belt was loose. I think that what happened was this. Whoever killed Monck knew of his reputation as fighter and was wary. So he holds the crossbow up, tells Monck to unloosen his sword belt and, as Monck began to unbuckle, fires. Monck is knocked off his horse, which bolts, and the murderer, probably on foot, slips away.'

Ranulf, listening, nodded his agreement. He put down his tankard and reached across the table to grab a piece of ham from under Maltote's nose.

Corbett shook his head at him in mock reprimand and went on, 'I wonder, though, what Monck was doing at the Holy Cross convent and why he galloped like a madman through Hunstanton. Why the haste and who was he meeting?' Corbett got to his feet. 'Come on, Ranulf, you can always eat later. Let's visit Monck's chamber before anyone else does.'

Ranulf softly cursed, grabbed a piece of cheese and bread, then he and Maltote followed Corbett out of the hall. Half-way up the stairs Corbett paused.

'Oh, by the way, did you discover anything while I was away?'

Ranulf shrugged. 'No one liked Monck. There again, Master, no one likes you. They don't take kindly to outsiders. In the village they want to see Gilbert hanged. Sir Simon appears to be a good lord of the manor. The Pastoureaux are harmless and the good sisters of the Holy Cross pompous and rich.'

'There is also the matter of the lights,' Maltote said.

'Oh, yes.' Ranulf spoke hastily, to prevent Maltote taking up the story. 'We went down to the dungeon to see Gilbert. We took him a jug of wine and our dice. He's got the courage of a rabbit, Master, he wouldn't kill anybody. But one thing we did discover. Apparently Gilbert goes poaching out on the moors. Sometimes, especially in good weather, he sees a lantern winking out at sea as if someone is signalling the shore.'

'We have heard that before,' Corbett replied. 'Catchpole said he had seen those lights.' He paused as Alice hurried by. She smiled nervously, rather flirtatiously, at him. Ranulf and Maltote stepped aside, Ranulf licking his lips at the way Alice's hips swayed under her murrey taffeta dress.

Maltote took advantage of the diversion to add his piece of information. 'Then we went to the inn in the village and talked to an old, rather garrulous fisherman. He claimed to have seen not only the lights from the sea but also answering lights from the cliff tops.'

Corbett raised his eyebrows. 'That is new,' he said. 'Catchpole saw no light from the land. Well, come on, perhaps Monck's papers may reveal something!'

His special key once again unlocked the door to Monck's chamber. The room was as he remembered it from his previous visit. Ranulf used his dagger to cut through the straps of Monck's the saddlebags. He emptied the contents out on the bed and Corbett began to sift through them.

The door swung back and Gurney strode in.

'You should have waited!' He exclaimed angrily.

'What for, Sir Simon?' Corbett asked. 'Your permission?'

'This is my house,' Gurney replied tersely.

'Sir Simon, I mean no offence, but we may find something here to tell us who killed Monck and to shed light on the mystery he was investigating.'

Gurney stamped out of the room, slamming the door behind him.

'That's interesting,' Corbett murmured. He grinned at Ranulf. 'Lady Alice must have realized where we were going and hurried to tell her husband. I wonder if Sir Simon was angry because of our lack of courtesy or something else? Anyway, let's have a look.'

They began to sift through the dead clerk's possessions. Two locks of hair, each in its small taffeta pouch, a wedding ring and a small, battered doll were sad mementoes of Monck's wife and murdered daughter. A short letter, the parchment yellow and cracking with age, proved to be a love note written twenty years ago by Monck's wife. Reading it, Corbett felt a surge of compassion for Monck.

'God rest you, Lavinius,' he whispered. He shivered as if an icy hand had gently stroked the nape of his neck. Would this happen to him? Would another clerk sift through his intimate possessions after some fatal ambush in a London alleyway or sudden attack on a lonely road?

'Master?' Ranulf shook him by the shoulder.

'Ranulf, take all this to our chamber. Just wrap it in a blanket. Everything.'

Maltote and Ranulf began to pile Monck's possessions on to the bed.

'What are these?' Ranulf pulled some grimy clothes from a battered saddlebag.

'Probably Lickspittle's,' Corbett said.

He took the tunic, shirt and hose from Ranulf. The shirt was blood-stained and, like the tunic and hose, still slightly damp. Corbett threw them in with the rest.

'Make sure you take everything,' he said. 'Sir Simon must be as curious as we are. And, Maltote, go down to the stables and see if any of Monck's possessions were brought back with the body.'

Back in their own chamber they sorted through what they had found. Among the purely personal possessions were a small book and some rolls of parchment. Corbett had taken these to the table and begun to study them when Selditch came in, eager to be of assistance.

'Sir Hugh, if it interests you, Monck was killed by the crossbow bolt. There's no other mark of violence on his body, apart from a slight bruising just under his navel.'

'How could that have happened?' Corbett asked.

Selditch pulled a face. 'Monck could have knocked into something before he left, or it could have been caused as he fell from the saddle. It's nothing serious.'

'And any possessions?' Corbett asked.

'Your servant has already taken them.' Selditch smiled bleakly. 'And, before you ask, there was no money. I suspect that Catchpole helped himself.'

Corbett thanked him and then went back to the parchments.

Some were roughly drawn maps of the area very similar to the ones he had seen before. There was also a short memorandum about King John losing his treasure in the Wash and some rough scribblings which proved more interesting. Monck had drawn up a list of questions:

Item – The lights at sea and the lights on the cliff top?
Item – Where could the treasure be hidden? The Hermitage? Or the caves beneath Mortlake Manor?
Item – Is Holcombe buried in the village churchyard?
Item – Where is Alan of the Marsh?

Corbett read on and smiled. There were similar questions about the reeve and the Pastoureaux and it seemed that Monck entertained suspicions of Gurney, Selditch and the sisters of Holy Cross convent. Corbett looked up.

'Alan of the Marsh,' he murmured.

'What's that, Master?'

'Alan of the Marsh,' Corbett said. 'I only found out about him because Gurney told me. So how did Monck know?' He sifted through the documents and found the parchment that gave him his answer. 'Monck may have been half-insane,' he said to Ranulf, 'but he was a good clerk. He found out that Holcombe's sister, Adele, married Alan of the Marsh. Certain property in Bishop's Lynn was handed over as her dowry. The grant, as was customary, was confirmed and included in the sheriff's report to the exchequer. Before he left London, Monck must have gone through the exchequer records and found the entry.'

'So?' Ranulf asked.

'Alan of the Marsh was described as living at Hunstanton,' Corbett explained. 'And that's why Monck came here. Alan of the Marsh was Holcombe's brother-in-law as well as his accomplice. Now, where would Alan be buried? And, more importantly, who are his descendants?'

When Corbett met him in the hall below, Gurney was of little help.

'Don't you think I haven't investigated that?' he said. 'Alan had no descendants. He disappeared about the same time as Holcombe did. Perhaps Father Augustine may be of some assistance? However, the burial, marriage and baptismal records of the church are in some chaos – the previous incumbent was not the most organized of men.'

Corbett left Ranulf and Maltote to sort through the rest of Monck's possessions and, saddling his horse, rode out to Hunstanton. He was hardly made welcome – the villagers gave him dark looks and turned their backs as he passed. Women dragged their ragged-arsed children indoors and the men, coming from the fields for their midday meal, glanced sourly at him and muttered amongst themselves.

Corbett found Father Augustine in a small sacristy beside the high altar. Robert the reeve, who was also the verger, was in attendance. He glowered at Corbett. The priest, though, was welcoming enough.

'How can I help you, Sir Hugh?'

'You have records here of baptisms, deaths, marriages?'

'We have, Sir Hugh. Indeed, we have been trying to put them in order. Why? How can these assist you?'

'I want to trace the name of a villager who lived here almost a hundred years ago. A man – probably fairly prosperous – called Alan of the Marsh.'

'Why?' Robert the reeve came forward, eyes wide, lips tightly pursed.

'Why not?' Corbett replied crossly.

'Because he's my relation. An ancestor of mine.'

'Is he buried here?' Corbett asked.

'No, he isn't. He's not really—' The reeve coughed in embarrassment. 'He's not really a relation, in the blood sense. My great-grandmother was married to him. She came from Bishop's Lynn. But Alan disappeared soon after their marriage. They had no children and my great-grandmother married again. Father Augustine can show you the records.'

The priest had already moved across to a large, iron-bound chest in the far corner of the sacristy and was rummaging among its contents. He brought out a great, leather-bound ledger and some scrolls and laid them out on the sacristy table. Robert the reeve was clearly determined to stay. He re-arranged candles, then began to polish the brass censer. Corbett tried to ignore him as Father Augustine opened the great ledger.

'Here,' the priest pointed a bony finger at one entry, the ink fading on the parchment, where a forgotten priest had recorded the marriage of Adele Holcombe to Alan of the Marsh on 8 November 1215.

'That will be the only entry there,' Father Augustine said. He closed the book and turned to a crackling, yellowing scroll. 'This is the burial register for the years 1215 to 1253.' Unrolling the scroll he found the entry recording the burial of Adele Holcombe, now Adele-atte-Reeve, in the graveyard. 'And this' – he offered another scroll – 'is the baptismal record.' He and Corbett read through it together but could find no reference to any children of Alan of the Marsh.

'Was Adele Holcombe's one of the graves disturbed?' Corbett asked.

'No, I don't think so.' Father Augustine looked at the reeve. 'Was it?'

Robert merely shook his head.

'Would it have been easy,' Corbett asked, 'for a woman like Adele to have her marriage to Alan annulled so she could marry again?'

The priest sat down at the table, resting his elbows on the arm of a chair. 'According to canon law, if a husband disappears and the marriage is childless, the wife can ask for an annulment after five years. Adele probably did this. Sir Hugh, I don't wish to be inquisitive, but why this interest in people long dead?'

'I am sorry, Father, for the moment I can't tell you. But,' he continued, 'that means Adele must have known that Alan was dead.'

'Not necessarily. She may simply have found another suitor after five years had elapsed and then applied to the bishop for an annulment. Such cases are quite common.'

Corbett looked at the reeve. 'Master Robert, can I ask you

a question? And you may deduce from it what you will. In your family, are there any legends or stories about hidden treasure?'

The reeve stared back pompously, though Corbett caught the flicker of guilt in his eyes.

'Master reeve,' he insisted. 'I suggest you be honest with me.'

The reeve clasped his hands together and stared up at the ceiling. 'There are legends.'

'Legends about King John's treasure?'

The reeve flinched as if Corbett had touched a sensitive spot.

'Master Monck asked the same questions.'

'He came here?' Corbett asked.

'Oh, yes,' Father Augustine replied. 'That's why we found the entries so quickly.' The priest's brow furrowed in puzzlement. 'He came, I think, on the second day after his arrival to make the same enquiries as you. Didn't he tell you, Sir Hugh?'

Corbett smiled wryly. 'Master Monck was a secretive man.'

'Was?' the priest and reeve chorused together.

'This morning Master Catchpole brought his corpse in. He was found on the moors, a crossbow bolt deep in his chest.'

The reeve shuffled his mud-stained boots and looked away.

Did you kill him? Corbett wondered. He recalled the black looks as he went through the village. Had Monck been murdered as a result of a village conspiracy?

'Master reeve,' he said quietly. 'You still haven't answered my question.'

Robert breathed in deeply. 'There are legends all over Norfolk about the old king's treasure. About a false guide called Holcombe whom Sir Richard Gurney hanged on the scaffold on the cliff top. There are also stories that Alan of the Marsh may have been his accomplice.'

'And how do these stories end?'

'They say Holcombe was hunted down.'

'And?'

'Either Alan of the Marsh was killed by the Gurneys who seized his wealth . . .'

'Or?'

'Or he hid away, trapped himself in a place he couldn't get out of and died of starvation.'

'Father, have you heard these stories?'

The priest smiled. 'As Robert says, they are common. But the whereabouts of Alan of the Marsh and the treasure are a mystery.' Father Augustine steepled his fingers together. 'I have even heard' – his long face broke into a grin – 'that the villagers here murdered Alan of the Marsh, seized his treasure and either hid it or distributed it.'

Robert the reeve made a rude sound with his lips.

'Did Master Monck examine Adele's grave?'

'Yes, he did,' the priest said. 'No one knew where it was and it took some time to find it. He even examined the coffin.' He shook his head. 'But there's nothing there.'

'A final question,' Corbett said.

'Yes, Sir Hugh?'

'Master Monck called here on the afternoon he died. Why was that?'

'He was asking once again about his clerk Cerdic. I couldn't help him. He spent some time here with me, speculating on what had happened to Cerdic.' The priest glanced slyly at Corbett. 'He also said some rather uncharitable things about your arrival and he was in a terrible temper. He left, saying he was going back to the Holy Cross convent.' The priest paused. 'It must have been well after dark. Do you remember, Robert, I called you to the church after making a sick call?'

'That's right,' the reeve confirmed. 'I was waiting here for Father Augustine when suddenly I heard hoof beats. I ran out of the church and Monck thundered by, riding his horse like the devil. He went through the village, scattering dogs and chickens, stopping neither for man, woman nor child.'

'Why do you think he was riding so furiously?'

'God knows. I thought he was going back to the manor or perhaps across the moors to the Pastoureaux.'

Corbett thanked them and went outside. He unhitched his horse and wondered whether to go to the Holy Cross convent. The day was drawing in. Large, fat raindrops, carried by the driving wind, wetted his face. Damn it, Corbett thought and, turning his horse's head, rode back towards the manor.

'I don't want to go to the convent and Dame Cecily's supercilious ways,' he murmured to himself. He stared into the gathering darkness. He was also being cautious – if Monck was murdered in an ambush, the same could happen to him.

Corbett cleared the village and made his way along the track. He glimpsed the scaffold dark against the sky and remembered the decayed flowers he had found there. They looked as if they had been lying there for weeks, so it couldn't be some neighbour of the Fourbours paying a small tribute. Corbett looked out to where the sea rose and fell in a sullen grey mass. The wind whipped his hair and the bracken on either side crackled with the movement of night creatures. Corbett shivered.

'You are a fool,' he murmured, 'to be out so late at night.' And he urged his horse into a gallop towards the welcoming lights of Mortlake.

Ranulf and Maltote were waiting for him, their boredom apparent.

'We found nothing, Master,' Ranulf confessed as Corbett sat on the edge of his bed and removed his riding boots.

'And I don't think we will,' Corbett said. 'We are finished at Hunstanton.'

'What do you mean, Master?'

'Tomorrow morning—' Corbett ran his fingers through his hair. 'Oh, what's the use. Look! Sit down!' He gestured at his two companions. 'When I was in the halls of Oxford – an experience I wouldn't wish on you, Ranulf – the masters used to make us debate a problem, teasing out the difficulties, the illogicalities. So what do we have here? About ninety years ago' – Corbett used his fingers to emphasize his points – 'a king loses a fortune in the Wash. The treacherous guide escapes the disaster with some of the treasure.'

'Holcombe?' Maltote asked.

'Yes,' Ranulf mimicked. 'Holcombe.'

'Holcombe's caught and hanged by Gurney's ancestor,' Corbett continued. 'His accomplice, Alan of the Marsh, disappears, as does the treasure or most of it. The Gurneys acquire some information about what may have happened to this treasure but, to protect the family name, keep it hidden. Selditch discovers this information along with three pieces of plate. He goes to London and sells these pieces.' Corbett raised his eyebrows at Ranulf. 'What else?'

'Strange lights at night, both on the cliff top and at sea,' Ranulf replied.

'Oh, yes.' Corbett stared at the ceiling. 'And we have a reeve who suddenly comes into unexpected wealth and nuns who are hiding something, whilst the Pastoureaux are as enigmatic as ever. What else?'

'Marina,' Maltote replied.

'Ah, yes, a girl is murdered. She received a secret message, probably sent by an old friend who had also been with the Pastoureaux.'

'We have the other murders,' Ranulf added, 'of Cerdic and Monck? What was Cerdic doing on the beach? And who was Monck riding like the devil to meet?'

Corbett got to his feet and stretched. 'Do you miss London, Ranulf?'

'Does a fish miss water, Master?'

Corbett smiled. 'As I said, we are finished here.'

'So, where to, Master?'

'Let's visit Bishop's Lynn. Who knows what we could draw out of the shadows?'

'Such as?' Ranulf asked, eager for the smells and sight of any city.

'Well, there's the baker's wife for a start, Amelia Fourbour. However, before that, Ranulf, I want you and Maltote to go to the convent and ask that smug prioress if the name Alan of the Marsh means anything to her. And, secondly, why was Master Monck visiting her?' Corbett went across to the lavarium to wash his hands and face. 'Now, Dame Cecily will lie through her teeth. She will only tell the truth when she's forced. Just watch her reaction.'

'And afterwards?' Maltote asked hopefully.

'Afterwards, we lock everything away, pack our horses and ride to Bishop's Lynn.'

'Could there be Holcombes alive there now?' Ranulf asked.

'Perhaps,' Corbett replied.

He walked over to the window, undid the shutters and watched the heavy rain lash the manor house.

'We've got to walk carefully,' he murmured, 'or the assassin will strike again.' He looked over his shoulder at his anxious-faced companions. 'If we don't,' he warned, 'Monck might not be the only clerk to die out on the moors!'

Chapter 9

Dame Cecily was not pleased to see Ranulf and Maltote the following morning. She made them wait in an antechamber before inviting them into her opulent chamber, where she and Father Augustine sat on high-backed chairs before the fire. Ranulf and Maltote had to squat on stools pushed forward by an old lay sister. Old Master Long Face was right, Ranulf thought. He winked mischievously at Maltote. The prioress preened herself, smiling sourly at them whilst flouncing her pure wool robes.

'What does Sir Hugh Corbett want of me this time?' she asked.

'Simple answers,' Ranulf replied, 'to very simple questions. Master Lavinius Monck was a visitor at your house just before he died?'

'Yes, yes, poor man.' Dame Cecily glanced coyly at Father Augustine. 'Our chaplain' – she emphasized the word – 'has already told us the news. What a tragedy! What terrible events!'

'Why was Monck here?' Ranulf asked.

'Well, far be it for me to read Master Monck's mind, God rest him! But he was still anxious to know why his servant Cerdic had come here.'

'And what answer did you give?'

'The same as I told Master Corbett. I don't really know.'

Father Augustine coughed, clearing his throat.

'Dame Cecily,' he declared, 'can't be held responsible for the people who visit her.'

'And why do you come here, Father?'

'I am chaplain to the priory.' The priest smiled at Ranulf. 'I have known this place many years. When I was a curate in Swaffham I used to come here in the summer as a rest from my pastoral duties.'

Ranulf didn't know whom he disliked the most – the preening prioress with her false, smiling coyness or this long-visaged, sour-faced priest. Ranulf always felt uncomfortable in the presence of clergy – they seemed always to be patronizing him or sharing some private joke at his expense. This time was no different. Deliberately he pushed his muddy boots forward towards the fire and stretched. He smiled as he saw the prioress quiver with annoyance at such boorishness.

'We are going to Bishop's Lynn,' he announced. He yawned, pushed his hands towards the fire, rubbed them, then smacked his thighs. 'You may be assured of one thing, mind you.'

'What's that?' Father Augustine asked sharply.

'Sir Hugh Corbett is a terrible man,' Ranulf declared. 'A digger for the truth, a searcher out of secrets, God's vengeance on murderers.'

'Then it's time he met with more success!' Dame Cecily snapped. 'Believe me, Master . . . ?'

'Ranulf.'

'Ah yes, Ranulf. I intend to write to the king. I object to the peace and harmony of my house being shattered by these peremptory visits!'

Ranulf smiled sweetly. 'With all respect, Dame Cecily, you

may write to the Holy Father himself, but Sir Hugh Corbett will come here when he thinks proper.'

The prioress's doughy face flushed with anger. Just a little more provocation, Ranulf thought.

'Of course,' Father Augustine intervened, 'Dame Cecily wishes to be helpful. But this is a nunnery.'

More like a molly-shop, Ranulf thought, peering around the luxurious chamber, with its velvet tasselled tapestries, gold and silver ornaments, shining furniture and beeswax candles.

'Does the name Alan of the Marsh mean anything to you?' he asked abruptly.

He could have hugged himself with pleasure. Dame Cecily started back in her chair and nervously toyed with the crucifix hanging round her neck.

'Well?'

'Alan of the Marsh?' Dame Cecily stammered. 'Who's he?'

'With respect, that wasn't the question. Does the name mean anything to you?'

'Of course not!' she snapped.

'You seem troubled by it.'

'Well, of course.' She forced a smile. 'Why should a man's name mean anything to a prioress in a convent? What are you implying?'

'Nothing,' Ranulf cheekily replied. 'So, I can report back to Sir Hugh that Alan of the Marsh means nothing to you?'

'I have never heard of him.'

Ranulf sniffed and got to his feet. Maltote followed suit.

'In which case, I'll bid you adieu.'

Ranulf stalked out of the chamber, softly chuckling to himself.

The old lay sister would have taken them straight back to

the stable yard but Ranulf, nudging Maltote, now had the devil in him.

'Madame?'

The lay sister paused, flattered by this pleasant, charming, red-haired, young man whose green, cat-like eyes danced with merriment.

'Yes?'

'I have never been in a convent before and this is such a beautiful place. Is it possible to be shown around?'

The lay sister's head went back in reproach.

'But this is a convent!' she gasped. 'A house of prayer for ladies!'

Ranulf shook his head. 'No, I don't mean within the house itself, but the grounds?' He dipped his finger into his purse.

The lay sister's eyes became greedy.

'I suppose I could take you back to the stables by the long route, perhaps show you the cloisters, the chapel and some of the grounds?'

Ranulf smiled. 'Madame, I am your servant.'

He grasped her cold, vein-streaked hand and raised it to his lips, making sure she gripped the coin in his hand. The lay sister simpered and, despite her age, quickly led them along galleries and passageways. She chattered like a squirrel as she showed them the cloisters and the chapel, guest house and refectory. After that they visited the herb gardens and orchard and walked back round the church towards the stables. Ranulf greedily stared at everything. Dame Cecily had been lying and Ranulf just hoped that he could take some evidence back to old Master Long Face that might be of use. They passed the lychgate of the small cemetery and Ranulf caught a flash of russet-brown. Ignoring the lay sister's pleas, he pushed the gate open and walked into the cemetery. He stared at the Pastoureaux working amongst the graves, gathering up piles of rotting leaves, cutting back the brambles and reeds. One of them turned, resting on his hoe, and pulled back his hood.

'Master Joseph!' Ranulf smiled. 'So, this is how you spend your time?'

The Pastoureaux leader smiled and walked towards him.

'We all do God's work, Master Ranulf. Why are you here?'

'Oh!' Ranulf shrugged. 'Like you, Master Joseph, I'm doing God's work but in a different way.'

Master Joseph's face became serious. 'We heard about Master Monck's death. Please accept our condolences.'

Ranulf nodded.

'Have you discovered anything about his death?'

'No, Master Joseph, we have not. It's as much a mystery as anything around here.'

'Will Sir Hugh continue Monck's work?'

Ranulf smiled and nodded. 'Of course. We are leaving soon for Bishop's Lynn, but Sir Hugh will return.' He stared into the man's face. 'I am sure,' he continued, 'I have met you before but I can't remember where.'

The Pastoureaux leader pulled back his hood and returned to his hoeing.

'Perhaps in another life, Master Ranulf! But I think your guide is becoming anxious.'

Ranulf looked over his shoulder. The old lay sister was comically hopping from one foot to another.

'I have shown you enough! I have shown you enough!' she bleated. 'The prioress would be angry. Please come!'

Ranulf and Maltote followed her. They collected their horses and left the convent. Laughing and joking over Dame Cecily's discomfort, they rode down past the church and into the village. They stopped at the "Inglenook" to sample some ale. Ranulf chattered a little with Robert the reeve and Fulke the tanner but their dark looks and surly replies showed they were not welcome. Ranulf and Maltote left and returned to the manor house, where Corbett was poring over a piece of parchment. Every so often he would scribble a little and, throwing his quill down, he'd sit, head in hands, and stare at what he had written. He listened quietly as Ranulf described what had happened at the convent. Corbett picked up his quill and tapped the table top.

'Bishop's Lynn!' he said. 'Are the bags packed?'

Ranulf nodded.

'Then we should leave. I want to be there by nightfall.'

Ranulf and Maltote went down to the stables. Corbett followed with the saddlebags. He stopped to take leave of Gurney who seemed agitated that they were going so abruptly. He insisted that they should take some refreshment and allow his cooks to prepare food for the journey. Corbett was reluctant to alienate his host any further and so he agreed. The steward laid out a table in the main hall and served a range of meats and cheeses, whilst Catchpole gave them directions on which roads to take.

An hour later they left, Corbett quietly cursing. The sky had become overcast and the cold, wet sea mist was creeping in over the cliffs. By the time they reached the crossroads the mist was swirling about them. Maltote and Ranulf debated on which road to take.

'Follow the directions on the post,' Corbett rudely interrupted. 'That's what Catchpole told us.'

He led them on. Within the hour Corbett had serious misgivings. According to Catchpole, the road ought to be broader and they should have passed through a series of small hamlets. However, because of the lowering sky and thickening mist, Corbett believed they were heading further inland across the moors. At last they stopped, cursing and muttering. The horses caught their unease and pawed the ground, snorting and whinnying against the black stillness of the moors. Corbett moved his horse round.

'How long have we been travelling from Mortlake?'

Ranulf shrugged and blew on his fingers. 'About two hours. Maltote, what's the matter?'

The young messenger was staring back the way they had come.

'Maltote!' Ranulf snapped. 'For God's sake, you are as skittish as a maid!'

Maltote turned back, his face white, eyes anxious.

'I don't know,' he muttered. 'After we left the crossroads I fell back. I am sure we are being followed.'

'Nonsense!' Ranulf scoffed.

'I am certain we were,' Maltote insisted. 'I heard the jingle of harness.'

'Hell's teeth, Master!' Ranulf snapped. 'We are lost and we'll freeze if we stay here.'

Corbett patted his horse's neck. 'There's only one thing for it. Let's return to the crossroads.'

'Look!' Ranulf cried. 'Perhaps all is well!'

He pointed into the mist, which shifted like steam above a cauldron. Corbett glimpsed the flare of light that Ranulf had seen. A farm, perhaps one of the villages. He moved his horse, leaving the path, crossing the rain-soaked moor in the direction of the light. His horse protested but Corbett urged it on. Again the horse whinnied. Corbett tugged at the reins but the horse was stuck fast. Corbett stared down in horror – his horse was really floundering, hoof and fetlock deep in the green mire around them. Corbett cursed and turned round.

'Get back!' he yelled to Ranulf and Maltote.

'Keep still, Master!' Ranulf urged. 'The more you struggle, the faster you'll sink!'

Corbett obeyed, stroking his horse's neck and talking softly. The horse threw its head back, the whites of its eyes rounded in terror. Ranulf dismounted and approached, bringing the rope he always carried to tether his horse or to use as a makeshift bridle. Maltote led the way, leading his own horse, feeling every step carefully before him.

'There's a sort of path,' he said, 'where the earth is firm.'

Corbett fought to control his panic as his mount began to flounder. The mud reached its belly. Ranulf and Maltote made their way gingerly along the firm strip of earth. When they were only feet away from Corbett, Ranulf threw the rope. Corbett managed to tie it around his horse's neck. Maltote tied the other end to the saddle horn of his own mount. Talking softly to it, he urged it back. The rope tautened. At first Corbett's horse did not move. The rope, growing tighter round its neck, only increased its panic. Corbett enlarged the noose, moving part of it over his saddle horn. Ranulf and Maltote tugged and pulled. Suddenly Corbett's horse broke free and scrambled on to the path. Corbett carefully dismounted and, following Maltote's advice, spoke gently to the horse until all of them, soaked in mud, were firmly back on the trackway.

For a while Corbett could do nothing except squat by the side of his horse, trying to calm his own terror. He was covered in mud and his horse was caked to its withers in marsh slime. Ranulf pushed some bread and a wineskin into his master's hand.

'You'd best drink!'

Corbett chewed the bread, but found it difficult to swallow so he spat it out. He then poured some wine into his hand. He sniffed and licked it carefully.

'What's the matter, Master?'

'What in hell's name do you think's the matter?' Corbett snarled. 'I am checking for poison!' He smiled in apology. 'However, it seems untainted.' Corbett took a generous swig and handed the wineskin back to Ranulf. 'Thank you,' he muttered. He stared at Maltote. 'If it hadn't been for you, we could have all died.' He got to his feet and gripped Maltote's hand. 'I'll not forget that. You or Ranulf.'

'And neither will the horses!' Ranulf joked, embarrassed by his usually taciturn master's thanks.

Corbett stretched. His legs were freezing cold and yet he felt strangely sleepy after being trapped in the mire. He stared through the swirling mist.

'We've got to go back to the crossroads,' he muttered.

'But that light?' Maltote asked.

'We were tricked,' Ranulf snapped. 'I have seen smugglers play the same trick on the marshes along the Thames estuary. They show lights and travellers make the mistake of thinking they mean safety. Some cruel bastards even make a living out of wrecking ships that way.'

'But how did they know we were here?' Maltote asked.

'I think the crossroads will tell us,' Corbett breathed. 'Come on!'

They led their horses along the trackway, back to the crossroads, but the gaudily painted wooden post was nowhere to be seen. Ranulf scrabbled around in the dark.

'It's fallen over!' he cried, his fingers feeling the wood.

Corbett threw the reins of his horse at Maltote and walked across.

'I doubt that,' he replied. 'I think it was loosened, turned round and pointed in the wrong direction. It then either fell or was pushed over by the heartless bastard who shone that lantern.'

'So, we were being followed?' Maltote asked.

'Probably,' Corbett said. 'But there was someone ahead of us, too. God knows there are enough who knew about our journey. It's a well-known outlaw trick – single out strangers in the area, lure them in the wrong direction and see what happens. Someone from Hunstanton got to the crossroads before us, changed the sign, waited for us to take the wrong path and tried to entice us into that marsh with a lantern. Don't forget, we delayed longer at Mortlake Manor and the villagers, or who ever it was, know every path and trackway in this area well.'

'But who?' Ranulf demanded. 'Who is the bastard? So we can go back and cut his throat!'

'It could be anyone,' Maltote replied, full of confidence after his master's praise. 'Sir Hugh is right. They went ahead of us and laid their trap.' He preened himself. 'We messengers are used to such stratagems. What do we do now, Master? Go back to Mortlake?'

'No. Maltote, you know which route we followed and the wrong path we took. So, up on your horse and ride like the wind. If you see lights, and it's a hamlet or village, come back!'

Maltote obeyed, the hoof beats of his horse receding into the distance. Corbett and Ranulf stood at the crossroads, and despite their efforts to keep warm, began to freeze.

At last Maltote returned.

'There's a small hamlet. I asked one of the peasants.' The

messenger pointed. 'This *is* the road to Bishop's Lynn. Shall we continue, Master?'

Corbett agreed. Surprisingly, he did not stop at the hamlet but, ignoring the protests of his companions, pressed on to Bishop's Lynn. The mist became denser, colder, more cloying and Corbett wondered if he had made the right decision. For a while Ranulf moaned loudly but eventually the darkness and the freezing cold silenced him. He slumped on his horse, pulling his cloak and hood about him in sullen resignation.

At last they reached Bishop's Lynn. Corbett's legs were numb. He was in no mood to argue with the city watch, who had already declared the curfew and closed the gates, and a display of warrants and Ranulf's angry shouts quickly had a postern gate opened for them. One of the wardsmen led them down St Nicholas Street to the town's most spacious tavern, the Lattice House on the corner of Chapel Street. Once again Corbett used his authority, this time to obtain stables for his horse and a chamber for himself and his companions. They all stripped and washed in bowls of steaming hot water, brought up by sleepy-eyed servants. Once dressed in clean clothes, they went down to the taproom for something to eat. All three were too exhausted to talk and the steaming bowls of meat and thick local ale soon made them heavy-eyed and drowsy. They returned to their chambers and flung themselves down on their beds.

All of them slept late. When Corbett awoke, he felt refreshed, suffering little, apart from a stiffness in his legs, from the previous day's misery. They broke their fast. Maltote went out to make sure the horses were clean and properly stabled and, at Corbett's instructions, took their muddy clothes down to the tavern's wash-house. The landlord, eager to make a profit from such important visitors, had promised that his servants would wash them.

'Maltote can stay here,' Corbett decided. 'Ranulf, we'll go down to the Guildhall.'

'What are we looking for, Master?'

'First, the roll of electors. I want to see if there's a Holcombe still alive in Bishop's Lynn.'

'And what else?'

'A miller known as Culpeper, whose daughter was recently murdered in Hunstanton.'

They left the tavern, leaving instructions for Maltote, and went up St Nicholas Street along to the Guildhall, which stood opposite the soaring towers of St Margaret's church. A beadle tried to stop them. Corbett explained who they were and, within minutes, an officious alderman was offering him every assistance.

'Yes, yes,' the man muttered, his face full of importance. 'We have tax rolls, electors' rolls, subsidy rolls. If there is a Holcombe, these will tell you.'

'And the miller known as Culpeper?'

'Oh, he's well known. But you won't find him at his mill.' The alderman pointed to the great fat hour candle burning on its stand. 'He'll be down at the quayside, near the custom house, supervising the barges taking flour downstream.'

Corbett left Ranulf to scrutinize the tax rolls.

'Don't forget the goldsmith, Edward Orifab,' he added, then walked down Purfleet Street towards the quayside. He found the city very noisy after the silence of Mortlake Manor. Bishop's Lynn was reminiscent of London, with its narrow alleyways, overhanging houses and the shouts of traders from behind their stalls and gaudily painted booths. The cries of children, as they skipped between the crashing carts, vied with the neighing of horses and the shouts of drovers, whilst the rank smells from the open sewer did nothing to dull the haggling and bartering round the busy market stalls. The taverns and alehouses were doing a roaring trade as this was market day. The peasants from the outlying villages were thronging in to sell their produce and buy provisions before the snows fell and the roads closed.

The weather had turned fine. The skies were cloud-free, though the lanes and alleyways were still soaked from the previous day's rain. Corbett had to watch where he stepped as he struggled through the crowd down to Purfleet quayside. At last he reached the riverside. The wharves were packed with a tangle of shipping – small herring boats, fishing smacks, merchant ships and even a great belly-bottomed cog belonging to the Hanse. The air was thick with the smell of salt, fish and spices and the quayside thronged with carters, port officials, merchants and sailors. Traders stood offering a wide range of goods, from ribbons to hot pies – Corbett found their shouting and talking in different dialects and tongues confusing. At last he espied a port official dressed in his brown fustian robe and carrying a white wand of office. After more deliberations, Corbett was eventually directed to the Green Wyvern tavern next to the custom house, where Culpeper and other members of his guild met to do business. In its taproom Corbett found Culpeper, a thick-set, burly man with watery eyes and vein-streaked face. He was already deep in his cups, chattering to his fellows. Corbett had to shout to make himself heard.

'You had a daughter, Amelia?'

Culpeper sobered up. He put his tankard down and pushed his face close to Corbett's.

'What is that to you?'

Corbett explained who he was and Culpeper rose drunkenly to his feet.

'I've drunk enough,' he muttered. 'And this is not the place to talk.'

He led Corbett back out on to the quayside and into the timber custom house. The miller slumped down on a wooden bench just inside the entrance and gestured at Corbett to do the same.

'I know it's early,' he slurred, 'but it's market day and the price of flour has risen.' He gazed bleary-eyed at Corbett. 'A man has to reward himself, as well as forget the past.'

'What have you to forget, Master Culpeper?'

'A daughter named Amelia. She was our only child. I lavished everything upon her – finery, trinkets, clothes – nothing was too good for her. But she was headstrong.' Culpeper turned away to wipe the tears from his cheeks. 'I went to Hunstanton, you know, to bring her body back. Her mother wanted that. Now we have locked away the past and I let it be.'

'Do you know why she was murdered?'

'God knows! Or at least he pretends to. Who would hurt poor Amelia, eh, Master Corbett? What a death, to be strung up like a rat on that lonely, horrible gibbet!'

'Why did you let her go to Hunstanton?'

The man blew out fumes of ale and placed his fat hands on his thighs.

'I had no choice. Amelia was finished here. A laughing stock, a shame to her family! Somebody once called her "used goods". Can you imagine that, eh, Master Corbett? A lovely girl being discarded like a piece of dirty cloth?'

Corbett remained silent. He could guess what was coming. No miller was popular because no miller was poor. Such a tradesman always provoked envy amongst those who had to buy his products.

'Amelia became pregnant,' Culpeper explained. 'What, oh, some ten, twelve years ago.'

'And the father?'

'We never knew. Never once did Amelia talk about him.'

'You honestly never knew?'

'No, it was always a great secret. You know the games young, lovelorn women play? She would say she was visiting friends or relations.' Culpeper blinked. 'Anyway, Amelia became pregnant, but she told no one about the father. The child was born, but died within days. Amelia became listless. She had not only lost her child but the man she loved. All she would say was that something had ended which could never continue.' Culpeper wiped the tears from his eyes with the back of his hand. 'The years passed. Amelia never referred to her love and he certainly made no attempt to communicate with her. Now, Master Fourbour was a constant visitor to our mill to buy flour for his bakery in Hunstanton. He knew about Amelia's past but offered his hand in marriage. She, surprisingly, accepted. I don't know why.' He shrugged. 'The rest you know.'

'Was Amelia happy with her husband?'

'Sir, Amelia was never happy. Fourbour loved her and I think she tolerated him. And, before you ask, she never gave any indication of the tragedy which befell her. Only recently, when going through certain belongings she had left behind, I found a piece of parchment in a small, velvet pouch. Here, you can look for yourself.' Culpeper fumbled in his wallet. He took out a small, dark-blue velvet bag and gave it to Corbett. 'I always carry it around with me.' His voice became choked. 'It's the only memento I have.'

Corbett undid the pouch. The parchment was a mere scrap, cut in the shape of a heart. On it was written *Amor Haesitat* above *Amor Currit*. The four capital letters were heavily emphasized.

'Love hesitates,' Corbett translated softly. 'Love hastens.'

'Do you know what it means, Sir Hugh?'

Corbett smiled compassionately at the miller.

'It's one of those keepsakes, Master Culpeper, loved by the young and those still in love. But it is also a puzzle.'

'You can keep it,' Culpeper murmured. He grasped Corbett's hand. 'Keep it!' he urged. He paused as two officials entered, chattering noisily as they went up the wooden, spiral staircase.

'Find her killer!' Culpeper pleaded. 'Bring him to justice. Let him hang like my poor Amelia!'

Culpeper put his face in his hands. Corbett patted him gently on the shoulder and sat till he regained his composure.

'Master Culpeper, does the name Alan of the Marsh mean anything to you?'

The miller shook his head.

'Or Holcombe?'

'No, Sir Hugh, why?'

'Nothing. You have heard of the Pastoureaux at Hunstanton?'

'Oh, yes, they come here.'

'Who do?'

'The Pastoureaux or, at least, their leader, Master Joseph. He comes to buy supplies, and sometimes negotiates with captains about his young men and women who wish to travel to the Holy Land. I often see him near the custom house.'

'Who else from Hunstanton comes here?'

'Sometimes Sir Simon Gurney and that surly man-at-arms of his, Catch—'

'Catchpole,' Corbett finished.

'And the people from the convent come to sell their wool. Oh, yes, and Sir Simon's physician, a fat man called Selditch. Why do you ask?'

Corbett got to his feet. 'I just wondered. You are a native of these parts?'

'Yes.'

'Does the name Orifab mean anything to you?'

The miller shook his head.

'Does much smuggling go on?' Corbett asked.

Culpeper's face widened into a grin. 'Sir Hugh, I shouldn't be telling you this, but that is the most lucrative trade around here. Everybody smuggles, but catching them and proving it is another matter!'

Chapter 10

Corbett left Culpeper and went back to the Guildhall, where Ranulf was sitting on the steps waiting for him.

'Any luck, Ranulf?'

'None whatsoever, Master. The last Holcombe died some forty years ago. However, I have found our goldsmith, Edward Orifab. He owns a large shop only a few alleyways from here. Our alderman gave me directions. But, Master, I'm starving!'

Corbett and he went to a nearby tavern and sat at the long table which ran from one wall to the wine tuns. Corbett looked at the cat stalking the counter where the meat would be cut and, seeing the greasy blobs of fat lying on the table, confined himself to bread and ale. Ranulf, however, who had a stomach as hard as flint, ate with relish a dish of meat.

Ranulf then led Corbett to a large goldsmith's shop in Conduit Street, its black beams and pink plaster freshly painted. There was a large stall in front manned by a journeyman and two apprentices, who informed Corbett that their master was not in. Corbett and Ranulf ignored their shouts and entered the shop. They found the goldsmith, a dour, vinegary-faced fellow, sitting at his counting table surrounded by chests and coffers. Corbett was reminded of a picture of a miser in a stained-glass window. He almost expected to see a devil appear to drag the man off to hell. Orifab hitched his fur-lined robe around him and sniffed, his gimlet eyes dismissing Ranulf and Corbett as not really worth attention.

'What do you want?' he demanded.

'Some manners for a start,' Ranulf replied cheerily. 'Didn't your mother ever tell you, manners maketh the man?'

'I'm busy,' the fellow retorted. He moved stacks of coins around the table.

Ranulf grabbed the table and shook it. The coins were sent spilling. Orifab leapt to his feet, lips curling like a dog.

'Master Orifab,' Corbett intervened. 'My name is Sir Hugh Corbett and I am here as the representative of the king. I need to ask you some questions.'

The goldsmith stepped back, knocking his stool over. He smiled, his head bobbing like a fawning dog.

'I didn't know,' he muttered.

'Well, you do now!' Ranulf told him – he enjoyed baiting the pompous and the wealthy in the presence of old Master Long Face.

'What is it you want? How can I help?' Orifab stuttered.

The goldsmith sat down and waved them to a bench in front of the table.

Corbett remained standing.

'Do you know Robert the reeve from Hunstanton village?'

Orifab pressed his lips together and shook his head.

'He came here,' Corbett continued quietly, 'a few weeks ago to collect a bequest.'

The goldsmith blinked and looked down at his coins.

'Yes, yes, I remember.'

'Who left that bequest?'

The goldsmith laced his fingers together nervously and stared longingly out of the window.

'It's a secret,' he mumbled. 'I can't tell you.'

'Fine,' Corbett replied and turned to go.

Ranulf pushed his face a few inches from the goldsmith's pale cheek.

'Master Orifab,' he hissed. 'Within a month you will receive a summons from Westminster. The barons of the exchequer will demand your presence and ask you the same question. I sincerely hope you give them a better reply than you gave Sir Hugh!'

'Wait! Wait!' The goldsmith jumped to his feet, alarmed at the prospect of a long and tiring journey to London. He waved Corbett over. 'I'll show you,' he whispered. 'But you mustn't tell anyone, particularly my wife.'

Corbett pulled a face at Ranulf. The goldsmith scuttled out to tell the journeyman to look after the shop. He then led Corbett and Ranulf down Tower Street, past Greyfriars, to a large house standing in its own grounds. Orifab pushed the garden gate open. He looked furtively around and knocked at the door. A pretty young maid answered and immediately beckoned them in. As soon as the door was closed behind them Ranulf took one look at a young girl scampering, half-dressed, upstairs and began to chuckle. As they went into a small antechamber, Ranulf grabbed Corbett's arm.

'Ever been to a molly-shop, Master?' he whispered.

Corbett narrowed his eyes.

'A brothel!' Ranulf hissed.

Corbett stared around the small room. It was luxuriously furnished, with dyed rugs on the floor, and a log fire spluttered in the small hearth. The chamber boasted at least four chairs, all with quilted backs, as well as a large, polished chest. Two tapestries on the wall, however, convinced Corbett that Ranulf was correct. Both were classical in style and both depicted young women in various stages of undress, boldly displaying their charms to lascivious-looking satyrs.

A tall, grey-haired lady came in. She looked rather dour, with her prim face, sharp features and long brown dress. She smiled at Orifab, but looked suspiciously at Corbett and Ranulf.

'You have brought us guests, Master Orifab?'

'No, Madam,' Ranulf replied, whilst Orifab shifted from foot to foot. 'We are king's men.'

The woman stepped back so quickly Corbett thought she was going to flee.

'There's no need for any alarm,' Corbett said. 'I couldn't give a damn what you do here. But, apparently, Master Orifab wishes us to meet someone.'

'Rohesia,' the goldsmith whispered. 'They wish to meet Rohesia. Mistress Quickly, I suggest you allow them to.'

He went up and whispered in the Mistress Quickly's ear. She threw one fearful look at Corbett and hastily left the room. A few minutes later she returned, accompanied by a tall, beautiful young woman. The newcomer wore a green taffeta dress, and her corn-coloured hair was covered by a wimple of the same colour, bordered at the edge with gold thread. Jewellery sparkled from her fingers and there were gold and silver bangles on her wrists. The tight-fitting dress emphasized her ample bosom and her slender waist. She looked as innocent and gentle as a young fawn. Corbett thanked God that Maeve would never know about this part of his mission.

'You wish to see me, Master?'

'By yourself.'

Mistress Quickly and Orifab hastily left the room. Ranulf closed the door behind them. Corbett waved the young woman to a seat.

'You are called Rohesia?'

'Yes, I am.'

'Do you know who I am?'

'No. Mistress Quickly didn't tell me.'

'I am Sir Hugh Corbett and I am here on the king's business. I come from Hunstanton. I want to know why you left considerable monies with the goldsmith Orifab for Robert the reeve from that village?'

The change in the young woman was remarkable. Her eyes became hard and unblinking, the generous lips became a thin, angry line and the golden hue of her face quickly dimmed.

'That is none of your business, sir.'

'It will go badly with you if you do not answer. Why did you leave money for Robert the Reeve?'

'A customer asked me to.'

Corbett rubbed his chin and stared long at her.

'I think you'd best come back with me,' he said quietly. 'Come back to Hunstanton.' He saw the tears glisten in the girl's eyes. 'I also bring you bad news. Marina has been murdered.'

Rohesia moaned as if in pain. She put her face in her hands and began to sob uncontrollably.

The following morning, having spent the rest of the day down at the quayside, Corbett, Ranulf and Maltote left Bishop's Lynn. They called again at the brothel, where the young woman calling herself Rohesia was waiting for them, swathed in a great cloak and hood. Corbett would not allow Ranulf or

Maltote to question her, nor discuss her between themselves, as they left the city and took the road north to Hunstanton.

Their journey back was uneventful. Corbett was relieved that they didn't have to travel through the village to Mortlake Manor. Sir Simon and Alice came out to greet them. Corbett curtly acknowledged their welcome – he still had his suspicions about who had tried to drown them in the marsh. He insisted that Rohesia be shown to a chamber and given refreshment but that no one other than himself be allowed to talk to her.

'I also want Catchpole,' he said. 'And any liveried retainers you can spare. They are to be armed and mounted and they are to accompany Ranulf to the Hermitage. He has his orders. He is to bring Master Joseph and Philip Nettler here immediately.'

'What's this all about?' Gurney demanded. 'This is my manor, Hugh.'

'Aye, but the king's writ runs here. I want both men brought to Mortlake immediately. Only then will you discover the reason why.'

Gurney reluctantly agreed and, within the hour, Catchpole and Ranulf, accompanied by a dozen armed retainers, thundered out of the yard. Maltote unpacked their bags. Corbett visited Rohesia and then went down to the great hall to wait. Gurney, irritated by Corbett's taciturn demeanour, left him alone and went out in to the yard in nervous anticipation of Ranulf's return.

Ranulf arrived, just before dusk, in a clatter of hoof beats and shouted exclamations. Corbett, standing with his back to the fire, steeled himself for the coming confrontation. Gurney joined him. Ranulf and Catchpole brought the two Pastoureaux leaders in. Both men had their hands tied and

Master Joseph's face was red with fury. Nettler looked pale and rather frightened. If it hadn't been for Ranulf, Master Joseph would have thrown himself at Corbett. His eyes dilated and specks of froth appeared at either side of his mouth.

'You'll pay for this, Corbett! You snivelling turd of a clerk! How dare you lay hands on me and send your servant to invade our private chambers?'

Corbett ignored him. He stared across at Ranulf, who smiled and nodded imperceptibly.

'Sir Simon!' Master Joseph turned as Gurney walked into the hall. 'This is against the law and Holy Mother Church! We put ourselves under your protection!'

'Oh, shut up!' Corbett roared.

Master Joseph looked so furious that he seemed on the verge of apoplexy.

'Shut up, Master Joseph! Or I'll use the considerable powers the king has given me and hang you from the rafters! Sir Simon, I should be grateful if you would release Gilbert and have him brought here. And I'd like my mysterious guest, the young woman from Bishop's Lynn, to be brought here also.

Master Joseph's shoulders sagged. He became quiet, narrowed his eyes and licked his lips nervously.

'What's all this about?' he muttered.

'What do you mean, Hubert?' Corbett asked.

The Pastoureaux leader gasped and paled.

'You are not Joseph,' Corbett continued. 'You are Hubert Mugwell, convicted ten years ago as a felon. So you'll shut up and listen to what I have got to say! Sir Simon, I'd be grateful if your retainers could hold both these men because I am sure they will become violent.'

Corbett walked over to the table, conscious of everyone watching him. He poured himself a cup of wine and sat on the edge of the table, sipping the wine carefully. Gilbert came into the hall. He hadn't shaved for days, but he seemed well enough, smiling vacuously around. Corbett told him to stand just within the door.

'You'll be a free man soon, Gilbert. Don't worry.'

Rohesia arrived next, still cowled and hooded. Corbett beckoned her across. He put his wine cup down, took her by the arm and stared at the pale, frightened face almost hidden in the cowl.

'Don't worry,' he said to her also. He led her across the room. Master Joseph watched anxiously, then gave a groan as she threw back her hood. Philip Nettler's terror was so great that he crouched down, arms across his chest, and began to whimper like a beaten dog.

'Lord save us!' Gurney cried. 'It's Blanche. You look beautiful. You're Blanche, the reeve's daughter.'

'Blanche,' Corbett began. 'Do you know this man who calls himself Master Joseph, the Pastoureaux leader?'

The girl's hand came out from beneath her cloak and her dagger stabbed towards 'Master Joseph's' chest. Corbett leapt forward in time to knock the dagger out of her hand, but he wasn't fast enough to top her slapping her other hand across the man's face in a stinging blow.

'You filthy bastard!' she screamed.

Master Joseph cowered, unresisting, between the two burly retainers who held him. Corbett dragged Blanche away.

'I want the hall cleared, Sir Simon.' He put Blanche's dagger on a table. 'And I want both prisoners chained, just in case.'

'Do you want everyone to leave?' Gurney asked.

'Apart from you, Ranulf and the prisoners, and Blanche, yes.'

Gurney gave the order. Catchpole came back with chains and secured the ankles and wrists of the prisoners. Blanche walked away and stood with her back to them, gazing into the fire.

Corbett picked up the dagger and thrust it into his belt. 'Let me start from the very beginning,' he said. 'Four or five years ago, through the Knights Hospitaller, the king learned that young free-born men and women of this realm were being sold into slavery, mostly for purposes of prostitution. They are prized especially for their fair hair and skin and they fetch high prices in the slave-markets of North Africa.' Corbett walked over to the table and took a sip from his goblet. 'This scandalous trade,' he continued, 'has been condemned by successive popes and Church councils – it is not only English men and women who are taken. Indeed, it is the one thing that Philip of France and Edward of England agree in opposing, though they find it impossible to stop. The trade is a very old one, but it has reached new levels since the Children's Crusade, nearly a hundred years ago, and whetted the slave-dealers' appetite.'

'I have heard something of that,' Gurney said.

'It was a strange phenomenon,' Corbett said. 'Thousands of children from all over Europe were persuaded by a shepherd boy named Stephen to follow him on a crusade to the Holy Land. Few, if any, reached it. Most fell into the hands of slavers and were sold in the markets of Algeria and Egypt.'

Gurney got to his feet. 'That is history,' he said. 'But are you saying that these two Pastoureaux leaders are involved in the present trade? They live in poverty—'

Ranulf's snort of laughter interrupted him. 'Go to the Hermitage, Sir Simon, and look into the private quarters of this precious pair. You'll find woollen blankets, goose-feather bolsters, silken sheets and tuns of fine wine brought specially from Bishop's Lynn. The rest of the community fasted but these two certainly didn't.'

'I'll wager,' Corbett said, keeping a wary eye on Blanche, who still stood by the fire, 'that Master Joseph and Philip Nettler also own some pleasant properties throughout the kingdom. Of course, there were also the occasional journeys to Bishop's Lynn to revel in the flesh-pots.'

'This is not true,' Master Joseph muttered. 'We had nothing to do with this. Sir Simon, you are right. How could we profit?'

'Easily enough,' Corbett said. 'You move around the kingdom, spending a year here, eighteen months there. Then you retire for a while to enjoy your ill-gotten gains, perhaps at some fine house in London or Lincoln. Then you re-emerge like a mummer in a play. You arrive in a lonely place such as Hunstanton, posing as some sort of St Francis of Assisi. You draw the young to you, with your dreams, ideals and visions of journeys to exciting places. The young stay with you for a while. You want to ensure there's no protest and there very rarely is. After all, many a peasant lad or lass is only too willing to escape the servitude of the soil. And why should their parents object? After all, it means one less mouth to feed when the winter comes.'

'But the ships' captains – they would have to be involved!' Gurney exclaimed.

'It's a thriving trade,' Corbett said. 'There's many a captain willing to engage in this lucrative business as it's so easy. No questions asked, no duty to pay and nobody to object.'

'The victims could,' Nettler whimpered. It was his only attempt to defend himself.

'Have you ever tried to escape from a sea captain who's paid good silver for you? From a brothel in Marseilles or Salerno, or from an Ottoman harem? And, if you do escape, where can you go? If those who own you don't track you down and kill you, others will. How can a girl from Hunstanton walk from Marseilles to Dieppe? She doesn't know a word of the language, and, if she did manage to tell her story, who would believe her? Our friends here would simply say that she had jumped ship or, tired of her religious vocation, had decided to further her fortunes elsewhere. And, even if she was believed, it might take years to prove. By then, Master Joseph would have changed his name again and moved on to some other part of this country or anywhere in Christendom. God save us, Sir Simon, you know how long it takes to obtain justice simply over a piece of cloth!'

'So, what went wrong?' Gurney asked.

'I went wrong.' Blanche turned, her face white with anger. 'And Sir Hugh Corbett is correct. Look at me, Sir Simon. I am too ashamed to go home and, if I did, who would believe me? And why should I bring shame on my parents? I joined the Pastoureaux. This bastard here, this hell-hound, negotiated my passage abroad. But I was fortunate.' Blanche swallowed hard. 'On board ship, I overheard the captain talking to the first mate. He didn't know I was hiding in the shadow of the stern castle, crouching like a dog, listening to my future.'

She went across and spat at Master Joseph.

'They talked about me as if I was a piece of merchandise. I

had had my suspicions, just vague ones, because of the way the captain would look at me sometimes, but I dismissed them as impure thoughts.' Her voice broke slightly as she stared at Corbett. 'Anyway, it was autumn and a fierce storm grew worse and the ship was forced to enter the Thames. I jumped ship near Queenshithe. Anyone from Norfolk is a good swimmer and I swam ashore.' Blanche laced her fingers together. 'At first I begged. The friars and some of the nuns were good.' She shrugged. 'But there are many hungry mouths in London. One night a sailor tried to take me. He was drunk. I stole his silver and bought myself some new clothes. Then I met a merchant in Cheapside.' She lowered her head. 'In a few months I had earned enough silver to travel back to Bishop's Lynn. I was too ashamed to go home. As I have said, who would have believed me? But I wanted vengeance. I'd have earned enough money to hire someone to kill this demon and his familiar!' Blanche played with the hem of her sleeve. 'One of my clients was a goldsmith. Through him I arranged for money to be sent to my family. And I got a message to Marina. I gave it to a pedlar. I promised him more coins if he came back and faithfully described both Gilbert and the old oak tree.' Blanche slumped down on a stool. 'I shouldn't have done that,' she added weakly. 'Marina tried to escape.'

Corbett walked across to Master Joseph and, bringing his hand back, struck him violently across the face.

'You deserved that,' he said quietly. He struck again, drawing blood from the man's lips. 'And that's for Marina, whom you undoubtedly murdered!'

'That's a lie!' Master Joseph screamed.

'No, it isn't, you bastard!' Corbett hissed.

He went over and looked down at Philip Nettler. 'You are

going to hang, you know, both of you?'

Nettler only whimpered in reply. Corbett crouched next to him.

'You'll hang,' he whispered. 'And when the king's justices hear about this they'll demand a most thorough investigation. You will be tortured until you tell us everything – the captains of the ships, destinations, where you have hidden away your ill-gotten gains. And only when they have finished with you will judgement be carried out? He killed Marina didn't he?'

Nettler nodded.

'Shut up, you whoreson!' Master Joseph yelled, and lunged at his erstwhile lieutenant.

But the chains that linked his ankles and the manacles on his wrists prevented any movement. The Pastoureaux leader fell to his knees. Ranulf dragged him to his feet.

'You killed that girl!' he said softly. 'She was fleeing from you. Fleeing across that mist-shrouded moor. God knows where to. Her family? The manor here? You knew something was wrong and you caught up with her. You raped and strangled the poor girl!' Ranulf pulled him closer. 'Perhaps my master may be good to me,' he whispered. 'Perhaps I'll be given the duty of escorting you down to London!'

Master Joseph's face broke into a sneer.

'You mustn't forget about Gilbert,' he jibed.

'Oh, yes, poor Gilbert.' Corbett left Nettler and came to stand beside Ranulf. 'You took that murdered girl's pathetic necklace and went to Gilbert's hut. By then the poor lad and his mother had fled, fearful of the whispered allegations against them. You threw the necklace down and coolly walked back to the Hermitage. You condemned an old woman to death by drowning and, if it hadn't been for God's grace, her son to death by hanging.' Corbett looked over at the white-faced Gurney. 'Don't you remember, Sir Simon, when you held the court in the parish church? Master Joseph abruptly left. I thought it was strange for a religious leader to forsake, so quickly, the corpse of one of his community. But, there again, why should he care? Marina wasn't worth a penny to him any more.'

'And how did you discover the truth?' Gurney asked.

'It was the money left to Robert the reeve that started me thinking. Why should some mysterious benefactor give money to a goldsmith in Bishop's Lynn for a poor reeve in a fishing village?' Corbett walked back and put his hands gently on Blanche's shoulder. 'Your father probably half-suspects.' He looked over his shoulder. 'Sir Simon, I am finished with these demons. You have room for them in your dungeons?'

Gurney nodded.

'Hold them there, but keep them separate. Nettler here may turn king's evidence and throw himself on the royal mercy. He may give us the dates, names, seasons. If he does, who knows what clemency we may recommend?'

Nettler looked up, a sly look in his eyes. Master Joseph swore and tried to lash out at Nettler, but fell with a crash of chains to the floor. Gurney was half-way to the door to call his retainers when Master Joseph struggled to his feet.

'Wait!' he shouted.

Corbett turned, eyebrows raised.

'A full and frank confession, Master Joseph?'

'Piss off!'

'What then?'

'Information.'

Corbett walked closer. 'What about?'

'The treasure.'

'What treasure?' Corbett asked.

The man raised his manacled hand to wipe the blood from his mouth and stared maliciously at Corbett.

'First, give me your word.'

'There'll be no pardon for you, Master Joseph, or Hubert Mugwell, whatever you wish to call yourself! You'll hang!'

'Oh, I don't worry about myself. I'll skip to the scaffold. Death doesn't worry me. I am going to hell where I'll dance with the devil and wait for you, Corbett!'

'What then?'

'I have a house, a woman and child at Lothbury. You'd eventually find out about them. They are not to be harmed or their goods seized.'

'That's where I have seen you!' Ranulf suddenly interrupted. 'Years ago. In London, in a brothel on the stew-side in Southwark. What did you call yourself? Some French name? Oh, yes, Alphonse. I was there. You were the Master of Revels.' Ranulf walked closer. 'I never forget a face, but I couldn't clearly remember' – Ranulf smiled apologetically at Corbett – 'because the memories of that evening are sweet. How many names have you had?'

Master Joseph sneered. 'More than your wits.' He looked at Corbett. 'Do I have your word, clerk?'

'It depends on the information.'

Master Joseph was about to refuse but he shrugged and shuffled a little closer. 'I have been here eighteen months. Everybody talks about the treasure. I did a little searching of my own, but found nothing. Then you and that other black-garbed, snivelling clerk came, asking about Alan of the Marsh.'

Corbett nodded. 'How do you know about him?'

'Give me your word about the woman and child!'

Corbett stared back, chewing his lip.

'I want your word! Your solemn word here in the presence of witnesses!'

'You have it,' Corbett answered.

'Go to the Hermitage!' Master Joseph said. 'There you will find out about Alan of the Marsh. I do have your word?'

Corbett nodded.

'Take them away!' he ordered.

Once the door was closed behind the prisoners, Corbett walked across to Blanche.

'It's finished,' he whispered.

The woman looked round. 'No, Sir Hugh, it's only just beginning. Master Joseph will hang. You will go back to London. But, tomorrow morning, I will return to a brothel in Bishop's Lynn.'

'You needn't,' Corbett replied.

The girl half-smiled. 'Yes, yes, I know. But you see, Sir Hugh, what can I go back to? Back-breaking work in the fields? Scornful glances until the day I die? No, I'll go back.' She smoothed the front of her dress. 'I'll think. Perhaps one day . . . But tomorrow morning I will return.' She glanced fleetingly at Gurney. 'You will give me an escort?'

'Of course.'

'And tell my father nothing?'

Gurney nodded.

Corbett watched her leave.

'The whole village will know,' Ranulf murmured.

'Of course they will,' Gurney replied. 'In a community like this, gossip crackles like flames amongst dry stubble.' He sighed and got to his feet. 'We'll leave you alone, Hugh. I'll send food to your chambers. You'll want that?'

'Yes.'

Gurney pointed to Ranulf. 'You'll come with me?'

'Where to?'

'The Hermitage. I've got to inform the so-called community that it's finished. Some can walk home, others I'll give money to.' Gurney glanced at Corbett. 'What about their possessions?'

'Let them take their own belongings with them,' Corbett suggested. 'The place will be stripped of everything else once the villagers get to know. I doubt if Master Joseph's wealth is there. It will take months for officials from the exchequer to track it down. A house here, money banked there. Our prisoner's a master criminal and I don't think he will hang as quickly as he wished.'

'Will his accomplice be pardoned?' Ranulf asked.

'If he sings a song the justices want, he'll probably spend some months in prison before being exiled for life.' Corbett laughed sourly. 'I am sure he'll know enough ships' captains to secure safe passage abroad.' Corbett placed Blanche's dagger on the table. 'But, Ranulf, you go with Sir Simon.'

Corbett left the hall. He could tell from the anxious whispers and looks of the servants that the story was already out. Gilbert was there, a free man. He was hopping from foot to foot and smiling vacuously at Alice, who was pressing food and a few coins into his hands. Corbett went up to his chamber. For a while he sat on the bed and thought about the young lives the Pastoureaux had ruined. Then he lay down, staring up at the rafters, puzzling over the heart-shaped parchment that Culpeper had given him in Bishop's Lynn.

Chapter 11

Corbett shivered as he heard the wind lash the heavy rain against the window. He had shaved, dressed and been down to the hall to break his fast after a restless night's sleep which had left him aching and heavy-headed. The excitement of the previous day, fanned by the gossips, had swept through the village. Gilbert had returned to Hunstanton like some hero returning from the wars and, if Catchpole was to be believed, the villagers had already looted the Hermitage. Members of the community had immediately fled, eager to be away and escape untainted from the heavy charges laid against their leaders. Blanche had already left with two of Gurney's retainers. Maltote went with them, grumbling at the prospect of riding through such cruel weather. Ranulf enjoyed the thought of the hapless messenger's discomfort, but Corbett soon wiped the smile off his face.

'You found nothing about Alan of the Marsh at the Hermitage?'

'No, Master.'

'Then take your horse and ride along the coast – not along the cliff top but along the beach. The tide will be out.'

'What am I looking for?'

'You will know when you find it.'

Ranulf stormed off, muttering and cursing about old

Master Long Face. Corbett returned to his brooding, before going down to the dungeons to question Master Joseph. The Pastoureaux leader, though, knew the strength of his position.

'The more I keep to myself,' he taunted Corbett, 'the more I have to bargain with.'

Corbett smiled to hide his despair. The rogue was right. Corbett knew that the exchequer officials would enter into any negotiations, make any concessions, if they thought they would augment the king's treasure. If a pardon for Master Joseph would make the king richer, that was the price they would cheerfully pay.

'Doesn't it rile you, Corbett,' the rogue jibed, 'to know that somewhere round here lies a great treasure trove?'

'Where is Alan of the Marsh?' Corbett snapped.

'I've told you, look in the Hermitage, if it's still there.'

Corbett got to his feet.

'Oh, clerk!' Master Joseph's bruised face was one long sneer. 'Do give my tenderest love to our plump prioress. Oh, and clerk!'

Corbett refused to look round.

'I wouldn't trust anyone if I were you!'

Corbett slammed the door behind him. He made sure the guard locked and bolted it before trying his luck with Philip Nettler, but he was equally taciturn.

'I'll speak,' he muttered, 'when I have the king's pardon signed and sealed in my hand. Until then, you can piss off!'

Corbett left the two felons and returned to his chamber. Gurney was down in the village and the house was quiet. The rain had begun to lighten, so Corbett pulled on his riding boots, collected his cloak, saddled his horse and rode out across the moor to the Hermitage. The building was now derelict, someone had even removed the gates. Corbett paused inside the yard and looked around. It was a low, grey, overcast day which reflected his mood. He had an uneasy feeling, born of years of experience, that someone was following him. He sat on his horse, the silence broken by the creaking of his saddle and the whinny of his horse. He looked over his shoulder, but the rain-sodden moors were empty. He dismounted, hobbled his horse and began to explore the building. Every single room had been ransacked. Corbett had witnessed similar occurrences in the king's wars along the Scottish borders. He always appreciated, albeit wryly, the plundering skills of local peasants. Doors, hinges, anything which could move had been taken, even rags, pots and bedding. Hardly anything remained, apart from the occasional smashed earthenware bowl, to show this had once been an active community.

Corbett visited the upper chambers and, despite their stark appearance now, realized that Master Joseph and Nettler had occupied the best chambers. The walls were white-washed and, by the marks on the floors, Corbett saw they'd enjoyed good bedding, furniture, even carpets. The windows, glazed with horn or glass, had simply been removed. Some of the tiles from the roof had also been taken, so watery patches were already beginning to form on the floor. Corbett went round, visiting every place. His unease grew, not only because of the wickedness which had been perpetrated here, but because of the empty stillness and the stomach-churning feeling that he was being watched.

He returned to check on his horse and stood looking at the lowering sky.

'Where is Alan of the Marsh?' he muttered, absent-mindedly patting his horse's muzzle. 'Think, Corbett!' he said to himself. 'Alan of the Marsh must have come here as a fugitive hiding from the Gurney of the time. He was looking for a place to hide.'

Corbett stared round the yard. He glimpsed a small, low, brick building, which looked as if it had been standing for an eternity. Corbett went across. It was an old malt house smelling musty and tangy, littered with pieces of wood and shards of pottery. Corbett tapped his boots and shifted the dirt with his foot; the floor was not beaten earth but stone. He began to kick away the piles of rotting straw and sighed as he found the trapdoor. He took the pommel of his dagger, knocked back the bolt and lifted the trapdoor by its rusty, iron ring. He paused to fashion a crude torch, lit it and carefully went down the rotten wooden steps. He held the torch up, away from him, the flames dancing in the light breeze. He was standing in nothing more than a pit, a small cellar. The floor was earthen and the torchlight revealed only the occasional spider's web. He heard the screech of rats as they scurried away.

'No secret passageways,' he muttered. 'Nothing but a dirty cell.'

Then he saw that on one wall someone had scrawled a crude A and an M and a drawing of what seemed to be a skull – two eyes and a nose connected by a triangle. Corbett studied the drawing carefully. He had no doubt that he had found the hiding-place of Alan of the Marsh and that it was he who had scratched the drawing on the wall. In which case the letters and the triangle must convey some secret message. The torch was burning low, so Corbett dropped it and went back up the steps. He was so immersed in his own thoughts that only the sudden awareness of a woman's perfume made him look up. He saw the heavy billet of wood coming down and screamed even as he collapsed unconscious on the steps.

When he came to, he was wet and cold and his head beat like a tambour. He could not understand why people were screaming at him and why his feet and legs were so cold and wet. He dragged himself forward. If only the people would keep quiet. He sat up, trying to calm his nausea. He looked down in stupefaction at the waves swirling around, looked up and saw white gulls circling like angels above him. Something was very wrong. He closed his eyes and shook his head. He had been in that cellar, now he was on a cold, deserted beach. The cliffs were in front of him. From where he sat, he could see the gallows where the baker's wife had been hanged.

He realized he had been knocked on the head, but what was he doing on the beach? And why now? A wave lapped against his waist. Corbett stared out across the swelling sea and realized with horror what was happening. The tide was coming in, not in creeping waves but in one of those surge tides so well known and so treacherous along this coast. The waves were angry, high and swollen, racing in with a fury Corbett had never experienced before. He staggered to his feet and began to stumble across the beach towards the path leading to the cliff top. The sea pursued him. He couldn't run fast – his legs felt heavy and his head was splitting with pain. He choked, retching, missed his footing and fell. The waves swept over him, their icy touch calming his panic.

He ran for his life. He remembered the local gossip and knew that his assailant in the Hermitage had left him there as another casualty of the fickle sea. Corbett staggered on. He could see the waves on either side of him rushing ahead. He could only breath in short gasps and the path seemed as far away as ever. His cloak was heavy with water. Corbett took it off, wrapped it round his arm and ran on. The sea, however, was winning the race, sometimes he was wading through waves thigh deep. The path seemed an eternity away. Then he heard the sound of hoof beats and his name being called. Ranulf was there, screaming down at him from his horse. Corbett tried to mount behind him, but a wave caught him and knocked him back. Ranulf leaned down and dragged him across his saddle, its horn pushing painfully into Corbett's chest and stomach. Then Ranulf rode like the wind, aiming straight as an arrow back towards the cliff-top path. They reached it. Ranulf dismounted and pushed his master into the saddle. He led the horse up the path, slipping and cursing, not stopping until they had reached the windswept gorse on the cliff top. Ranulf threw the reins down and collapsed on to the grass. Corbett leaned over the horse's neck and vomited. Ranulf wordlessly got to his feet and, looping the reins round his wrist, trudged back towards Mortlake Manor.

Gurney was standing in the yard, talking to his retainers, Selditch beside him. Both took one look at the sea-soaked Corbett and Ranulf's angry face and hurried up.

'What has happened?'

'Someone tried to kill my master,' Ranulf snapped. He squared up to Gurney. 'A knock on the head before being tossed on to the beach like a piece of flotsam, to be swept away in a sudden tidal surge. And what would you write to the king then, Sir Simon, eh? Some unfortunate accident?'

Gurney, although he had once been a soldier, paled and stepped back at the fury in Ranulf's green eyes. Selditch hurried to help Corbett out of the saddle.

'Piss off!' Ranulf snarled. He stared around the yard. 'Listen, all of you, and listen well! And you can tittle-tattle about this in the tavern. If my master dies here, I, Ranulf-atte-Newgate, will come back!' His voice sank to a whisper.

'I'll return! With every man I can lay my hands on as well as the king's writ! Believe me, sir, people here will still remember my visit when we are all dead and gone!'

Ranulf then helped Corbett out of the saddle. He put his master's arms round his shoulders, helped him up to their chamber and laid him gently on the bed. Alice came up with a cup of blood-red claret, heavily spiced. She smiled deprecatingly when Ranulf made her sip it. He took a drink himself then, closing the door in the lady's face, went back and forced the cup between Corbett's lips. As his master slept, Ranulf stripped him of his clothes, washed him, laid him between the sheets and covered him with blankets. Ranulf then locked the chamber and went down to the kitchen. He ordered the servants to heat small bricks which he placed in Corbett's bed. He demanded chicken gruel and other foods to be prepared.

For the rest of that day and most of that night, Ranulf tended Corbett. He fed his master when he woke and, when he slept, dressed the savage bruise on his head. At last Ranulf was satisfied. Corbett had been beaten unconscious and was badly bruised, but most of his wounds were spiritual: the shock of being left on the beach and that wild murderous race against the oncoming tide. In the morning Corbett woke, pale-faced but rested.

'I'm not dead yet, Ranulf.'

Ranulf grinned. 'You can't bloody well die yet! I am only at the bottom of the greasy pole of preferment.'

Ranulf watched his master anxiously. He owed everything to him. In his more sober moments, Ranulf was as fearful as Maeve of Corbett's sudden death at the hands of an assassin. The manservant went downstairs and brought back a bowl of thick soup and some bread. He let Corbett eat. Sir Simon and Alice also came up and self-consciously asked him how he fared. Corbett was polite but watchful. Maltote returned, eager to tell Ranulf about the brothel and how he was sure he had lost his heart to Rohesia. One look at Ranulf's dark face and Maltote realized how serious the threat had been to his master. The messenger paced up and down, clapping his hands, muttering they should immediately go back to London. Ranulf roared at him to shut up and sit down, or he'd brain him with a stool!

'Who did it, Master?' Maltote asked.

Corbett shook his head and described his visit to the Hermitage.

'All I remember is the smell of perfume and that piece of wood coming down at me. The next moment I was on the beach. How did you find me, Ranulf?'

'You told me to go there, Master.'

Corbett closed his eyes and put his head back on the bolster.

'Tell me about it.'

'I rode further along the beach,' Ranulf answered. 'What a God-forsaken place it is, Master. I have seen enough seagulls to last me all the days of my life.'

'But what did you find?' Corbett asked testily.

'A small skiff or boat pulled high on the beach,' Ranulf answered. 'There's also a path, one of those sandy tracks leading up to the cliff top. I went up this. Something happens there, the place is used. I went back down. I examined the boat, nothing remarkable except one thing. The boat's seaworthy but, I am sure, in the stern, was a dark patch which looked like blood.' Ranulf shrugged. 'Though it could be something else. I then rode further along but I didn't like the look of the sea, angry and swollen. I rode back. I panicked myself because the faster I galloped, the sea seemed to be racing me. I intended to go up the path leading to the Hermitage.' Ranulf pulled a face. 'Then I saw you running.' He paused at a knock on the door and Selditch came in.

'Sir Hugh,' he stammered, his fingers clutching at his large, protuberant belly. 'Is there anything I can do?' He waved his ink-stained fingers in the air like an old woman.

'No, no,' Corbett answered quickly before Ranulf could reply. 'Master Selditch, I feel well and I thank you.'

The physician disappeared.

'I wouldn't trust him!' Ranulf snarled. He sniffed the air. 'He wears some sort of perfume, Master, as does the Lady Alice.'

Corbett stared at the door and grinned at Ranulf.

'Thank God you came!'

His manservant shrugged. 'Looking back, you would have probably reached the path in time. Your thick skull saved you. The murderer, God damn him or her, never counted on your regaining consciousness.'

Corbett plucked at a loose thread in one of the blankets.

'If you hadn't come, Ranulf, whatever you say, I would have drowned. You are not to tell the Lady Maeve.' Corbett stared across the room. 'I studied at Oxford, I became a clerk in the royal service. Sometimes I feel like a busy spider spinning webs or destroying those others weave. Yet, I admit, I don't understand human nature. What would my death have achieved? What would it profit to make Maeve a widow? And my child fatherless? The king himself would come here or send someone else and so it would go on until the matter was resolved.' Corbett rubbed his face. 'Perhaps I should hand over my seals! Say the day is done and go back to my manor house?'

Ranulf hid his alarm and studied his master. In many ways

he knew Corbett was right. Old Master Long Face was a chess player and very good at it, but in the hurly-burly of the narrow streets he was an innocent.

'If you went, Master,' Ranulf replied slowly, 'the only difference would be that more murderers would walk away, wiping their lips and proclaiming their innocence.' He half-smiled. 'Leighton Manor may be quiet, Sir Hugh, but so is the graveyard.'

Corbett touched the top of his bruised head gingerly and winced.

'The shrewd voice of the common man,' he murmured.

'When you fall into the gutter, Master, you have to be as cunning and as crafty as those you hunt.'

Corbett looked at him sharply. 'What do you mean, Ranulf?'

'Well, take our fat physician friend. Or Sir Simon Gurney. What happened when some of King John's treasure was found?'

'They sold it.'

Ranulf sat on the edge of the bed.

'And what do you think would happen, Master, if they found the rest?'

Corbett narrowed his eyes. 'Are you saying they're searching for it?'

'Well, they know about the secret of the treasure. Don't you think they would like to find it?'

'But if they did and failed to inform the king, that would be felony, even treason.'

'Oh, of course, they'd inform the king,' Ranulf replied. 'And, according to the law, demand their portion. What is it, a quarter of any treasure trove? Now Sir Simon, his wife and physician may be innocent and as white as the driven snow.

They may have no hand in these murders. Or, there again, they may be as guilty as Cain.' Ranulf laughed drily. 'But I'll never accept that they are not looking for the treasure.'

'Continue,' Corbett murmured.

Ranulf grinned sheepishly over his shoulder at Maltote.

'It was our young messenger here who gave me the idea. Maltote comes from peasant stock. His father was a villein on a manor something like this. Now, you know the manor system, everything is recorded, everything is written down. Surely, our fat physician, with his love of antiquities, has discovered something about Alan of the Marsh?'

Corbett threw the blankets back and gingerly climbed out of the bed.

'I'm going to shave and dress,' he declared. 'Then I want Selditch up here.'

An hour later, when Corbett was ready, Ranulf ushered Selditch into the chamber. The physician's nervousness only increased when he saw Corbett dressed and waiting.

'Master Selditch,' Corbett began, 'I'll come swiftly to the point. I suspect Alan of the Marsh was a tenant of these parts, and perhaps even Holcombe. What have you discovered about both this precious pair?'

The physician was about to refuse to answer. Corbett leaned over and gripped him by the hand.

'I want to know,' he said quietly. 'I want to know everything. Otherwise I will seize all of Sir Simon's records – his list of rents, taxes, dues and imposts. I'll spend days going through them. If I find there is something you haven't told me, as God is my witness, you will rue the day!' Corbett touched the top of his head. 'Yesterday I was nearly murdered. My patience is running out!'

Selditch fluttered his fingers nervously.

'Holcombe was a tenant farmer outside Bishop's Lynn,' he replied slowly. 'Alan was a native of these parts. There's really very little in the records.' He shuffled his feet.

'How did Alan earn his bread?' Ranulf asked.

'He was steward of the manor.'

'And what does that mean?' Corbett asked.

'He would ride round collecting the manor lord's dues and carry messages and orders.'

'So, he would know the countryside?'

'Oh, yes.'

'And all the hideaways and the secret places?'

Selditch nodded.

'Is there anything I should know?'

The physician blinked. 'According to one of the rolls of the manorial court,' he answered slowly, 'two years before King John lost his treasure in the Wash, allegations were laid against Alan of being a smuggler.'

Corbett groaned and hid his face in his hands. He looked up.

'Is there anything else?'

Selditch shook his head, so Corbett dismissed him.

'What's the matter?' Ranulf asked anxiously as the physician closed the door behind him.

'Oh, for God's sake, Ranulf! Can't you see for yourself? Alan of the Marsh and Holcombe planned to steal King John's treasure. A hasty plan, probably concocted once Holcombe knew that he had been hired to guide the treasure train across the Wash. The plan is, however, successful. Holcombe steals the treasure and meets his accomplice at some lonely place. Now they hide most of their plunder; some they take, perhaps to raise ready cash.' Corbett paused to marshal his thoughts. 'Holcombe, however, is suspected.

He's hunted down by the Gurneys, who question then execute him and bury his corpse ignominiously with the little treasure he was carrying.' Corbett paused and smoothed the table with the top of his hand. 'Now, of course, it's all supposed to be a secret but gossip and rumours spread. Alan of the Marsh decides to flee. He hides the treasure.' Corbett glanced at Ranulf. 'What would he do next?'

'Try and leave the country?'

'Correct. Now, he is a smuggler like many in these parts. He faces, however, a number of difficulties – hiding, securing a passage, then moving the treasure without anyone knowing. Very dangerous, because he knows he's a wanted man.'

Ranulf shrugged. 'Perhaps he just died?'

Corbett shook his head. 'What about the other possibility? What if Alan of the Marsh was successful? What if he fled abroad, taking the treasure with him to live a life of luxury beyond the Rhine or in southern France? Don't you realize, Ranulf, we could be chasing will-o'-the-wisps.'

'So, why all the mystery?' Ranulf exclaimed. 'Why the murders?'

Corbett rubbed the side of his face. 'I can't answer that. All I do believe is that someone else, or a group of people, is also looking for the treasure.' Corbett sighed. 'However, they too may be chasing will-o'-the-wisps.' Corbett picked up a piece of parchment. 'What we must do is establish a pattern. Yet, what do we have? Dead flowers left under a gallows. A poor baker's wife murdered. Cerdic Lickspittle decapitated, his remains tossed on the beach. Graves being pillaged and Monck murdered out on the moors.'

'Well, at least,' Maltote interrupted 'we have arrested the Pastoureaux and discovered the person responsible for Marina's death.'

Corbett chewed the quick of his thumb.

'Yes, we have,' he muttered. 'But those bastards may also have been looking for the treasure.' He went back, lay on the bed and stared up at the timbered ceiling.

'And we mustn't forget the lights, the strange signalling between ship and shore,' Ranulf added.

'No, no,' Corbett murmured. He turned. 'I have an explanation for that, though it's hard both to swallow and digest. Anyway, leave me for a while.'

Ranulf and Maltote went down to the hall, whispering excitedly about their master's strange mood. Corbett chewed his lip and stared at the ceiling. For some reason he kept thinking of the love-message given him by Culpeper the miller: *Amor Haesitat, Amor Currit*. And was there something else? Something he had seen or thought about, whilst running across that beach? Corbett closed his eyes. And what had Ranulf told him about that boat beached and hidden away? He smiled as he remembered his logic, a common axiom in the schools: 'If you reduce all matters and reach one conclusion, that conclusion must be the only acceptable one. Consequently, you have discovered the truth.'

'Well, let's test it,' Corbett murmured.

He swung his legs off the bed, grabbed his riding boots and cloak and went out, shouting for Ranulf and Maltote.

They collected their horses from the stables and rode out on to the moor to the Hermitage. Maltote tended the horses whilst Corbett and Ranulf went into the old malt house. As soon as they were inside, Ranulf sniffed.

'I can smell the perfume. It's rather strong. Very similar, I am sure, to what Lady Alice wears.'

'Yes,' Corbett replied. 'I smelled it just before I was struck on the head. Come on, I'll show you what I found.'

He gathered some dry straw and led Ranulf down to the cellar. Corbett placed the straw at the base of the wall and struck a tinder but, when it flared into life, Corbett stared in disbelief at the wall. What he had previously seen had now disappeared, scorched off.

'Someone used a torch,' he murmured. 'Someone lit a torch and brushed the wall.' Corbett pointed to the burn marks and described what he had seen.

'Whatever it was,' Ranulf spluttered, 'it must have been important.'

Corbett and he returned to the yard.

'Let's say,' Corbett declared, staring up to where the seagulls circled, raucously screaming at being disturbed, 'Let's say we had stolen the gold. Where would you hide it?'

'Well, not in a place like this,' Ranulf answered.

'Why is that?'

'Any place visited by others is dangerous. Sooner or later, someone may be fortunate, or skilled enough, to discover where you hid the treasure.'

'But to bury it out on the moors,' Corbett said, 'is dangerous too. You might be seen burying it and there's always the possibility that you might forget exactly where you concealed it.' He mounted his horse. 'But now, Ranulf, on to a different sort of digging – let's go and upset the prioress.'

They arrived at the Holy Cross convent, where Dame Cecily kept them waiting for a while in an antechamber. When they were eventually ushered into her room she greeted them with such a false smile that Ranulf felt his stomach lurch.

'Well, how can we help you now, Sir Hugh?' she simpered. 'I was so shocked to hear about the Pastoureaux. Such a dreadful business. What evil men!'

'Yes, they were smugglers,' Corbett said. 'They smuggled out human flesh for sale in all the devil-ridden markets of the world.' He leaned forward. 'Smuggling is a sin, isn't it?'

The prioress blinked, her doughy face paled.

'Yes, it is a sin,' Corbett continued, 'and a crime – in the evasion of taxes and the infringement of royal authority, so that's how you can help me. You can tell me why you are a smuggler?'

Dame Cecily grabbed the desk to steady herself.

'What is this?' she spluttered.

Ranulf wished that Maltote were here instead of guarding the horses in the stable yard. Dame Cecily's mouth opened and closed.

'Are you accusing me of smuggling?'

'Yes, I am,' Corbett replied, hoping he was correct in his deductions.

'And, pray, what do I smuggle? '

'Yes, you should pray!'Corbett snapped. 'You should pray that the king has mercy on you. You should pray for royal clemency and the forgiveness of your bishop.' He leaned forward. 'You are a smuggler. You own sheep, you have shearing-sheds, you load the wool into bales and your carters take it down to the custom house at Bishop's Lynn. Now, let us say you have three hundred bales. Two hundred and fifty go through customs and are loaded on board ship at Bishop's Lynn. The ship leaves harbour, probably on the evening tide. Standing off the coast it heads towards Flanders. But instead of sailing across the Channel it anchors off the Norfolk coast and takes aboard the other fifty bales. Whether it sends a boat to the shore or whether a boat is rowed out to it from here, I don't know. You are paid in cash and pay no duty. The ship's captain makes a healthy profit in Flemish ports.'

'This is ridiculous,' the prioress exclaimed.

'No, it's the truth. So now we come to the death of Dame Agnes. She was the treasurer of this priory and every so often she would go for a walk on the cliff top. She would take a staff and a lantern. Most people viewed her as eccentric. In reality, she was signalling to a ship. I believe you even have a small boat in the cove to help you in your nefarious business arrangements.' Corbett got to his feet and walked over to stare at a painting. 'One night, however, tragedy occurred.' He turned, raising one hand. 'Oh, I agree, no foul play was involved, but Dame Agnes was getting old. Perhaps the cliff was beginning to crumble or the wind was too strong? Anyway, the good sister stumbled and fell to her death.' Corbett looked over his shoulder and smiled. 'She was the treasurer to this house and, in time, will be replaced. Your smuggling activities will undoubtedly continue, once snooping royal clerks disappear.'

'You have no proof,' the prioress snarled.

'But I have,' Corbett lied. 'I have interviewed one of the ships' captains. He has confessed all.' Corbett walked back, playing with the hilt of his dagger. 'Perhaps I should also question some of your retainers, particularly those who are so well paid for rowing that boat out?'

Dame Cecily could take no more. She put her head down and sobbed.

'Madam,' Corbett said quietly.

Dame Cecily raised her tear-stained face. 'We have always done this,' she whispered. 'And, Sir Hugh, can you blame us? The taxes are so heavy. Our profits are cut.'

Corbett glanced around the luxurious chamber.

'You could make economies,' he murmured.

Dame Cecily composed herself. 'What will you do, Sir Hugh? Inform the king?'

'Not necessarily,' Corbett replied. 'Provided two conditions are fulfilled.' He saw the hope flare in the prioress's black-button eyes.

'Which are?'

'First, that the smuggling must cease forthwith. Secondly, that you tell me what you know of Alan of the Marsh.'

Dame Cecily burst into tears, her shoulders shaking so much that even Ranulf felt sorry for her.

Chapter 12

'Madam,' Corbett asked. 'Why should a man who died so many years ago trouble you?'

Dame Cecily rose to her feet. She grasped the ring of keys hanging from the belt at her waist and walked over to a large, iron-bound coffer. She opened it, brought out a small roll of yellowing parchment and handed it to Corbett.

'Read it, Sir Hugh. It is a piece removed from the chronicles of our convent that only the prioress of the day is permitted to see.'

Corbett took the parchment over to the window, where the light was stronger. He saw that the convent's chronicle must be a roll of parchment made up of pieces stitched together. The portion he held in his hand had been carefully removed so that the loose ends of the chronicle itself could be re-stitched, leaving no sign that a piece was missing.

Dame Cecily moved towards the door. 'I'll return,' she said. 'I have something else to show you.'

Corbett shrugged and began to read, studying the blue-green lettering, quickly translating the Latin.

'Does it mention Alan of the Marsh?' Ranulf asked.

'No, it doesn't.'

'Then what use is it to us?'

'It is very useful indeed. Listen to this. It's dated August

1217, almost a year after King John lost his treasure in the Wash. In that month a fugitive took refuge in the convent. He reached the chapel and grasped the high altar, claiming sanctuary, which the prioress of the time granted. The fugitive demanded food and water and claimed his right to remain for the statutory forty days. But listen to this, Ranulf. It becomes more interesting. Sir Ralph Gurney came to the convent looking for a fugitive who was held responsible for the disappearance of a priest called James. The lady prioress told him that she had no knowledge of such a felon.' Corbett walked to the table and tossed the parchment down.

'Is that all?' Ranulf cried.

'It's enough,' Corbett answered. 'But I am sure Dame Cecily can tell us more.'

'Who is this priest, Father James?' Ranulf asked.

'God knows!' Corbett replied morosely.

'Why did they put such an item in their chronicle?' Ranulf persisted. 'And then remove it?'

Corbett clapped him on the shoulder. 'A good question, Ranulf. I suspect that something happened between the fugitive claiming sanctuary and the arrival of Lord Simon's great-grandfather. The two events were routinely recorded, but it's what linked the two that led to this portion of the chronicle being removed. Perhaps Dame Cecily may provide that link?'

Eventually the prioress returned. She hurried behind her desk and brought from beneath her robe a velvet bag tied at the neck. She undid this and brought out a gold chalice, which shone and sparkled in the candlelight. Ranulf gasped at the sheer beauty of it.

'Pure gold!' Ranulf breathed. He watched enviously as the prioress handed it to Corbett. 'Look at those diamonds!'

Ranulf pointed to the precious stones which encrusted the lip and stem of the chalice.

Corbett weighed the cup in his hand.

'I've read your manuscript.'

Dame Cecily sat down and sighed in resignation.

'And now you know all our secrets, Sir Hugh.'

Corbett put the chalice back on the table. 'I think so. Alan of the Marsh was the fugitive. He was well known to Holy Cross convent. After all, he was steward of Mortlake Manor and would often have dealings with the good sisters here. Indeed, Alan may well have had a hand in the smuggling which' – he laughed abruptly – 'seems to be one of the occupations of this house. However, he was also a thief. He and his accomplice Holcombe had plundered the royal treasure. They would have escaped unnoticed if it hadn't been for the vigilance of Sir Richard Gurney. Holcombe was taken and hanged. Alan went into hiding.' Corbett picked up the chalice and stared at it. 'Now Alan of the Marsh was like the unjust steward in the gospel. He was trapped by the law and his own greed. He couldn't escape through the ports with so much treasure – no ship's master who discovered how much wealth he carried would allow him to live. Corbett stared at the white-faced prioress. 'Now, for a while Alan hid out at the Hermitage but the net was closing in fast. He searched around for a place to hide.'

'He came here?' Ranulf asked.

'Yes, he came here. He knew the law of sanctuary and the then prioress would not deny him.' Corbett put the cup down. 'Am I speaking the truth?'

Dame Cecily nodded.

'So,' Corbett continued, 'while Alan was in hiding at the priory he and the prioress entered into a secret pact. I am sure

Alan pointed out that if he was captured he would have to tell the authorities about the smuggling activities of the good sisters here. Of course, he bribed as well as threatened. He had stolen this precious chalice from King John's treasure. He offered it to the prioress as the convent's reward for hiding him.' Corbett glanced at Dame Cecily. 'I gather this is used at Mass?'

'Yes,' she murmured. 'We say it was a bequest.'

'Now, everything proceeded satisfactorily,' Corbett continued. 'The convent kept its smuggling activities hidden and gained a very valuable chalice. But what happened to Alan of the Marsh?' Corbett rubbed the side of his head, still sore after the blow the previous day. He got to his feet and stretched. 'What will happen if the king learns about all this, eh? Well, I'll tell you, Dame Cecily, he would send my Lord of Surrey here to tear this place apart, in the hope of finding his grandfather's treasure trove.'

'But that's all we have!' Dame Cecily wailed.

'Oh, no!' Corbett murmured. 'You also have Alan of the Marsh.'

Dame Cecily's face fell. 'But the man is dead!'

'Oh, I am sure he's dead.' Corbett put his hands on the table and leaned over. 'Don't you see? The prioress who sheltered this fugitive and took the chalice is hardly going to let Alan leave, is she? Why not keep him here? Why not see if she could wheedle more gold out of him? Tell me, Dame Cecily, what would you do if you were confronted with such a problem?'

'I don't know,' she spluttered. 'I'd be terrified.' She squirmed in her chair. Corbett sat down.

'Let's look at it as a logical problem, then,' Corbett said. 'You know the convent better than I do, Dame Cecily. Where would you hide a man in a community of women?'

She shrugged. 'He could have become one of the workers on our farm?'

Corbett laughed. 'I hardly think so. First, Alan of the Marsh was well known in the area. Secondly, the then prioress must have been very eager to keep him away from prying eyes.'

'I don't know!' Dame Cecily wailed. 'As God is my witness, Sir Hugh, I do not know!'

Corbett steepled his fingers. 'Do you still have the right of sanctuary?'

Dame Cecily swallowed hard.

'Well, do you?' Corbett snapped.

'Our house surrendered it.'

'When?'

'In 1228.'

Corbett smiled. 'And before that, when someone claimed sanctuary, where would they have stayed?'

Dame Cecily rose to her feet. 'Sir Hugh, I think you had better come with me.'

Corbett raised his eyes at Ranulf as they followed the anxious prioress out of her chamber, along the galleries, across the cloisters and into the empty chapel. Corbett stared around in amazement at the soaring nave, wide transepts and beautifully carved rood screen. Dame Cecily took them into the sanctuary, where the floor was of Purbeck marble and the white altar glistened in the light of burning candles. The sanctuary was dominated by long, stained-glass windows and, high in the wall, on either side, stood stalls of gleaming oak. An intricately carved wooden statue of the Virgin and child stood in the far corner. Dame Cecily genuflected before the winking sanctuary lamp.

'Look over there!' She pointed.

Corbett stared at the wall; he noticed that one small section of it, level with his eyes, had, at some time in its history, been plastered and carefully painted. There was a similar, but much larger, patch at the base of the wall.

'What was this?' Corbett asked.

'An anchorite's cell,' Dame Cecily said. 'A small recess built into the wall with a small door for the hermit to crawl through and a squint hole through which she could see out. In the early days of our house there would always be an anchorite living in that cell. She would fast and pray, participating in the services by peering through the squint hole. The sisters would leave bread and water outside the door. As the years passed, this practice ceased.'

I am sure it did, Corbett thought, staring at the prioress's plump face, her gold trimmed head-dress and pure woollen gown.

'And what happened then?'

'After a while there was no anchorite and Hunstanton became a lawless place.'

At least Dame Cecily had the courtesy to blush with embarrassment.

'The convent was designated a place of sanctuary. Fugitives could shelter here, within the chapel for forty days, after which they would have to give themselves up.' Dame Cecily drew in her breath and stared at the wall. 'There are rumours,' she murmured as if speaking to herself.

'Rumours about what?' Corbett asked.

'Ghosts. I have never liked this place.'

'Then let's exorcize these ghosts,' Corbett replied. 'Ranulf, go with the prioress. Bring back hammers and chisels and let's see what we can find. Oh, and Dame Cecily, let's keep this secret between ourselves. So, when you return, lock and bar the chapel.'

Dame Cecily waddled away, completely subdued, Ranulf walking beside her. Corbett went and stared up at the face of the Virgin; the baby she held stared serenely back with innocent eyes.

'Sweet Lord!' Corbett breathed. 'The sights you have to see.'

He took a taper from a small recess and lit a candle on the iron stand before the Virgin. Kneeling down, he prayed that he would finish this business and return safely to Maeve and Eleanor in London.

He sat back on his heels, revelling in the peace and serenity of the chapel. He started as the door was abruptly thrown open and Ranulf came swaggering back up the chapel, a leather bag clutched in his hand. Behind him, Dame Cecily locked and barred the chapel door and came hurrying up. Ranulf undid the bag. He brought out a long, wooden mallet with a great iron head. Corbett pointed to the plaster near the floor.

'Start there, Ranulf. I am sure you'll find a door.'

Ranulf pulled his sleeves up and set to with a relish. Corbett and the prioress walked away. Dame Cecily moaned softly as Ranulf swung the great mallet backwards and forwards against the wall in a cloud of dust and fragmenting plaster. Corbett, coughing and spluttering, told him to stop. Corbett examined the wall.

'We'll soon be through,' he commented. 'Continue!'

Soon the chapel was full of white dust. The floor was covered with fragments and shards of brick as Ranulf pounded like a man possessed. However, it was onerous work; Ranulf rested on the mallet, sweat running down his face.

'Whoever did this,' he coughed, 'did it in a hurry.' He pointed to the wall. 'Two lines of soft brick covered by a white plaster and painted to blend in with the rest of the chapel.'

He grinned mischievously at the now stricken prioress and continued with gusto. Corbett, covering his mouth and nose, watched the hole grow, a yard from the floor and about two foot across. At last Ranulf stopped. They all had to walk away coughing and spluttering, allowing the dust to settle. Dame Cecily took one look at the damaged wall and sat down groaning. Corbett went to the altar, took two candles, lit them and gave one to Ranulf.

'Now, let's see what secrets are here.'

They entered the recess, Corbett held the candle up as Ranulf squeezed behind him. The anchorite's hole was cleverly constructed, actually built within the walls of the chapel. Corbett had seen similar recesses at both Westminster Abbey and St Paul's Cathedral. This one was about six feet high and just over two yards broad.

'Where we came in,' Ranulf murmured, 'was the door. Somewhere about here should be the squint hole.'

Corbett lowered his candle and gasped. He crouched and pushed his candle closer. A skeleton lay sprawled in the corner, the bones yellowing. At first Corbett thought fragments of flesh were clinging to them but, as he crawled closer, realized they were only tattered cloth and a battered leather belt. Corbett grabbed Ranulf's candle and put it on the floor. A small dagger, the blade broken, lay glinting in the dust next to the skeleton. Corbett raised his candle. Alan of the Marsh (for Corbett knew it was he) had apparently attempted to dig his way through the wall – a pathetic attempt, as the broken dagger proved. On the wall, above the skeleton, was a crude drawing very similar to the one Corbett had seen in the Hermitage. The clerk stared round carefully; there were no other remains and the small, shabby purse attached to the belt was empty.

'God have mercy!' Corbett whispered. 'God have mercy on the poor bastard!'

He crawled out after Ranulf and handed the candles to the prioress.

'It's Alan of the Marsh,' he announced. 'Or, at least, his skeleton.'

The venerable lady had suffered enough shocks for one morning and, if Corbett hadn't caught her, she would have fainted to the floor. He gently assisted her across the sanctuary and into one of the stalls.

'What can I do?' she murmured. 'What can I do? Sir Hugh, what happened there?'

'What I suspect happened,' Corbett answered, sitting in the stall next to her, 'is that Alan of the Marsh fled here and sought sanctuary, hiding in the anchorite hole. He made his pact with the then prioress, handing over the cup and promising to keep silent about the smuggling activities of this house.'

'Was he walled in alive?' Dame Cecily interrupted.

Corbett noticed the trickle of sweat running down from beneath her coif.

'The walls are thick enough to drown any groans or cries,' Corbett explained. 'However, Alan was first drugged, probably with some sleeping potion or poisoned drink. Once he was unconscious, both the doorway and the squint hole were blocked and sealed.' Corbett shrugged. 'The prioress then had the anchorite hole bricked over. It was probably done at night, in a few hours, and the poor man was forgotten.'

'But surely someone would have noticed?'

Corbett shook his head. 'When I first came here you told me the building work was not finished until 1220. There would have been scaffolding and builders around. Just imagine. Alan of the Marsh is put there late one afternoon. The prioress brings him some food and drugged wine. She locks the door and immediately orders it to be bricked up. No one but she knows there's someone inside. Many, many hours later, Alan of the Marsh regains consciousness. He makes a pathetic attempt to escape.' Corbett stared at the statue of the Virgin Mary. 'I am not saying it happened like that. But I think it's the nearest we'll get to the truth!'

Dame Cecily rose and grasped Corbett's hand. 'Sir Hugh, for the love of God, there are long chests, boxes in the sacristy. Could you remove the skeleton? Please! I, we are not responsible for that poor man's death. I'll have prayers offered for the repose of his soul. I'll make reparation.'

Corbett saw that the prioress was so agitated she was on the verge of fainting again.

'One more question?' he asked.

She nodded.

'Does anyone else know the story of the fugitive?'

She shook her head. 'No one knows. The chronicle is kept hidden. Only the prioress is allowed to read it. As for the chalice' – she shrugged – 'it is now part of our treasure. No one comments on it.' She touched Corbett's wrist; her fingers felt cold as ice. 'But, please,' she murmured, 'get rid of that terrible thing!'

Corbett and Ranulf took the skeleton out and placed it in a long, wooden box they found in the sacristy. They sealed the lid and, preceded by a trembling prioress, carried the coffin out into the deserted cemetery. In a small outhouse Ranulf found a pick and shovel. A shallow grave was dug and the coffin lowered. Once it was finished, Dame Cecily gave Corbett her solemn word that, at an appropriate time, a cross would be erected there and Masses sung for Alan's soul.

'The poor bugger will need it!' Ranulf whispered as they went back to the stable yard to collect their horses.

Corbett paused. 'I wonder!' he exclaimed.

'Wonder about what, Master – the chalice?'

Corbett grinned. 'No, let the convent keep that. I am wondering about the priest, Father James, and Alan of the Marsh's involvement in his disappearance.'

Ranulf kicked the ground with the toe of his boot.

'I don't know; there's a deeper mystery here. I still think we should take that cup.'

Corbett laughed softly. 'It's a chalice, Ranulf, a sacred vessel. It is where it should be! Edward would only give it to Surrey. Now come, let's go!'

They found Maltote warming himself in the smithy. He demanded to know why they had been so long. Ranulf shook his head, raising a finger to his lips as a sign for silence until they had left the convent.

Once out on the moors, Corbett halted and looked back at the convent.

'Nothing,' he murmured, 'is what it seems to be. Who would guess that a house dedicated to prayer and God's work could harbour such dreadful secrets?'

'We have done some good,' Ranulf replied with a smile. 'We have exorcized a ghost, discovered the truth and given that arrogant woman a lesson she'll never forget as long as she lives!'

And, as Corbett urged them on, Ranulf pulled back to whisper to Maltote what they had discovered at the convent. Corbett rode ahead, lost in his own thoughts. He didn't take the path back to the manor but rode to the cliff top. He paused for a while, staring down at the beach, watching the waves sweep in and recalled how he had nearly met his death there. He sat, letting the spray-soaked wind whip his face and hair whilst brooding on what he had learnt.

'Master, where to now?' Ranulf called. 'What do we do next?'

Corbett stared down at the grey mass of heaving sea.

'Master,' Ranulf persisted. 'Is it finished? Do you know where the rest of the treasure is?'

Corbett turned his horse's head and winked at them.

'It's beneath our noses,' he replied cryptically. 'Right beneath our noses and has been all the time. But, come, it's back to Mortlake Manor. We have to trap a murderer!'

He spurred his horse into a gallop across the moor, on to the path skirting the village and into Mortlake Manor.

Once there Corbett became infuriatingly absent-minded. He went to the buttery for something to eat and drink and then back to his chamber. He took out pumice stone, ink horn and quill and a small roll of parchment and began to write furiously, listing everything he knew. He refused to answer Ranulf's questions. Now and again he would look up, stare into space and tap the quill against his cheek. He'd make some exclamation and go back to his writing. Only once did he break off, to ask Ranulf to bring to him the dead Cerdic's shirt. He scrutinized this, muttered to himself and went back to his writing. Ranulf had seen him like this before.

'Old Master Long Face is in one of his moods – he's as

miserable as sin,' he whispered to Maltote. 'He is setting his traps.'

At last Corbett was finished. He rose and stretched, trying to force the cramp from his tired back.

'What now, Master, what now?' Ranulf asked.

'Go down to the hall. Give Sir Simon my regards. Tell him that I would like to dine tonight with him and his wife. He is to invite those who attended our first dinner here.' He paused. 'And one extra guest.'

'Who?'

'Fourbour the baker.' Corbett went across to the table and poured himself half a goblet of wine. 'And tell Sir Simon we'll be leaving tomorrow. I'll sleep for a while. The arrangements will take some time. Just make sure that Sir Simon does what I ask.'

Corbett drained the wine cup, lay down on the bed and fell asleep. It was dark when Ranulf woke him.

'It's late,' Ranulf whispered. 'The meal will commence within an hour. You'd best prepare.'

Corbett swung himself off the bed and groaned as the wound on his head made him wince.

'Ranulf, make sure you are armed!'

Corbett got ready slowly, then he and his companions went down to the hall.

The great table had already been prepared. Sir Simon and Alice were sitting in their chairs before the fire. They plied him with questions – what was the matter? Why was he leaving so abruptly? – but he returned no answers. He sat toying with the ring on his finger and staring into the fire.

'Has Monck's corpse been removed?' he asked.

It was Alice who replied. 'Yes, it's been taken to the village church; Father Augustine will sing the requiem tomorrow.

Though perhaps it would be best if Monck was buried here.'

'I think so,' Corbett said. 'He had no family and my Lord of Surrey is not mindful of such things.'

'When will you leave, Hugh?' Alice asked.

'Early tomorrow morning, I hope,' Corbett replied. He smiled thinly. 'Perhaps I'll stay for Monck's requiem Mass. I'll make arrangements with Father Augustine. He is coming here tonight, is he not?'

'Of course. And Fourbour the baker.'

Selditch came bustling in, chattering about a patient he'd been treating in the village. Father Augustine arrived next, looking rather angry at being summoned from what he called his 'onerous duties'. He refused to sit but stood by the hearth.

'The gossips are busy in the village,' he said.

'Sir Simon, I suggest that the prisoners be removed as quickly as possible. Poor Robert the reeve!' He glared at Corbett. 'Everyone knows the truth. We should have kept the girl here.'

'I have no authority to do that,' Corbett replied. 'And what future is there for her here? The gossips would kill her, if not physically then at least spiritually. You know that, Father.'

The priest was about to object but at that moment the steward called them to dinner. They took their places at the table. The atmosphere was stilted and tense, and became even more so when Fourbour hurried into the hall, apologizing profusely for being late.

Gurney ushered him into his seat, Father Augustine said grace and the meal was served. The Gurneys were puzzled, rather frightened. Catchpole, who had swaggered in after grace had been said, sat stony-faced. Selditch was secretive, Fourbour tense and fearful. Father Augustine still showed his vexation at being summoned to the manor. Corbett toyed with his food until Gurney could tolerate the atmosphere no longer. He banged his wine cup on the table and glared down at the clerk.

'Hugh, you asked us all here. Give us your reasons.'

'*He* asked us!' Father Augustine exclaimed. 'What is all this?'

'I thought you'd be interested in what I have to say,' Corbett replied. 'First, I know who has been responsible for all the murders.'

'The Pastoureaux, surely?' Fourbour bleated.

Corbett smiled grimly and shook his head. 'Oh no,' he said, 'that's just vicious rumour.' He rolled a crumb back and forth on the table top. 'More importantly, I think I have found the lost treasure of King John.'

Chapter 13

Corbett's hearers sat dumbstruck, eyes staring, mouths gaping. Selditch was the first to recover.

'Where is it?'

'I will tell you that later,' Corbett replied.

'This is preposterous!' Gurney exploded.

'Where, Corbett?' Selditch repeated. 'Where, for God's sake?'

'Certain questions first,' Corbett said. 'Lady Alice, your perfume?'

'What about it, Hugh? What on earth has that got to do with . . . ?' Her voice trailed off.

'I smelled it,' Corbett replied, 'yesterday, when I was attacked in the Hermitage. It's a fragrant perfume' – he smiled thinly – 'that I have always associated with you.'

'For Heaven's sake!' Gurney shouted. 'Are you implying that my wife attacked you?'

'No, Sir Simon. I simply said I smelled her perfume.'

'It means the same thing,' Catchpole grunted from down the table.

Father Augustine, seated beside Alice, looked askance. 'Are you saying Lady Alice was in the Hermitage?' he demanded.

Corbett sighed in exasperation. 'Lady Alice, has any of your perfume ever been stolen?'

'Of course not!'

'How is it kept?' Corbett asked.

'As small sachets of wool, linen or velvet soaked in the fragrance. For Heaven's sake, Hugh!'

'Have you ever given any of it away?' Corbett insisted.

Alice's fingers flew to her lips as the memory came back to her. 'Why yes, I did! Some time ago. Do you remember, Master Fourbour, I went to your shop? Your wife looked so pale and cheerless that I felt sorry for her. Poor thing! God rest her! I was talking to her and she remarked how fragrant my perfume was. I gave her some sachets. She put them in her purse.'

Fourbour's face, usually pasty-coloured, had now gone deathly white.

'I remember that, Lady Alice,' he stammered. 'But, for God's sake, sir,' – he glared at Corbett – 'what are you implying?'

'I am implying nothing,' Corbett replied. 'I was just clearing up a small puzzle. You see, the perfume was carried by Mistress Fourbour's murderer. Wasn't it, Father?'

The priest's hands gripped the table. He looked suddenly more gaunt. His eyes never left those of Corbett.

'What are you saying?'

'Let me tell you a story,' Corbett said, 'which began before any of us were born. A king tries to take his treasure trove across the Wash. A traitor called Holcombe steals some of the treasure. He rides away to share the ill-gotten gains with his brother-in-law, Alan of the Marsh, who is the steward of the then lord of the manor here, Sir Richard

Gurney. Alan knows the wastes of Norfolk – he knows where men, horses, even treasure, can be hidden. He is also a smuggler, so he knows the secret ways out of the kingdom. But something goes wrong – Holcombe is tracked down, executed and ignominiously buried.' Corbett gave Gurney a half smile – a sign that he would not betray his secrets.

'Alan of the Marsh, too, dies, but not before bequeathing a precious object to the sisters of the Holy Cross.' It was, he told himself, at least the partial truth. 'King John,' he went on, 'dies a short while later in Newark. The treasure is lost and the two perpetrators had met their just fate. The years passed and both the treasure and its thieves become the subject of legend.' He stopped and looked across the table at Father Augustine. 'Now, Alan of the Marsh was a local man, but Holcombe hailed from Bishop's Lynn. Before his capture, but after he had stolen the treasure, he returned to his family home. He must have chattered. His family became aware that he was a robber, being hunted by the Gurneys who later captured and killed him. The stories about his daring robbery entered into family legend and were passed on from one generation to another. Now, about forty years ago, the Holcombe family in Bishop's Lynn died out in the male line. But there was a daughter. She married.' Corbett caught his lower lip between his teeth. 'Father Augustine, what is your surname?'

'Norringham!' the priest spat back.

Corbett sipped from his wine cup. 'Norringham,' he repeated. 'So it was a man called Norringham whom the Holcombe daughter married. Now, I conjecture that this Norringham died young, leaving a baby, who grew into an intelligent young boy whose mind became full of stories about his mother's ancestor, John Holcombe, and King John's treasure. This boy, called Augustine, became a priest. He served, I suggest, as a curate in Bishop's Lynn, probably at St Margaret's, before being moved to Swaffham.'

Corbett had very little evidence, and no proof, for any of this. The priest's silence, his failure to deny any of these allegations, seemed, though, to confirm them and Corbett was encouraged.

'Now,' he continued, 'whilst this priest was a curate in Bishop's Lynn he fell in love with a young, headstrong girl called Amelia Culpeper—' He turned to the baker. 'Yes, Master Fourbour, your future wife. The girl became pregnant, but the child later died. Now Amelia Fourbour never told anyone about her lover. Why should she? Perhaps she knew it was impossible from the start? How could a priest break his vows to marry her? Moreover, she could make no accusation without publicizing her own shame. Who knows, perhaps she loved this man to distraction and could not bear to do anything that might hurt him.' He stared at Father Augustine and this time the priest's eyes did falter.

'Hugh,' Gurney interrupted. 'Are you sure of what you are saying? What proof do you have of this?'

'I have proof,' Selditch intervened, his fat, normally cheery face now solemn. 'Proof of a sort. When Father Augustine came here, he discovered my love of antiquities. He questioned me closely about the history of Hunstanton and Mortlake. I thought he had similar antiquarian tastes to my own, but as soon as I had passed on everything I had learned, he lost interest.'

'Oh, I have stronger proof than that,' Corbett said.

'Amelia was a secretive, devious woman. Only once did she let her guard slip. She made for herself, on a heart-shaped scrap of parchment, one of those keepsakes so popular with lovers – you know the kind, where the lovers' initials are combined. But, to preserve her secret, Amelia made of her keepsake a kind of puzzle. Her own initials, A.C., for Amelia Culpeper, she concealed as the first letters of the words *Amor Currit*. Those of her lover, A.H., were hidden in the words *Amor Haesitat*. They stand for Augustine Holcombe. Although, Father, your real name was Augustine Norringham, you are prouder of the Holcombe side of the family tree. The Holcombes have a more interesting history – perhaps a grander one. You undoubtedly told Amelia all about it.' He looked again at the priest. 'And perhaps she thought that *amor haesitat* aptly described your behaviour towards her.'

Father Augustine bowed his head.

'Now time went on,' Corbett continued. 'You became parish priest at Swaffham, near enough to Hunstanton and Mortlake to do something about the dreams and stories you had grown up on. You visited the convent of the Holy Cross, serving there as a chaplain during the summer months. The sisters were pleased and old Father Ethelred was only too glad to have someone to help out. You saw and used their chalice and remembered all the stories you had been told. You realized that the cup was very old and very precious.'

The priest raised his head then, malice blazing in his eyes.

'You are very clever, Sir Hugh,' he murmured. 'But you tell a preposterous story. Are you going to say that I murdered Amelia Fourbour? Have you forgotten that no signs or marks were found around the scaffold?'

'I have not forgotten,' Corbett replied. 'But let me carry on with the story. You were a priest in Swaffham – a royal town, a busy place, where the income was good, the benefices rich. So why come to Hunstanton, to a poor fishing village? Had you done something disgraceful? I doubt it. I think that you petitioned the Bishop of Norwich for Hunstanton and that he was only too willing to give such a lonely little parish to someone so keen to take it on. So you come to Hunstanton. You make enquiries of Master Selditch. You make friends with Dame Cecily and learn all you can from her. You go through the parish records, looking for references to Holcombe and his accomplice, Alan of the Marsh. You had your own pool of knowledge, from what your mother had told you. You leave flowers at the scaffold on which your ancestor was hanged – a small gesture of respect to someone who was going to make you very rich.'

'I've seen those flowers sometimes,' Catchpole interjected. 'Bunches of wild flowers, placed at the foot of the gibbet and replaced when they rotted.' He jabbed a finger at the priest. 'Yes, Sir Hugh is right. It started when you came and ceased when Master Monck arrived.'

'You knew your ancestor had been hanged,' Corbett continued. 'But where was he buried? What had happened to him? And to his accomplice, Alan of the Marsh? And, above all, where could the treasure be? You began investigating your own churchyard, violating old graves, thinking that perhaps the treasure was in a coffin or that at least you might find some sort of clue in one of those derelict tombs. You could do that without any recrimination or accusation. Who would dream that the parish priest was the person pillaging the graves? And any strange happenings or occurrences could always be blamed on the Pastoureaux.'

'Of course,' Selditch said. He stared, appalled, at the priest. 'It was you who advised Sir Simon to give the Pastoureaux the Hermitage. You told your parishioners to treat them well.'

'Of course he did!'

Corbett watched Father Augustine intently. The priest's hands had disappeared beneath the table. He had also pushed his chair back and was now staring into the darkness as if only half-listening to what Corbett was saying.

'Priest!'

Father Augustine's eyes flickered.

'You were patient, weren't you?' Corbett continued. 'You knew it might take years but, there again, you had no distractions – until Amelia Culpeper came to the village.' Corbett looked down the table at Fourbour the baker, who sat, wide-eyed like the rest, listening to his tale.

'God save me, Master Fourbour! I mean no offence,' Corbett declared, 'but God knows why Amelia Culpeper married you. She may have been attracted to you. She may have wished to escape the malice of her neighbours in Bishop's Lynn or perhaps she knew that Father Augustine was in Hunstanton. Whatever the reason, she came here.'

'But she didn't like him!' the baker cried. 'She said she only went to church on sufferance!'

'Amelia Culpeper must have been a remarkable woman,' Corbett said. 'Her public attitude to Father Augustine was only pretence. Don't you remember telling me how she liked to go for walks or rides? I am sure that she went to see her long-lost lover, Father Augustine.'

'I can't believe this!' Fourbour whispered.

'It's true,' Corbett told him. 'There must have been several lover's meetings. But Amelia's very presence was a threat to everything Father Augustine had worked for. The night she died Amelia took a horse and rode out to meet him on the moors. Father Augustine had invited her, though he had also made preparations. Remember, the night was dark, wild and blustery. He had already prepared for murder, coating the rope and noose on the scaffold in black pitch to camouflage it against any prying eyes. Tell me, priest, what do you use on the wooden crosses in the cemetery?'

The priest smiled, a fox-like grin, as if savouring some secret.

'That same pitch,' Corbett answered for him, 'you used on the scaffold rope.' He paused and stared around. Father Augustine was gazing coolly around the hall. There was an air of controlled menace about him that made Corbett uneasy. The others, including Ranulf and Maltote, sat like a group of children waiting for a minstrel to finish his tale.

'We are waiting,' Father Augustine said softly.

'Aye, just as Amelia must have waited,' Corbett said. 'I suppose you were all loving towards her that night. Everything was ready. The noose had been coated with pitch earlier in the day. You'd use twigs to remove any sign of your presence there. And you went to meet Amelia.' Corbett watched the priest. 'You went on foot. You'd share her horse – Amelia would like that, perched on the saddle before you, two lovers riding into the night. You'd take her to the place where your ancestor died. Amelia knew all the legends.' Corbett glanced at Fourbour. 'Hence, her veiled remarks to you about Hunstanton being richer than it knew.'

The baker covered his face with his hands as Corbett continued.

'God knows what happened then? Perhaps you paused for a while, murmuring endearments into Amelia's ear? She was distracted, delighted by what she heard. Your hand goes out. You clasp the swinging rope, slip the noose around her neck and move the horse away. It would have been so simple.'

He turned to Selditch. 'I believe Amelia's neck was broken?'

'It was,' Selditch agreed. 'The head was loose. Her neck must have snapped like a piece of thread!'

'Perhaps she struggled,' Corbett continued, trying not to be distracted by Fourbour, now sobbing till his shoulders shook. 'Perhaps she fought against the noose, but it would have been over in seconds. There's a rope round her neck, the horse she was sitting on moves away, she drops—' Corbett drew a deep breath. 'You check her wallet, but there's nothing in it except some sachets of perfume, which you remove. You ride to the edge of the village. You pass some peasants. They see the baker's horse and a cloaked figure sitting sidesaddle and think it's Amelia Fourbour. Now the church is on the edge of the village—' Corbett paused and tried to catch Ranulf's eye, whilst quietly cursing his own ineptitude. No longer the humble parish priest, Father Augustine had a definite air of menace. Does he have a knife, Corbett wondered, remembering de Luce, canon of St Paul's, who had inflicted the knife wound whose scar he still bore.

'On the edge of the village,' Corbett continued, getting to his feet, 'you slipped off the horse and disappeared into your church.' He began to walk towards the priest, but he was too late.

Father Augustine sprang to his feet and, before Corbett

could shout a warning, took the few steps that put him to stand beside Alice.

'Sit down, Father!' Corbett commanded.

'Sit down! Sit down!' Father Augustine mimicked.

He had his head lowered, chin pressing into his chest. Catchpole regained his wits and made to rise but the priest's hand came sweeping out of his cloak and he pressed the point of his dagger against Alice's soft throat.

'Keep still, my lady!' Father Augustine murmured.

'Don't be a fool!' Corbett shouted.

'Don't be a fool!' Father Augustine mocked. 'You stupid, miserable-faced clerk! You can tell that bastard' – he nodded towards Ranulf – 'to put his hands on the table. Come on!'

He pressed the point of the dagger against Alice's neck. A small prick of blood seeped out. Alice moaned. She tried to force her neck away but the priest held her fast.

'Gently, Ranulf!' Corbett snapped. 'He'll kill!'

'Yes, I'll kill!' the priest said. His eyes darted around like those of a trapped animal. 'You don't understand. None of you do. That treasure is mine. It has been since the first day I heard about it. It was like a demon inside me. I thought I could forget it. I became a priest.' Father Augustine tapped the side of his head. 'But the voices kept telling me. The ghosts of my ancestors, chattering away, like a tune you hear and never forget. I tried to forget it.'

Ranulf moved but the priest pressed the dagger harder against Alice's throat.

'For God's sake!' Gurney hissed, glaring at Ranulf.

Corbett gazed despairingly at Alice's face. Grey with fear, she was on the verge of fainting. The priest's dagger shifted towards her windpipe, leaving a red mark and a small bubble of blood where her throat had been nicked. Father Augustine was now talking as if to himself.

'I tried,' he muttered. 'I really did try to stop the voices. I thought the love of a woman would help but she betrayed me, she became pregnant.' He raised his head and his lips curled. 'The stupid bitch wanted me to leave the priesthood.' He gazed at the hapless baker. 'You were welcome to the stupid sow!'

'I loved her!' Fourbour whispered. 'You wicked, evil man! I really loved her!'

Corbett pressed Fourbour back into his seat. He shook his head imperceptibly at Ranulf and Catchpole, both of whom were tense, waiting for his signal. The priest glanced at Selditch, but the physician's trembling and sweat-soaked face showed he was no fighting man.

'Leave the woman!' Corbett pleaded.

'Oh, I will!' The priest smiled. 'We'll go together, Corbett. Perhaps you deserve some of the treasure? Like me, you may have discovered its whereabouts, but I found it first.' His voice sounded like that of a spoilt child. 'Yes, I found it first. Those stupid, fat nuns! One day at Mass I couldn't believe my eyes. I stood at the altar and I saw a chalice from the treasure of King John!' He gazed round-eyed at Corbett as if expecting his approval. 'I knew then that my voices were correct. God was showing me, in His own way, that the treasure was really mine. My fingers itched to take that cup. I began my searches – of graves, of the Hermitage. And then that bastard Monck arrived! He thought he was so perceptive, but it was his servant I feared. The man went to Mass at the convent. He saw the chalice.'

Alice – her eyes becoming glazed, the muscles of her face tense – was motionless with terror.

'Release the woman, please!' Corbett begged.

'I'll soon be finished and then I'll be gone,' Father Augustine told him. 'You see, Cerdic saw the chalice and he babbled like a child. He wanted to please his master, so he came to see me. He wanted to know more about the chalice and the voices told me to do it. I slit his throat. Whish!' The priest drew his finger across his throat. 'And what did I do then, clerk?'

'I suppose you bundled the body on a horse and took it to a cove where there was a small boat and rowed down the coast to the beach beneath Hunstanton. You cut off the head and stuck it on a pole and slung the body on the beach just below the high-tide mark. The rising tide washed away your footprints and any sign that a boat had been beached.'

Father Augustine nodded. 'Ingenious,' he murmured. 'I left the head upon a pole. I thought the Pastoureaux would take the blame. I climbed into the boat and rowed a little way out, watching the incoming sea smooth out the shingle and remove any signs that I had been there – though most of Cerdic's body remained dry.' He pointed at Corbett with his free hand. 'You should have died there. I watched you go out to the Hermitage. I heard how that rogue Master Joseph had taunted you. I took Amelia's perfume.' Father Augustine blinked. 'But we are wasting time. Come here, Sir Hugh, quickly! I'll soon let this bitch go!'

Corbett walked around the table, touching Ranulf gently on the shoulders as a sign to stay still. The priest, however, saw this.

'Stand up!' he ordered.

Ranulf got to his feet.

'And the crossbow!'

Ranulf looked at Corbett, who nodded.

'Very carefully,' the priest snapped, 'put it on the table!'

Ranulf obeyed.

'And the bolts! Come on, you've got more than one!'

Ranulf placed the two squat crossbow bolts on the table.

'Clever, clever boy! Now, take the bolts!'

Ranulf picked them up.

'And throw them down the hall.'

Ranulf obeyed.

Alice whimpered, slumping in a half-swoon. The priest grabbed her by the arm and ordered Corbett nearer.

'Take her other arm!' he ordered.

Corbett obeyed. He and the priest, who still held the knife to Alice's throat, dragged the half-swooning woman down the hall, walking backwards. The priest shouted curses and warnings at the rest to stay seated. Corbett curbed his own panic and resisted the desire to do something stupid, quickly dismissing thoughts of pulling Alice away, for he dare not take the risk. The priest's knife was still digging deeply into Alice's throat. Corbett knew the man was both insane and evil enough to kill her without a second's thought.

At the hall door a group of servants, who had been half-dozing in the passageway, suddenly jumped to their feet. They stared in horror at the macabre procession. The priest ordered them into the hall and they scurried in like frightened children. Father Augustine pulled Alice towards him, circling her neck with one arm, the knife now under her chin.

'Lock the door!' he yelled.

Corbett swung the two great doors closed, pulling down the beam across the iron slats. He turned as the priest backed down the passageway.

'For God's sake!' Corbett hissed. 'What on earth do you think will happen? Gurney will hunt you down and, if he doesn't, I will!'

Father Augustine ignored him.

'My ancestor survived for a year!' He snapped. 'Alan of the Marsh was never caught.'

'How did you kill Monck?' Corbett asked.

'Oh, that was simple. He said he had been examining Cerdic's clothes.' The priest grinned. 'Like you did. What did you find, Sir Hugh?'

'Candle grease.'

'Well, Monck found the same. He said it was from a church candle, beeswax. I, of course, denied it. I blamed those bitches up at the convent. He left in a hurry, believing they were the culprits. I told him that both Cerdic and I had suspicions about their smuggling and the chalice. When he came out of the convent I was waiting for him. Quite easy. A crossbow bolt in his chest. I put him back on his horse. I thrust his boots back into his stirrups and fastened his own belt round the saddle horn to keep him upright. I pricked the horse with my dagger and sent it galloping like a rider from hell through the village. The horse must have raced on to the moor until Monck was shaken loose and fell off. No one would believe that he had already been killed when his horse galloped through the village. Except you, of course!'

Corbett watched the movement behind the priest.

'Yes,' he said. 'I, too, saw the candle grease and the bruise on Monck's belly where the saddle horn had dug deep. I also noticed his belt was rucked and twisted.'

'I should have killed you!' the priest hissed.

He dragged the now unconscious Alice further along the passageway.

'You were very clever,' Corbett flattered, hoping to distract the priest. 'I suppose you told Monck to go to the convent but not to voice his suspicions to Dame Cecily.'

'Oh, yes.' Father Augustine smirked. 'Of course, once he visited that fat bitch, Monck would know Cerdic had been to see me.' The priest yanked Alice closer to him. 'You, of course, were different. There were three of you. I immediately recognized you, Corbett, for what you are, the king's hunting dog.' The priest smirked. 'I heard about your visit to Bishop's Lynn and changed round the signpost. You wouldn't have been the first travellers to die in some God-forsaken Norfolk marsh.'

'That's when I began to wonder how Monck may have died,' Corbett said. 'Maltote freed me. He threw me a rope to put round the horse's neck so as to pull it from the mire. I widened it to loop round my saddle horn.' Corbett took a step nearer, watching the shadow behind the priest, further down the passageway. 'I really have a lot to thank you for, Father Augustine. After all, only when I raced for my life along the beach did I see the skull etched in the cliffs.'

'Oh, so you know about that?' Father Augustine stared in surprise.

'Yes, and how did you?'

'Now that's my secret,' Father Augustine hissed. He raised his hand and tapped the side of his head. 'And it's all in here. I memorized then destroyed the fruits of my searches.'

He began to walk backwards again, dragging a now unresisting Alice.

'Where are you taking her?' Corbett asked.

'Oh, I am taking her nowhere. I want to ask you one

question. After that I am going to kill her and I am going to kill you. The treasure? The skull and the triangle? Let's see if we agree!'

'First, look behind you!'

The priest smirked. 'Don't be stupid!'

'Very well,' Corbett snapped. 'Kill him!'

The smirk faded. Father Augustine turned slightly. As he did, Ranulf fired the crossbow. The bolt smashed into Father Augustine's skull just above the right ear. The priest staggered forward. The knife slipped. Corbett raced forward, pushed him aside and pulled Alice out of his slack grip. The priest stood, a look of stupefaction on his face. He coughed. A trickle of blood spurted out of the corner of his mouth. He sighed, then collapsed to the ground. Corbett laid Alice down gently on a window seat. He felt the side of her neck and the blood beat in her wrist, her hands and face were ice cold. He looked up as Ranulf came padding down the corridor, his face white with fury. He pulled the priest's head back by his hair and Corbett saw the glint of his knife.

'Leave him!' Corbett snapped. 'The bastard's dead! Open the doors and get Sir Simon.'

Ranulf threw the priest's head back, re-sheathed his knife and did as Corbett asked. The next hour all was confusion. Alice was taken back to her chamber with Selditch in attendance, though the physician had to ease his own discomfort with a constant supply of wine. Catchpole was despatched to the priest's house to see what he could find. Gurney instructed his servants to remove the corpse, then sat like a man bemused in front of the fire. He gazed bleakly at Corbett.

'You shouldn't have brought him here. For God's sake, man, why not just arrest him?'

Corbett looked over his shoulder to where Ranulf was supervising the servants.

'What could I do, Sir Simon?' he asked, sitting down. 'Confront him in his own church? God knows what weapons are hidden away there. He could have killed me like he did Cerdic or Monck.'

Corbett described how Father Augustine had murdered Monck. Gurney whistled under his breath.

'All that for some treasure!'

'Why condemn him?' Corbett replied. 'You were looking for it as well. How would you feel if you really thought that treasure was yours, paid for by the blood of your ancestor?'

'But he was priest!'

'He was mad. Even at the end, all he could think of was the treasure. He could no more have escaped from his dream than a prisoner in the deepest dungeon.'

'Do you think he knew about the Pastoureaux?' Gurney asked.

'Possibly. He used them as a shield for his own activities, that's why he mutilated Cerdic's body.' Corbett paused as an ashen-faced Selditch joined them.

'Lady Alice is resting now. I gave her a sleeping potion.' Selditch shook his head. 'If it hadn't been for your servant, Ranulf . . .'

Corbett stared at the flames of the fire, listening as his manservant argued with Maltote over some minor matter.

'There's not a room,' he said, 'that can hold Ranulf.'

'He went through the window like a cat,' Gurney murmured. 'One minute he was sitting down, the next he'd collected both crossbow and bolts.' Gurney sighed. 'Hugh, do you really know where the treasure is?'

'Oh, yes,' Corbett replied. 'And tomorrow morning, as soon as dawn breaks, I'll show you.'

Fourbour the baker came up. The baker was more shocked from grief than from the revelations about Father Augustine. He grasped Corbett's hand.

'I thank you,' he muttered. His eyes brimmed with tears. 'You're sure she wouldn't have suffered long?'

Corbett refused to meet his gaze. 'I don't think so.'

'If only she had told me!'

Corbett looked away. The baker was still mumbling the same forlorn regret as he left the hall.

'Isn't it strange?' Corbett whispered. 'Amelia loved but did not recognize what she was loving?'

'What's the role of the sisters of the Holy Cross in this?' Gurney asked crossly.

'Sir Simon, that's a matter between you and the prioress.'

'And the treasure?' Gurney persisted. 'You say it's near here?'

'I think so,' Corbett replied. 'And I suspect Father Augustine knew where it was. We have to wait till morning, for the tide to turn. What still concerns me is how Alan of the Marsh could, by himself, hide it all.' Corbett raised his fingers to his lips and stared at the flames. 'That's one puzzle. The other puzzle is where did Father Augustine get his information from? Monck found out about that from the royal records and I from your ancestor's confession. But how was Father Augustine so knowledgeable?'

Corbett sat back in the chair. He absent-mindedly heard Ranulf and Maltote say they were returning to their chamber.

'Sir Simon,' Corbett asked. 'How long has the village of Hunstanton been here?'

'Since time immemorial.'

'And so's murder,' Corbett replied. 'And, I suspect, there's still one more to resolve!'

Chapter 14

They gathered in the cold hall just after dawn, tired and haggard from lack of sleep. Gurney said that Alice was now resting. They broke their fast and listened as Catchpole described his visit to the priest's house.

'There's nothing much there,' he said. 'Clothes, a few possessions, nothing remarkable at all.' He dug into a sack and brought out a sheet of parchment and looked sheepishly at Corbett. 'I can read a little. Most of the manuscripts were parish accounts but there was this.'

Corbett took the parchment and smoothed it out. It bore a marked resemblance to what he had seen amongst Monck's possessions – maps of the area, some crude and rough, others finely drawn. Then a cipher, words abbreviated, question marks beside them. Nothing startling except a name, *Jacobus*, written time and again. In one place it was *Pater Jacobus*.

'Ah,' Corbett murmured. 'Father James.' He glanced at Ranulf. 'We learnt about him at the convent.'

'I think—!' Selditch exclaimed.

'What?' Corbett asked softly.

'I have heard of him too!' Selditch confessed, and waddled off, shaking his head.

Selditch returned, breathless, carrying a small roll of

vellum tied with a piece of faded silk. He unrolled it and handed it to Corbett.

'Study it carefully,' he said. 'It's an index of letters written by Sir Simon's ancestor in January 1218.

Corbett studied the faded contents, the headings of letters the Gurneys had written in January 1218. However, one fairly long entry was a complaint to the Bishop of Norwich alleging that, 'since the disappearance of Father James', the diocese had offered no priest to the parish church of Hunstanton.

Corbett looked up. 'Disappearance?' He rubbed his chin with his fingers. 'I doubt it. This is our final murder.' He put the parchment down. 'You see, if Alan of the Marsh hid his portion of the treasure where I think he did, he would have needed an accomplice. Somebody who helped him carry and hide it. Someone above suspicion.' Corbett smiled weakly at Sir Simon. 'In this case, once again, the parish priest – Father James.' Corbett tapped the document. 'This is another reason why Father Augustine came to Hunstanton. He probably knew about Father James. He saw the chalice at the convent and wondered if there were similar treasures hidden away in the village church. I wager he searched that priest's house from top to bottom and, of course, it was another reason for ransacking the graves. He may have been looking for hiding-places or even some document written by Father James.'

'Subtle and devious,' Sir Simon said. 'Secrets hidden in a graveyard are fairly safe.'

'I agree,' Corbett replied. 'Father Augustine must have pondered all the possibilities. He did his own investigation and found out that Father James disappeared at about the same time as Alan absconded and Holcombe was executed. He realized that this was more than mere coincidence. And the devil once again came to Hunstanton. Father Augustine must have prayed that that little parish church or its churchyard held the key to the great mystery.' He stared at his companions. 'You can imagine his fury when he was unable to discover the treasure? This turned to madness when Amelia Fourbour arrived, followed by Monck and, finally, myself. The whole world was turning its hand against him. Ah well, let's finish this story.'

They collected their cloaks and went out into the yard, where Maltote and others had their horses ready. A few minutes later they left the manor and took the path towards the convent. The morning was cold and blustery and rain clouds were sweeping in above a sullen sea. On the cliff top they dismounted and left their horses with the retainers. They slipped and slid down the path to the beach. Corbett stared across it and shivered.

It looked so peaceful, with the desolate sand and shingle soaked by the receding tide. Gulls, their cries wafted by the wind, circled above them. Corbett found it difficult to believe that only a few days previously, he had raced along this beach for his very life.

'There's no need to worry,' Sir Simon murmured, putting up his hood against the blustering wind. 'Father Augustine knew what he was doing when he struck you on the head and left you here. Our priest studied Hunstanton. He knew that strong gales and heavy seas would create a sudden surge.' He smiled thinly, narrowing his eyes as they watered in the salt-soaked wind. 'Just as they did when my ancestor and King John tried to cross the Wash.'

'Come on!' Corbett urged. 'The sooner the better. I have brought you here to show you a sketch.'

They walked across the beach. Corbett looked back towards the cliffs, trying to find the exact spot where he had run for his life. The others watched in exasperation, for it was biting cold and the wind soon froze their faces and hands. Corbett, however, kept walking up and down talking to himself. At last he stopped.

'There!' he cried. 'Look everyone! Look at the cliff face!'

Gurney did, and merely shrugged. Ranulf, however, sharper-eyed, studied the white, rocky outline and exclaimed in surprise.

'It's the skull!' he said. 'It's what my master saw at the Hermitage and . . . !' His voice faltered away as he remembered his master's promise to Dame Cecily.

'Sir Simon!' Corbett exclaimed. 'Look, the cliff is rocky chalk. Now, forget what's to the left and to the right. Just study the grain of the cliff in front of us. There's a ripple in the chalk which forms into a skull, yes?'

Gurney followed his directions.

'Yes, yes, I see it,' he said. 'That part of the cliff juts out. If you stare at it long enough, the top part is like a skull and tapers to a jaw.'

'And the bushes?' Corbett added. 'They're the eyes!'

'No, they're not bushes, they're small caves,' Ranulf interrupted. 'Now, draw a triangle – one line connecting the two eyes, two more downwards from the eyes. See where they meet.'

Gurney followed Ranulf's description and exclaimed in surprise.

'It's a clump of brushwood which is the mouth of the skull! Hugh, are you saying the treasure's hidden there? Those caves are really nothing more than potholes.'

'We shall see,' Corbett said. 'But, if my suspicions are correct, behind that bush, which forms the mouth of the skull, there's a larger cave.'

He walked back up the cliff path, pleased to be away from that desolate beach and the sea thundering behind them.

'Maltote!' Corbett returned to his young messenger. 'You brought the equipment I asked for last night?'

Maltote nodded and pointed to a large sack slung behind his own horse. Corbett led the party along the cliff edge. He tried not to look over the lip of the cliff, a dizzying drop, made all the worse by the buffeting wind and the low clouds massing above the land. Ranulf was more sure-footed. Going to the edge of the cliff, he walked along like a cat, staring down, impervious to the dizzying drop. He gestured with his hand for the others to go back. Corbett was only too pleased. He, Gurney, Selditch and Catchpole clustered in a group, whilst Maltote and the retainers began emptying the sack.

'Be careful!' Corbett called.

Ranulf grinned, gesturing to them to stay still. He shouted something about the cliff edge being no worse than the rooftops of merchants' houses. Suddenly he slipped, the wet soil beneath him crumbling away. Corbett groaned and closed his eyes. When he opened them, Ranulf, none the worse, had regained his poise and was continuing his search. He stopped, took out his dagger, drove it into the soil and walked back to them.

'We are just above the bushes,' he said. 'Though I can see no cave. However, the rock face dips. Perhaps the recess lies deeper in?'

Corbett called Maltote over and they supervised the pegging of a rope ladder very similar to those used in ships or on castle walls. Once this was firmly in place, two guide ropes were pegged on either side.

'It's safer that way,' Ranulf insisted. 'If something happens to the ladder, the guide ropes provide further grips.' He grinned at Corbett. 'I'll go first. You are coming?'

Corbett nodded.

'Then follow me. But slowly and don't look down!' He took off his sword belt and slung it over his shoulder. 'Maltote, you stay here. Watch the strain on the pegs!'

Ranulf grasped the rope ladder and began to walk backwards. He lowered himself over the edge of the cliff and disappeared out of sight. Corbett prayed. He heard Ranulf's shout. Grasping the rope ladder, he too went over the edge of the cliff. He shut his eyes, lowering one foot then another. He gripped the ladder with both hands. Now and again he stopped as a buffet of wind caught him. He thanked God that the wind was coming from the land and not the sea. Even so the rope ladder swayed dangerously, and Corbett grasped the rope tighter as he continued his descent.

'Not far!' Ranulf shouted.

The voice seemed to come out of the rock face beside Corbett.

'Here, Master!'

Corbett turned to his right and saw Ranulf's outstretched hand. He grasped the guide rope more securely, and then Ranulf's hand.

'Let go!' his servant ordered.

Corbett did and, a little bruised where he had brushed the face of the cliff, he was abruptly pulled into an underground cavern. It was dark and wet. Ranulf walked deeper into the darkness. He took two candles out of his jerkin, struck a tinder and lit both. He came back and handed one to Corbett. The clerk stared around and glimpsed the pools of water on the floor.

'Is it safe?' he muttered. 'Can the tide creep in here?'

'We're too high,' Ranulf assured him. 'But the cave catches

the spray and the rain, hence the dampness. You've seen the cliff, it's chalk-layered, it must soak up a lot of water.' Ranulf's voice echoed round the cavern.

'Hell's teeth!' Corbett muttered. 'I'm tempted to tell the king to search for his treasure himself!'

Ranulf, however, was eager to continue. 'There's no one else coming?' he asked.

Corbett shook his head. 'I think it's best if we do this by ourselves.'

They walked further down the cave. At one point Corbett stopped to examine strange drawings etched on the walls – men, armed with spears and shields, hunted strange creatures he had never seen before. The paintings were done in black, red and blue dyes.

'Does that have anything to do with the treasure?' Ranulf asked.

Corbett peered closer. 'I doubt it. I've heard of these drawings in caves along the southern coast, painted by peoples long dead.'

Corbett followed Ranulf. His nervousness increased as the tunnel narrowed. Would it end in a rock face, he wondered? Had he misunderstood Alan of the Marsh's drawing? Or was that some subtle ploy to disguise the true hiding-place? Ranulf, also, lost some of his jauntiness. Soon they were forced to walk in single file, the walls closed in, the rock above them seemed to swoop down to trap them. They entered a narrow passage, no more than a foot across. Ranulf squeezed through. Corbett heard his exclamation and followed to find they had entered a spacious underground chamber.

'This must be it,' Ranulf murmured.

They walked forward, the pool of light from the tallow candles going before them. They separated, Corbett going to the right, Ranulf moving over to the far corner. Corbett's heart sank. Would there be anything here? Ranulf's shouts answered his question.

'Master, it's here!'

Corbett went over to where his manservant stood. At first he could see nothing but a pool of candlelight but Ranulf crouched, pushing the candle before him. Against the rock face were four or five large sacks. The cloth was beginning to crumble and Corbett glimpsed the precious objects they contained.

'The royal treasure!' Ranulf exclaimed. He moved his candle and Corbett saw the outstretched arm of a skeleton, head drunkenly flung to one side. 'And its guardian, Father James!'

Corbett went across and studied the skeleton carefully. The flesh had long decayed, the bones were yellow and brittle. The man's leather boots and belt and a few scattered scraps of cloth were all that remained. He pointed to the back of the skull, where the bone had been shattered.

'I think,' he said, 'that Alan of the Marsh and Holcombe divided the treasure. This is Alan's portion. A smuggler, he would know about this cave. He needed another person to help him so he called on his parish priest. They brought the treasure here, climbing down to it in the same way as we did. After which Alan killed the priest, striking him on the back of the head with a rock.'

Ranulf listened impatiently. He pulled one of the weather-beaten sacks over. The fabric, thin with age, ripped and the precious contents – silver plate, golden ewers, jewelled hanapers, diamond-studded goblets – cascaded out, clattering and clanging on the cavern floor.

'Hell's teeth!' Ranulf knelt down. He picked up a silver

plate and glanced up at his master, his eyes shining. 'Must we take it all back?'

Corbett prised the silver plate from his hand and tossed it to the ground.

'What else can we do? Steal a portion? Sell it on the market in London?'

Ranulf stared back.

'Can't you see?' Corbett explained. 'We would be drawn into the same circle of deceit and murder as all those who've died for this. No, all the treasure will be brought out. Ranulf, I'll leave you here. Fresh bags will be sent down. You will fill them with every item. They will be sealed and placed in some chamber at Mortlake Manor until the exchequer sends officials north.'

With Ranulf's help, Corbett climbed back to the cliff top, where he spent the rest of the day, freezing and cursing in the icy, bitter wind. One by one, Ranulf filled new bags with the treasure. They were pulled up and placed in the waiting cart. At last the task was finished. Corbett bound and sealed each bag. He was uneasy as he glimpsed the greedy look of some of his companions, recognizing in the wetting of the lips, the narrowing of the eyes, an itchiness to grasp something precious and keep it for oneself. At Mortlake Manor the treasure was transported to an upper room. The door was locked and Corbett took the key. Two of Gurney's retainers were placed on guard. Maltote was ordered to take a change of horses and ride as swiftly as possible to Walsingham with the news.

'The sooner the king has his hands on this,' Corbett muttered, 'the better!'

Later the same day, Corbett and Ranulf attended the burial of Monck's corpse in the village churchyard. Then Father

Augustine's sheeted corpse was placed into an elm-wooc coffin and swiftly interred. Gurney promised that, as soon as a new priest arrived, Masses would be offered for the repose of both men's souls. After the burials, Corbett walkec through the priest's deserted house. Rumours about Fathe Augustine had swept through the village and, as wa customary, the peasants had swarmed into the house to take anything precious which caught their eye – mattresses bolsters and candlesticks. Gurney followed Corbett anc stared grimly around.

'The place should be purged, cleansed!' he said. 'Thank God the treasure's found and the chaos of the last few months will disappear!'

Corbett made his farewells and left the churchyard. He rode back to Mortlake Manor, leaving Gurney to confer with the verger about how the church should be administered until a replacement priest was found. Whilst Ranulf packed thei belongings, Corbett paid a courtesy visit to a white-faced anc rather nervous Alice, still resting in her own chambers Gurney returned in the evening, insisting that Corbett anc Ranulf be his guests at a small informal banquet. The mea turned out to be a desultory affair. A taciturn Gurney and hi household tried to hide their relief at Corbett's impending departure. Ranulf, though, had no inhibitions – he drank deeply and declared loudly that, no offence to presen company, it would be a long time before he returned to Norfolk.

'The exchequer officials will be here soon?' Gurney asked yet again.

'If I know the king,' Corbett told him, 'he'll probably come here himself. They'll take the treasure as well as your two prisoners in the dungeons, the Pastoureaux. Both wil

›robably be sent to London to stand trial. I'll pay for the cross ›bove Monck's grave,' he added.

Gurney demurred. 'No, no.'

Corbett, however, insisted and took several coins out of his ›urse. 'A stone for Monck, a cross for the priest and Masses ›or their souls.'

The meal ended shortly afterwards. Corbett and Ranulf ›ent back to their own chamber, the latter chattering like a ›quirrel about what he would do once they were back in ›ondon.

Corbett listened with half an ear. He lay down on his bed ›nd pulled the blankets over him. For some reason he ›ouldn't forget Amelia Culpeper. He recalled that lonely ›caffold on the cliff top, and pictured Amelia Culpeper, with ›er arms around her lover, failing to notice the noose being ›ipped over her head. Or had she, he wondered, in the last ›ew seconds of her life, realized – and submitted.

The next morning Corbett hurriedly dressed. He broke his ›ast and took his farewell of Gurney and of Alice. Followed ›y a rather silent Ranulf, who was still suffering from the ›ffects of last night's drinking, he rode along the cliff top. The ›orning was calm, the clouds had broken and pale sunlight ›inted on the sea. At the scaffold Corbett reined in. He ›ared up at the jutting beams with their ugly, rusting hooks.

'What's the matter, Master?' Ranulf asked crossly. 'And ›hy are we going to Bishop's Lynn?'

'Just think, Ranulf, all those deaths, all that violent ›trigue. Do you know whom I pity most? The baker's wife, ›melia. She didn't care for any of this. She loved that evil ›astard Augustine to distraction.' Corbett stared over his ›oulder at Ranulf. 'He had a treasure few of us will ever have ›ut he rejected it for bags, coffers of plate and sacks of coins.'

The wind agitated his horse and Corbett patted his mount gently, though his eyes never left the scaffold.

'I have asked Sir Simon to burn the scaffold,' he said quietly. 'He's agreed. He'll put a cross up in its place, asking travellers to pray for the repose of the soul of Amelia Culpeper.'

'I wager he's sad about losing the treasure,' Ranulf said, pushing his horse alongside. 'That fat physician looked as if he had lost a groat and found a farthing!'

'Oh, they'll get their just reward,' Corbett replied. 'Sir Simon knows the law. The treasure was found on his land. He's also promised to keep quiet about the chalice at the convent.'

'And that's the end of it,' Ranulf announced.

'Is it?' Corbett asked. 'Do you really think that, Ranulf? No, no, we are just like judges who have risen from the bench after delivering sentence. Alice will never be the same, nor will the villagers. They won't forget the priest. Fulke the tanner will never forget Marina, his daughter. Poor Fourbour will never forget his wife. Poor, simple Gilbert will spend the rest of his life wondering why the people who drowned his mother now pat him on the back and buy him stoups of ale. Dame Cecily will count the cost of all this as will Sir Simon. Finally, of course, they have all smelt the lure of gold.'

'But we have found the treasure,' Ranulf interrupted.

'No! We only found Alan of the Marsh's share. Where did Holcombe hide the rest, eh?' Corbett stared out over the moors, where the morning mist still hung in thin grey wisps. 'Some of the treasure's still here. As long as the stories persist, so will the searching.' Corbett stared once more at the scaffold and crossed himself. 'Ah well, and now for Bishop's Lynn!'

'Why there?' Ranulf asked.

'I want to talk to the miller about his daughter. I want to tell him that he, too, owned a treasure of great price.'

Corbett dug his spurs into his horse. Behind them the scaffold creaked as the wind rose and the dark angel swept in from the sea to sing its eternal song above the desolate moors.

Author's Note

There are several strands to this story, all based on fact rather than fiction. The Pastoureaux or Shepherd's Movement in France, and the rest of Europe, is well documented in the 13th and 14th centuries. A lay visionary movement which went terribly wrong, the Pastoureaux acquired the reputation for being nothing better than gangs of criminals. For a brief time, they even enjoyed royal patronage until their true nature was revealed. They became involved in robbery, rape, rapine, pillage and extortion. In England their presence led to violent affrays at Shoreham in Sussex. Eventually, condemned by Church and state, the Pastoureaux were hunted down and their leaders hanged. Their followers dispersed until the next new cults appeared, as they did with alarming regularity during the medieval period.

The church had always condemned slavery. However, the kidnapping of young men and women from Western Europe for sale in the markets along the Mediterranean and Middle East was a well-known medieval scandal. It was much more sinister and wicked than the white-slave trade of Victorian imperialism. Time and again, popes thundered their condemnation and kings issued orders, but the trade continued to thrive. The most flagrant example of this is mentioned in the novel, the Children's Crusade, a visionary crusading movement which led to death and abuse for thousands of the children involved. They never reached Palestine, but became the prey of mercenary ships' captains and greedy slave-masters.

King John's debacle at the Wash in the autumn of 1216 is, of course, well documented, though historians heatedly debate the exact location of the disaster and the causes behind it. Treason and treachery have never been ruled out. After all, here was an autocratic king with his army and household who decided to cross one of the most treacherous coastal areas of Britain without any proper reconnaissance or guide. There was no need for such haste. King John was not being pursued and the march should have been more properly organized. The loss of his treasure in the Wash probably resulted in John's demise a few weeks later.

The lost treasure constantly attracted fortune-hunters to the area. The imperial regalia were never recovered but, during the 13th century, items of this treasure do reappear on treasury lists and we know that both Henry III and his son Edward I regularly organized official searches for this treasure. The Wash, Hunstanton, the moors and the coastline can still be visited, though there have been marked geographical changes since the 14th century. Nevertheless, the main features are as described in this novel. The Hermitage is based on the ruins of what used to be called St Dunstan's Hostelry for travellers wishing to cross the Wash. The cliffs are there, as is the village of Hunstanton. So, of course, is the lovely, bustling town of King's Lynn. Before anyone writes in to me to point out my mistake, King's Lynn was actually Bishop's Lynn and only renamed during the reign of Henry VIII.

And the treasure? Local stories and legends say that most of it is still hidden away. The museum at King's Lynn is supposed to have one or two items but the rest could still be hidden in those lonely marshes where the SONG OF A DARK ANGEL can still be heard!